Unforgiven

Unforgiven

A Western Double

Levi Johnson Mountain Man Scout

Book Seven

Ash Lingam

Unforgiven
Paperback Edition

Wolfpack Publishing
1707 E. Diana Street
Tampa, Florida 33610

www.wolfpackpublishing.com

Paperback ISBN 979-8-89567-569-4
Ebook ISBN 979-8-89567-745-2

Contents

Unforgiven

1. Rusty & Angus 5
2. The South Pass 16
3. What's Cooking? 26
4. Shoshone 35
5. Guns & Bullets 45
6. Betty Crockett 53
7. Rivers Brothers 59
8. Gypsies 67
9. The Outlaws 75
10. Army Stragglers 81
11. Rainfall 86
12. The Captain 96
13. The Compound 105
14. Trail to Oregon 113
15. Snake River 126
16. Rocky Mountains 135
17. Full Moon 141
18. Leaving Safety 147
19. Three Cabins 154

Hell on High Water

1. Wild Horses 165
2. White Ghost 173
3. The Discovery 182
4. Back to Safety 191
5. Higher Ground 202
6. Ambush 210
7. Tricky Games 218
8. The Magician 226

9. Three Cabins 238
10. The Attack 247
11. The Alarm 257
12. The Red Lake 266
13. Black Crow 274
14. The Tunnels 279
15. Ghosts & Spirits 287
16. Proposals 295
17. Jump the Broom 302
18. Peace & Quiet 308
19. 13th Awakening 312

A Look at Book Eight: 315
About the Author 317

Unforgiven

UNFORGIVEN

LEVI JOHNSON MOUNTAIN
MAN SCOUT 13

"Remember, remember, this is now, and now, and now. Live it, feel it, cling to it. I want to become acutely aware of all I've taken for granted."

Sylvia Plath

Rusty & Angus

"Come on, you old fool, we can't sit here all night, or it'll be morning before ya know it," Rusty Steel grumbled. "We've got to get out of camp and into the brush before daylight, or somebody will see us go. You know as well as I do that every thief in the Rockies is looking for the folks that did well at the Rendezvous. I don't intend to let some no-good; ungrateful lowlife steal our money."

He pulled on his long gray beard as he peered into the night, looking for imminent danger. No matter where you turned in the wilderness, there was always the chance of trouble just around the corner. As he moved, the bear claws on his necklace clicked lightly. The big black dog on the ground growled for no apparent reason.

"Nature can't be hurried, dagnabit," Angus replied as he pulled his britches up, tied his belt, and walked through the shadows. "You best stuff that necklace in your pocket. You make more noise than a bullhorn at a funeral. It's ninety miles as the crow flies back to the foothills. Then we'll be on home ground and won't have to worry. Still, it's another five days from here to there. After that, it's uphill for another week. That last stretch to the cabins is the stinker, but by then, we'll be so glad to be home it won't bother us none."

"You know as well as me the necklace brings me good luck," Rusty retorted. The canine teeth from the same bear hung from his bracelet. "You're one to talk, too. You wear more Indian beads and doodads than your Crow wife."

"It was mighty unlucky for the grizzly you killed to make that necklace, so how do you figure they'll be lucky for you, fool?" Angus chuckled. "You know my woman; Pine Needle gives me all my beads and necklaces. She says it makes me look more like a Crow warrior. All right, I'm ready. Are you sure you got the animals on your own, Dennis? I wouldn't take kindly to somebody stealing all our mules. You've got Crow Chief Hachta's critters, too, pilgrim."

"It was lucky for me I killed the grizzly and he, not me," Rusty retorted. "That's why the bear claws and teeth are good luck—because I survived, so you're the fool. Just like they're good luck for Indians. You would get me in a dander before we leave. You know I like to move through the forest like a ballerina and not like a couple of bulls."

"I'd rather be taking the mules back than the gold," Dennis whispered. His bulging white eyes and his gold front teeth shone in the moonlight. "Don't worry, boys. The Crow Indians know the Rendezvous is over, so they'll be looking for our return. Remember, half of that money is theirs. We won't have to worry about hostile Indians stealin' the mules once we're in the mountains anyway. The Blackfoot had already been run off by the mountain men when they found out they killed or kidnapped some seventy White women. That riled the fellas lookin' for a wife since the lot was recently widowed. Still, seven of 'em got married. The Crow will be keeping their eyes peeled for anybody else out there, but that won't turn the White thieves back. It'll take more than that to scare 'em off the smell of gold."

Dennis waited in the dark, sipping hot coffee. The moon cast a silvery sheen over all the shapes and angles as far as they could see. Rusty and Levi had made a deal with Fred Country from the Rocky Mountain Fur Trading Company and sold him over a thousand pounds of cold-water beaver pelts at the Rendezvous at nearly two bucks a piece. They made over two thousand dollars. Now, all they had to do was make it back to the cabins, alive and with their earnings. They were a long way from home, but they knew the mountains like the backs of their hands after living in the Rockies for decades. The dodgy part was the land between the Rendezvous on the Green River and the foothills of the mountains.

The ninety miles in between would be where they would run into trouble if there was any trouble to be had. This part of the country would be swarming with outlaws out to steal the hard-earned cash from the trappers' pelts and furs. Half the men living in the mountains were making their way home as quickly as possible. They all knew the risk.

"Well, there's no sense waiting anymore," Rusty said.

"We'll see ya when we see ya, Dennis. It's a harder climb up the mountains than it is down. At least the mules have light loads."

"I bought tobacco, coffee, lard, sugar, cornmeal, and tobacco," Angus said. "We've got everything else we need for this winter except for meat and that we'll hunt and salt when we get back to the compound."

"It's gonna be strange coming back home without Bob, Pete, and Sam," Dennis said, but when he turned, the two grizzly old mountain men had disappeared.

One moment, Angus and Rusty were standing right beside Mountain Dennis, and the next, they vanished into the shadows and hard places to see. They didn't make a sound as their moccasins silently raced across the moonlit land. Occasionally, bushes rustled, but other than that, they were all but invisible as they hurried through the night. Despite their ages, they moved as quickly as the very Indians that owned the land. Years of living in the wilderness had honed their skills, and now they were just as good at moving unseen as their Crow and Blackfeet counterparts.

By the end of the day, they entered denser brush. The mountains were visible in the distance. Both men stopped as soon as they passed a stand of trees and dropped to the ground. The sparse vegetation was giving way to more and more trees and bushes. As they neared the Rocky Mountains, the going would get more challenging, but blending in with their surroundings and finding good places to hide would be easier. Their lungs heaved like broken steam engines, and sweat stained their backs, underarms, and faces. Neither man said a word, but they both knew what the other was thinking. Angus pulled off a waterskin, took a long draw, and passed it to his friend. Ten minutes later, they were racing toward the Rocky Mountains. Rays of sun slanted through the leaves like rain and streaked their faces.

They used mud to cover their skin to make them harder to see. Little leafy twigs and branches protruded from their bushy hair and beards. Only the whites of their eyes gave them away, but even they were hooded. They ran like a pair of elk eastbound with a rifle in each hand and their belts full of pistols.

As the afternoon waned and darkness neared again, they slowed their pace. The moon wouldn't come up for a few hours, so they dropped back to a walk, but still, they carried on. They walked until they knew they would have to rest. The mountain men found places in dense growths of bushes; they could wiggle their way in so deep that even a bear would have difficulty getting to them.

For anybody else, they were invisible. This way, they could get four or five hours of sleep without putting out a guard. Their best bet was to remain unseen as long as possible. But something told them that would be harder to do than they had assumed. Five hours later, they awoke as the moonlight lit the trail. They turned and began to run again for the Rocky Mountains. Only there could they slow their pace and not worry.

Rusty put his arm out to stop Angus in mid-stride. Just as soon as he did, McFarlin saw it too. Cinders circled on thermal currents and rose into the sky. They were visible for seconds just over the circle of bushes and stubby trees. Somebody had made a camp just ahead of them, but they weren't making much attempt to hide, so they knew they weren't from the mountains or Indians. The mountain men and buffalo hunters would only be so careless if they were in large numbers and heavily armed. Rusty locked eyes with Angus—they wondered if the thieves had seen them leave or maybe they just saw them make the sale. They also knew their friends were making the same or a similar trajectory, and they would be carrying gold, too.

Gossip was rampant across the wilderness, where people didn't have much to do but talk. So, if something juicy did pop up, it multiplied in number or size with every mouth and ear it touched, just like the Squirrel woman. When there were eighty, the mountain men exaggerated the numbers until the rumors said there were a thousand. That left a lot of disappointed men and trappers.

The angry mountain men were well-practiced at staying alive. Rusty and Angus crept like strange creatures across the side of the thieves' camp. Every movement was intentional and slow. They arched their backs like wild animals, gracefully moving through the night.

Both men dropped to the ground without a sound and began to crawl forward to see who it was and what they were up to. Sure, they could give them a wide circle and avoid contact, but it was better to get an idea of what they were doing before they made their way home. If there was a bunch of men camping and they weren't buffalo hunters or trappers, they were probably trouble. If that were the case, Angus and Rusty would feel better if they knew what and where they were. Maybe even a clue of what they planned to do. In most situations, they had experienced the one with the element of surprise won the day, so they had to stay hidden.

They took an hour to advance on the camp while

crawling on their bellies. They slithered forward as slow as snails. The mountain men didn't know if any of the men in the group they spied were trackers, but they doubted it. They were more likely to be up to no good. When they were close enough, they worked their way into the bush nearest the camp. The darkness was dense in the foliage.

The campfire burned, and flames crackled and popped. The buffalo chips fueled red-hot coals but left little smoke. Rusty looked at Angus, and they both knew they had brought the chips with them to avoid a smoky fire. These people didn't want to be noticed because there was firewood was available. But that would make a brighter fire and lots of smoke, making them easier to spot.

Rusty used his fingers to part the bushes and had a peek. He was shocked to see five men around the fire and another two mountain men gagged with tied hands and feet. He looked at Angus with raised eyebrows. They knew the captured mountain men who lived halfway down the mountain. They sat back-to-back with ropes wrapped around their bodies and blinds over their eyes. They couldn't see but could hear everything that was said even though they spoke softly. Rusty and Angus were so close they could hear, too.

JIMMY AND JOHNNY sat before three men. They were the other members of the Rivers Gang. The brothers' limp hair held a hint of ginger and hung to their chests. As Johnny talked, his hazel eyes looked as cold as ice. There were signs of danger in his face. All the men except his twin could see it, but it was in Jimmy's eyes, too. They were indeed two peas from the same pod.

Behind them were bales of stolen furs from trappers on the way to the Rendezvous. These, of course, they killed just like everybody they robbed. Dead men couldn't tell tales. Bundles of hair like woolly balls were wrapped in rope—Indian's scalps. Guns leaned against stumps and lightning-racked trees. Their fire sent tiny cinders swirling skyward into the night.

"Are ya sure you told me everything you saw?" Johnny asked. "Don't make me knock it out of ya, so tell me it all in one go. I hate it when you beat around the bush and hold things back. Why are you such a slippery turd?"

"Like I told ya, I saw the old fella comin' out of the Rocky Mountain Fur Company's tent right before the meet ended," Riley Bloodnstab said. "In the morning, they shifted their pelts to the trader, and later when he came back, I figure they paid 'em in gold like the others. If not in coins, then in nuggets. It's all the same to me when it comes time to spend what we stole." He pulled on his buckskins like he wasn't used to wearing them. The hide was stiff and wasn't well cured.

"All we have to do is fan out during the day, and we're bound to run into a few more of these rich mountain goats." Johnny smiled, pushing back his black hat. "What do they want with all that money living lost in the mountains anyway?" The red coals reflected in his eyes. It made him look evil.

"I came back to tell ya as soon as I saw all four groups of men leave that same tent weighed down with gold," Riley said. "I doubt any of 'em run before first light except for the two fools we caught yesterday, but they ain't done us no good so far. We might as well just kill 'em. Now, all we gotta do is stay between the trappers and the Rockies. We can clean 'em out as they pass by. You saw how those first two stumbled right into us. Lucky for us, they were drunk. It just made it all that much easier. I bet if we'd been ready, we could have picked a dozen off during the Rendezvous. The clever ones left early without making any noise."

"We've still got the trappers that waited for Polecat Jack's shootin' match," Johnny said. "The good trappers were all there. A man's got to make sure he don't bite off more than he can chew at one meal. It'll be light in a few hours. We can strike out an hour before dawn to make sure none of 'em get by us. Jimmy, give Riley your binoculars. With mine, that'll give us an edge. We'll be able to see them way before they can see us, even if they are clever."

"What are we gonna do with these two fools we got tied up?" Portland Paul asked. The beanpole of a man shuffled his feet when he walked. He had a long purple scar that disfigured his face, running from his hairline, down his forehead, over his cloudy eye, and across his cheek to his chin. He had been laid open like a filleted salmon.

Riley eyed the other gang member and asked, "Why can't we? I don't see any reason not to. We didn't find ten cents on 'em."

"Until they tell us where they hid their gold, they stay right where they are," Johnny spat. He took two strides to the tied men. He kicked the closest trapper in the gut, making him umph and growl through his gag. "Or maybe we ought to hang one of ya, so you'll know we mean business. Get me a rope and make a noose."

The mountain men struggled against their bindings, but they were tight. Which one would it be? Johnny pulled out a large knife. The fire reflected off the blade as he cut the ropes binding the two together. Jimmy slipped a noose around the closest captive's neck. His friend sighed in relief.

"I don't think that tree is tall enough to hang this fool," Rory said. "It might not hold up to the weight either. We're wastin' time."

"Gemmy, that rope," Johnny growled. He made a slipknot on the other end and climbed astride his horse.

As soon as he slipped the loop over the saddle horn, he gigged his horse's flanks. The slack rope suddenly pulled tight and jerked the buckskin-clad man to his feet. He tried to run, but he stumbled, and the noose pulled tight, making his face turn as red as a tomato as his body bounced over rocks and brush. Soon, his head would pop off.

No more did the horse begin to pound its hooves when a shot rang out, and the animal dropped to the dirt. Johnny flew off his horse, hitting the ground hard, knocking his breath out of him. He tried to gobble air as he pulled his pistol and swung it toward the bushes, but he didn't see anything but a whiff of gun smoke floating on puffs of air. In two seconds, it was gone.

The bushes rustled as two-gun barrels poked through the leaves and branches. Jimmy moved his right hand across his stomach, then folded his arms across his chest. His hidden hand was wrapped around his pistol's grip.

"I know you're out there, so state your business and walk into the light nice and slow," Johnny called out. His voice betrayed his sudden surprise and even a little fear.

More rustling leaves and branches, but nobody answered. Yet the outlaws knew somebody was out there and didn't expect them to be Indians—another gunshot rang out and then the hammering of boots on the ground. Somebody screamed in pain.

The South Pass

"I just do my best not to make a straight line crooked," Virgil Lovejoy said as he flipped the flapjacks in the skillet. The first traces of sun began to break over the end of the prairie. "That's been my objective in life, and maybe it ain't completely kept me out of harm's way, but I ain't dead." He smiled with full lips and a mouthful of white teeth.

Virgil Lovejoy insisted on cooking for the sheriff and his new scouts on the trail up from the Rendezvous to the South Pass in Wyoming. He always prepared the meal for the captain anyway. Even though Levi Johnson was his best friend, the captain, and he had some deep link leading from his fall and resulting amnesia. It was true he did miracles with the simplest of ingredients, and none of them could compare to his skills.

He carried a small bag of spices, which he used sparingly, but it made all the difference in the world. Of course, he could also shoot outlaws or hostiles at a dead run, regardless of whether on foot or a horse. Now he was attached to the travelers Joseph Walker escorted west to Oregon City. Before Joseph offered him a job, he was a successful buffalo hunter, which left him a wealthy man. At least in his eyes and for him, that was enough.

Still, when he was offered another fifty dollars to go exploring, he couldn't pass any more than Levi and Will could. He went more for the money and the others more for the adventure. They might have even gone without wages. At forty years old, Virgil only went where it paid his living. Now that he had a little money stashed away, he preferred to keep working and hold on to as much as he could for a rainy day.

Of course, Dahteste, the woman Crow war chief, and her husband Levi Beaver Johnson worked as scouts, and Captain Will Forrester worked as a guard. Something that he was obviously taking very seriously. Lately, the captain took to most chores passionately. He seemed in a perpetual state of change. He was as gentle as a lamb with them, but when challenged, he was the most dangerous man in the group and sent chills up even his best friend's spine. Still, despite his West Point education, he was happy with his rough and rugged friends. They were the only ones he had.

Of course, Sheriff Joseph Walker knew the skills of both men in battle. They had proved their worth against the Squirrel family. Even Levi's wife joined in and killed three of the feudalistic clan members. Twenty men of the strange family died, but so did a few of their friends. It was a bittersweet victory due to the losses of Portland Pete, Syracuse Sam, and Yosemite Bob. They were buried under the shade of an old oak along the Green River near the latest Rendezvous. The three old mountain men who had lived in the Rockies together for so many years now rested together under three white crosses near the foothills. The mountains were visible in the far distance.

What they all found strange was that the weather, the grizzlies, nor the local Indians were responsible for their demise. It came from an unexpected source. They had crossed paths with dangerous settlers. In the wilderness, you just never knew what enemy would take your life or at least make you fight for it with every ounce you could muster to survive.

The crew sat close to the fire to ward off the morning chill as they sipped coffee while staring into the cinders. Soon, the sun would rise, and the blistering heat would return. Men and women warmed their hands with hot tin cups as steam barreled off the liquid.

"So, this is the first day for y'all on our way westward," Joseph said to his new friends. "I'm afraid the city folks are less than happy with us, but I wouldn't put too much stock on their opinion. By the time we get to Oregon City, they may well have forgotten it all. Tougher times are ahead, folks."

"It was a long ride," Dahteste said. "Seven sleeps in all."

"Has anyone seen the captain?" Levi asked as he eyed Virgil. "Did he come back from his walk last night?"

"I reckon as soon as he smells breakfast, he'll head in," Virgil replied without looking up. Worried eyes hid under the shade of his hat. "The captain seems to change with the direction of the wind ever since I found him with a serious wound in his head. Lucky for him, the horse threw him into the rock wall and not over the cliff. I can't say the same for the horse."

"Could you really see the bone?" Levi asked, concerned.

"Not only could I see his skull, but I could also see the crack in it," Virgil said. "Hadn't I found 'im, I doubt little he'd have fallen prey to animals. They can sense when there are wounded critters about. I reckon that brain of his has been through so much change it must be more confused than we are about what's happening to him."

Betty Crockettt wasn't working for Sheriff Walker but preferred to stay with the people who saved her. Her married name was Betty Squirrel. The mountain men had saved her from her husband, along with the leader of the clan, Jack Amble. The Squirrel men used their women like cows to have more offspring. They married two, three, or more wives to a single husband, and all shared the same bed. All this was done against the women's will.

Puffs of dust followed the soldier's boot heels as he appeared out of the morning haze and walked into the camp with a rifle cradled in his arms. With the sun at his back, it made him appear to have an orange aura about him. The captain seemed at peace for a change. His features were relaxed, and his shoulders were limp. He even stopped grinding his jaw.

"Do you ever sleep?" Betty smiled, blinking her blue eyes.

The captain was caught off guard and blushed a deep red. The striking beauty with yellow hair stared at him questioningly. Will pushed blond hair from his face, and deep blue eyes stared back.

"What's the matter, Will?" Betty laughed. "Cat got your tongue?"

Will sighed and replied, "I was making sure nobody sneaks up on our camp at night." Now he smiled, too. It was contagious, and he couldn't help himself.

"So, when do you sleep?" Betty asked.

"I sort of sleep with one eye open," Will said slowly. "Out there somewhere in the dark. If I do dose off, I wake up at the slightest noise. It's to ensure the Indians don't sneak up on us at night. I won't accept the loss of any more friends."

Betty looked at the captain's empty bedroll. She had awoken during the night, and each time she looked, it was vacant. Miss Crockettt wondered what made the ex-Army officer tick. He was clearly a complex man. He had even frightened them when they came to their camp after the Blackfeet warriors had repeatedly attacked them. They lost over seventy women in the raids. Some were stolen, others stood their ground and fought, only to die on the battlefield and be scalped.

But when he rode up on his black stallion to their burning wagon train and said he was there to save them, Betty suddenly felt like he was the first man she had ever met she felt she could truly trust. She didn't even know why, but she just did.

Betty passed her cup to Virgil, who kindly filled it to the brim. He nodded his head and smiled approvingly.

"Come over here and sit," Betty offered the captain her cup of coffee and patted her blanket as she scooted over to make room.

Their eyes met for a fleeting moment, but to them, it felt longer. Captain William Forrester couldn't hold her stare. He could ride into a skirmish with wild Indians or, even worse, crazy settlers without showing an ounce of fear, but when it came to something as simple as locking eyes with a beautiful woman, it gave him pause and made him uneasy.

Betty seemed to delight in the captain's discomfort. She held the back of her hand to her mouth as she stifled a laugh. "Come on, don't be shy. Plus, there's no place else to sit close to the fire. Or do you find me particularly ugly? I know some of the Squirrel women were. Mainly the ones that were born into the family, so they were pure Squirrels through and through. I'm not a Squirrel by birth. I'm a Crockettt, just like my Uncle Davy was."

"Did you know your uncle well?" Captain Forrester asked. "With his recent death, he's probably one of the most famous men in America. It's hard to believe that Santa Ana really killed him and all the rest. I read that not a single man survived. The Alamo must have been a dreadful sight."

"I knew him as well as you can with a family of thirteen children." Betty laughed. "My grandfather and grandmother were prone to produce a child nearly every year. Davy was often on one of his adventures or back in Washington, DC. He first was a colonel in the Tennessee Militia. Then, he was voted into the House of Representatives in the State Capitol. He was as busy as a bee but still made time to come home to Limestone in Green County, close to the Nolichucky River. He's the perfect example of a man without a formal education making his way to the top despite his lack of schooling. He taught himself."

"A man like him succeeds without an education, and I failed in my mission despite my West Point schooling," Will huffed.

"The Comanche was what made the mission fail,

and not you, Will," Levi said to his friend. "We were lucky to survive at all. There's nothing scarier than a Comanche warrior up close. If it weren't for our skills, we would have succumbed to them too. I reckon we did as best as any man in the same situation could have. Many an expedition has been launched into the wilderness and never returned at all. At least we're still alive."

Joseph emptied his cup in one gulp, pushed his hat from his forehead, and then wiped the back of his hand across his mouth. He looked at the scout, suggesting a reply with his expression.

"I'm on it, boss," the smallish man with a prominent personality replied. Freckles dusted his nose and cheeks, making his green eyes shine.

"I'll give you a hand with the horses, Rory," Levi said. "Will could use a few minutes rest, and Virgil's done made breakfast. Y'all and the captain can keep Betty company."

The massive six-foot-seven mountain man towered over the bowlegged cowboy from Kansas. They disappeared into the morning haze. Soon, it would burn off, and blistering heat would follow.

"I'll go get this moody bunch of Easterners ready to travel," Joseph said as he scraped his boot along the dusty earth and kicked dirt into the fire, making it smolder. "I hope they're in a better mood today than they were yesterday. If they ain't, I reckon the next few hundred miles will cool them out."

Just like the Indians who populated these plains, they pulled up stakes and were prepared to travel in an hour. Of course, this was despite the complaints of the twenty men and women in long black and gray frocks. Their five servants moved about, preparing to leave with their eyes glued to the ground. They couldn't be worse dressed for the country they were about to cross. The five Black people who met the travelers' every need never uttered a word. They just nodded their heads when ordered to do something.

Dust rose around the horses' hooves and seemed to cling to their clothes, skin, and lungs. The missionaries mopped their faces continually. The soft blue of a cloudless sky met with the purplish color of the mountains in the distance. It was the only redeeming factor with the ragged, wild look of the plains.

Above them, in a never-ending grade, was the saddle. The South Pass was the most accessible place to cross the Rocky Mountains. In twelve short months, it would be christened the name The Oregon Trail.

After a half day of travel, the travelers already dozed in their saddles and had listless looks on their faces. The captain pressed his heels into the black stallion's flanks and rode out front. The weather was unyielding, and the rugged terrain grounded their nerves into the ground. By noon, they felt like they had been traveling all day.

"Everything is so much farther away than it looks," Levi said.

"Just because it looks like we'll get there today don't mean we reach the top for days." Joseph chuckled. "The top is almost 7,500 meters high. At least it's not too steep. I reckon a bunch of wagons could make this pass. Next season, I plan to have the first wagon train organized as soon as the government makes the announcement of free land public."

They threaded their horses through the sparsely growing scrub bushes and mesquite trees. The vegetation got thinner as they slowly advanced up the almost unnoticeable grade. Still, there was plenty of grazing for the animals. But by late in the day, the horses and mules began to suffer the slow climb in the blistering heat.

Dahteste sniffed the air and looked at Levi. He did the same and shrugged his shoulders as he narrowed his eyes. She peered into the distance. It looked like a low hovering cloud. She slid off her Appaloosa, dropped to her hands and knees, and put her ear to the ground. "Tatanka..." she whispered. "Buffalo."

Rory rode out front, gigging his horse to a whirlwind pace. He charged right at the advancing bison. He hoped against all odds that the herd was small enough to turn. And what were they doing out there on the South Pass in this heat?

He flinched when a gunshot rang out beside him. He saw the captain and Levi on either side as the horse's hooves hammered the earth. They both had pistols in their hands. Breaker pulled two pistols and fired them simultaneously. A Crow war cry came from an Indian woman on a spotted horse. Virgil came racing from behind, banging two skillets together, making more racket than the pistols and screams.

One moment, the herd was headed straight for the travelers. And the next, it suddenly veered off just short of the humans. Virgil stood guard on the Easterners, but they did not attempt to hide themselves by hunching their shoulders or crouching down. Both were natural instincts.

The missionaries didn't even realize the danger they were in, but the mountain men did. They had escaped certain death by a hair. Betty swallowed repeatedly with a wide-eyed stare. She was aware of how close they had come to tragedy. It seemed to follow her around like a pesky fly.

She shook his head wearily, clearing her throat before speaking. Her voice trembled as she walked her horse over to the black stallion, lay her hand on the captain's arm, and blinked as she bravely fought back tears.

What's Cooking?

As the end of the day neared, they didn't seem any closer to the top. The saddle at the summit was over twenty miles wide and was marked at either end by two large rock formations. The steady grade seemed to go on forever. They all wondered how long it would take to get to the ridge, making the lowest point of the Continental Divide with the slow-moving city dwellers from back East. They were making half the expected time, and they didn't respond when Joseph tried to urge them to move faster. But the heat was too much for people of such fair skin. So, they continued to plod on like snails.

Dahteste kept a sharp eye out for signs of hostile Indians. Here, she doubted she would run into any Crow, but Blackfeet Indians, among others, could always be somewhere hiding, spying. There were many other tribes, too. Arapaho, Arikara, Bannock, Cheyenne, Gros Venture, Kiowa, Nez Percé, Sheep Eater, Shoshone, and Ute lived on these plains. Of the group of travelers, she was, of course, the best at spotting other Indians.

She was a warrior, so she even knew their habits and where they would prefer to hide.

Joseph Walker dropped back and pulled up beside Pastor Smith's horse. It was short and stout like its rider. The preacher ignored him as he poured water on a scarf and dabbed it on his face. The missionaries had all fallen silent from the long, fiery day. As they approached the South Pass, the weather got warmer. Heat rolled over them like an ocean wave. A perpetual haze of dust followed them like a plague, accumulating in every wrinkle of their clothing and skin, making them all the hotter.

"Y'all might wanna consider gettin' rid of those long black coats, sir," Joseph said. "The same with your womenfolk and their gray frocks. You best be careful with the water, too. I know it's hot, but we've gotta use it sparingly and for drinking only. When you wet your face, it just turns the dust into mud anyway. When it cakes on your face, it'll be even hotter in the end."

Pastor Smith shot the sheriff a dirty look and didn't bother to reply. The head minister of the group of missionaries didn't respond to employees or servants. He was the one who gave orders and no one else—at least not among this group. He wet his scarf again and wiped the back of his neck, unabashedly defying Joseph's orders. He intended it to be a warning message to show Joseph who was the boss.

Pastor Rufford Smith came from back east in Boston. He decided to dedicate his life to being a missionary, which obliged the closest members of his flock to follow. The short man with a stern face rarely smiled. It almost appeared he considered it a sin. He was short and fleshy with fiery gray eyes and heavy bushy eyebrows, short hair, a clean-shaven face, and wore a wide-brimmed beaver hat. His voice was so soft you had to focus to hear him.

Pastor James Brown was Smith's right-hand man and was the second in charge of the church elders, other preachers, and their wives. The ginger-haired man was Irish born but immigrated to Boston as a young boy with his father's family. They all had snow-white skin from a life of cities. The sun was like poison to their fair complexions.

The mountain men's skin was dark and weathered from the sun. But for them, it was like every other day. They didn't ponder on the heat, or it bothered you more. Men like Levi pushed the discomfort from their minds and thought about something else while never losing focus on their job. They had all been much more uncomfortable in other situations anyway. For the mountain men, this was just another adventure.

The preacher didn't even notice the wry look on the sheriff's face. He had to stifle a laugh. Rather than be offended, he found the man acted like a buffoon. Maybe back in the big city, things were different, and he was probably an influential man. From how they all acted, they must all be important people in their churches and communities. Despite their most honorable intentions to spread the word of God, they forgot their apathy for their fellow man. That and the fact they were well out of their depth—so much so that they didn't even know it.

People who worked for them they referred to as employees and seldom called them by their names. Whether this was intentional or not remained to be seen. The mountain men wondered if they even knew their servants' names—people they had brought with them from Boston.

The servants walked beside their employers but didn't seem to suffer the weather conditions or the hike half as much as the missionaries did. The church they came from condemned slavery. They employed the very people who were enslaved in the past. They didn't really have bad intentions and did many good things. Still, they paid them a pittance but couldn't make them stay if they didn't want to. Maybe when they got to Oregon City, some would decide to strike out independently and find out what absolute freedom felt like.

The city preachers and their wives were like ducks out of water on the trail. They arrogantly made their way across the West, never once stopping to try to understand the country they were in or the people who were guiding them. For them, they were simply six more employees. They had it all figured out. Most of them thought more about where the trail would lead them than where they were right then. It was a mistaken attitude to have in such a hostile land.

Virgil eyed Dahteste riding beside Levi and chuckled. "She's no bigger than a minute."

Joseph snickered. "Yeah, and about as shy as a buffalo." They followed the two, knowing they would spot any danger out on point. Still, with Levi's size and Dahteste's presence, they were indeed a strange-looking couple. "It's odd what love will do to a man and a woman. Sure, Levi acts half-Indian anyway, but still, with him so big and her so small. It's strange how she sounds bigger than she is when she talks."

Levi and Dahteste rode moccasin to moccasin. His

horse pranced beside the Appaloosa. The sun shone off his wife's black hair and darkened his skin.

"Easy now, boy," Johnson said. "We'll be stoppin' soon enough."

He towered over his wife as he sat on his fourteen-hundred-pound horse. The mountain man was two-hundred-twenty pounds of solid muscle. He made an extraordinary appearance beside the wild Indian war chief. Four pistol handles protruded from his wide belt, and a long rifle was cradled in his arms. His wife beside him had her bow, a quiver of arrows strapped across her back, and a lance in her hand. They both wore light buckskin suits and from head to toe. Knee-high moccasins protected them from the brush and thorns. Rays of the sun flashed off Levi's bear claw necklace.

Virgil Lovejoy stopped and caught his breath as he used his bandana to wipe sweat from his face with a brown hand. He removed his hat and used it to block the sun while he peered into the distance. A faint wisp of gray smoke curled skyward in a thin line. Against the sun's glare, it was hardly noticeable. Above that circled a dozen large birds.

"Vultures," Virgil whispered. "More trouble, I reckon. This country sure is prone to violence of one sort or another."

But Levi and Dahteste had already seen them circling low. Whatever it was, it must be dead or near dying, or they would be flying higher in the sky until it was safe to have their meal.

"Maybe it's a dead buffalo," Levi said, but he knew it was wishful feelings.

They touched the flanks of their horses and bolted

toward the predators. The captain followed as he stared at the wavering heat with a frozen gaze.

Captain Forrester rode past his friends with his saber in hand. When he got close, the nauseating smell was almost unbearable. He wheeled his horse around and pointed his thumb over his shoulder.

"You might not wanna see this, ma'am," Forrester said.

Betty Crockettt had followed them out of curiosity, but she was just about to see something that would be scarred in her memory for life. The missionaries continued lethargically upward and onward, ignoring their employees. They didn't show the slightest interest. As soon as Miss Crockett got sight of the scene, revulsion suddenly hit her, and she looked away. Bile climbed to her throat.

A man was suspended from an arc of three thin poles stuck into the ground and lashed together at the top. He had been hung head-down just two feet over what was a fire. The bottom half of his body was burned black, and the skin flaked off. The black rawness crept up to his hands tied to his thighs. The top half was covered in red, angry blisters. There was no doubting what he had been through. His Army boots were all that was left recognizable. The pigging string was still wound around his ankles at the top. His dead body swayed slightly in the constant breeze. The air was full of buzzing flies and the potent smell of death.

"This poor soul's dying was a slow process," the captain said. "It must have been about as painful as any way possible. I've never seen such a thing done to a man."

Footprints surrounded the fire where the Indians

danced. Blood-covered rocks where they had poked the skewed body with their lances. The captain looked from Levi to Joseph without blinking, but his jaw muscles were as tight as a drum as he ground his teeth.

"I've never seen such ruthlessness," Betty said in awe. She turned her head and covered her nose with her hankie.

Will turned to the woman, took her bridle, and gently led her horse away. "This isn't something you need to see, darlin'. You've already seen too much."

The captain didn't even notice he said it, but despite the dreadful scene, Betty did hear it—darling. Even though she knew he did so unconsciously, she liked it just the same—maybe even more since the captain found it so challenging to be forward with a woman. Backward was more like what he was. But she would remember it fondly later, just like she would sadly remember the horrible sight.

The captain and Joseph studied the crime scene stoically with impassionate eyes. Levi tried to show the same calm as Rusty would. He had to swallow back the food that threatened to climb up to his mouth despite his brave façade. Of course, he and the officer had seen their fair share of death, but they didn't count on this. Sorrow cut to the bottom of his stomach. Anger burned in his wife's eyes.

"What tribe did the hostile Indians come from?" Levi asked his wife as he stared at the dead body.

"Whatever tribe did this left no arrows, or I would know by the type of feathers they use and their design. The only things left behind were their footprints and this poor White man. I've never seen this done before, but I have heard of this type of torture in several tribes. Maybe Blackfeet again or even Shoshoni."

They clutched their rifles and pistols and fingered the hammers, ready to caress the triggers as they looked around. They had a knowing need to get even, but they didn't feel that gut feeling when hostiles were nearby. Most men and women that survived as warriors had such feelings. It was almost like a sixth sense.

"I'd say they've long gone," Levi said as he stepped down. "The fires goin' cold."

"I wonder where a soldier came from way out here," the captain said as he made an ugly pause and sighed, angered. "Maybe they brought him here for a reason, but I couldn't say that I could imagine why."

"I can see the anger in your eyes right down to your soul, Captain," Virgil said. "Don't you worry that violence begets violence?"

Virgil had a Bible in one hand; the other held a pistol. He didn't feel as sure as the more experienced frontiersmen that nobody was waiting for them out there, but then again, he had yet to fight hostile Indians. He and his two employees had been lucky back in the Rocky Mountains. They had never seen anything even close to what he saw today.

"Let's get this poor man cut down and in the ground," Virgil said impatiently.

"We have to wait for a spell first," Joseph said.

"I can't stand here and watch another moment," Virgil said. "If you won't take him down, I will."

The captain lay his hand on his friend's shoulder. "The body is too hot to touch, Virgil. If we cut him down now, his flesh will fall off the bone, and we'll need a shovel to scrape him up. I believe he'd prefer if we wait so we can get him to his grave in one piece."

Rory Breaker sat back and watched from a distance. He held a pistol in each hand and kept a sharp eye on their surroundings.

Joseph looked over his shoulder and yelled, "You best bring both shovels, Rory. We'll be makin' camp over there where the missionaries are tonight. They don't need to see or know what happened here. Tell 'em a horse came up lame. We can dig the hole when the sun gets near the horizon, and it's not so hot. By then, the body will have cooled down."

Minutes later, they heard the sound of spades piercing the ground, followed by the sound of dirt being tossed in a pile.

Shoshone

Their legs ached from the long hours in the saddle. The new scouts were used to traveling in the mountains and not on the plains. Sure, they all came overland by way of Kansas, but some were more used to such a long ride than others. For the cowboy Rory, it was just another day. The woman war chief gazed ahead, welcoming the arid land stretching as far as the eye could see. They continued climbing the never-ending grade toward the wild and rugged trail to the top.

The sun was fading fast, and the missionaries began to nod to sleep in their saddles. They were oblivious to anything other than the sun. Things appeared to waver in the distance as the end of the day neared. They all knew relief was just around the corner. Soon, the fiery, angry disk would fall off the edge of the earth, bringing the chill that was inherent to such arid places.

Without warning, Dahteste jumped off and hid behind her spotted horse. "Do like me, quick," she said. "Maybe we can trick them, and they think the horses are wild and riderless or buffalo."

Levi kicked his leg over the saddle horn and slid off, then ducked behind Trigger. He peeked over his rump in the direction Dahteste pointed, but he didn't see a thing.

"Whatcha see?" Levi whispered. "I don't see nothin'."

"Something startled the quail," the war chief replied, nodding in the distance as she wrapped her fingers around her pistol—a click—the metallic sound of a hammer. "Whoever burned the bluecoat won't be far away. It doesn't look like people live out here, but they do. We just can't see them. In such a vast place, there are many places to hide. It is very different from the Rocky Mountains. Still, our people have traveled these lands White men say they discovered for thousands of years." She smiled. "Your people came here yesterday."

"Maybe we should ride ahead and make sure it's gonna be safe for the missionaries," Levi said. "We best tell Joseph to have them arm themselves. We have to assume they outnumber us until we know how many there are."

"Now you sound like the captain," Dahteste said, but he took it as a compliment. "We better warn the travelers before we disappear. The captain wouldn't like that, would he?" She smiled again.

They wheeled their horses and rode helter-skelter for Joseph and the rest of the travelers. What happened to the poor soldier was overkill, to say the least. They still had no idea what a lone soldier was doing way out here in the wilderness. What were they capable of doing to the missionaries if they were cruel enough to burn a man over a low fire so they could watch him die for hours?

When they pulled up to a sliding stop and dropped off their horses out of breath, the captain, Virgil, and Joseph already had their rifles in their hands. They had all been unnerved by the brutality of the murder of the soldier. They all remembered the leather squeaking against his boots as he swung back and forth.

"Shoshoni," Dahteste said as soon as she gobbled some air and her heartbeat settled. "They call themselves Nuwe, or the People. For them, everybody else are animals. They are who killed the White man."

"How do you know?" Levi asked. "We didn't see anybody."

"I smelled them," Dahteste said, matter-of-fact-like. "They have a strange diet, so they smell different. When a Shoshoni brave kills an enemy warrior, he cuts out his heart. They probably ate the soldier's heart once it was cooked. My people don't eat other humans. It is unforgivable. But some tribes eat their enemies whole."

Virgil visibly shuddered and asked, "And why would they do such a morbid thing? What have I gotten myself into?"

"They believe if they eat their enemies' hearts, they will gain their strength and capture their spirits. The Tonkawa are worse," Dahteste said in a whisper. The Shoshoni were too far away, so they couldn't hear, but she didn't want Minister Smith and his flock to know what was going on. This was terrible news, and they all knew it.

"We need to find out how many there are so we know if we can stand up to 'em or not," Levi said. "I don't see anywhere close by to hide. I'm afraid we're left with our tails in the wind, and we're about to have our feathers ruffled."

"And the missionaries are just about to have their metal tested," Captain Forrester said. "If we have to fight, we'll need every one of those expensive guns they brought from Boston."

"And somebody will have to be on the other end shootin' the guns," Levi huffed. "I hope they're up to it. I've seen harder men freeze up when facing daunting odds."

"I doubt it'll be the only time on this trip, either," Joseph said. "The local Indians ain't used to seein' White or Black folks around here. Normally, everybody's skin is red, so it don't surprise me they take offense. Even back where you folks live in the Rockies, they're more used to seeing mountain men, and still, at times, things run off the rails. It'll be safer when we're a hundred wagons or more. Then we'll intimidate them and them, not us."

"Not if they kill us today," Virgil huffed. His brow furrowed, and he ground his jaw. "I don't know one tribe from another, but this bunch seems particularly angry."

"Slow down, Virgil." The captain smiled. "There might be only a few out there, though it's best to be prepared for anything. There's no sense worrying about something you don't know and can't change anyway. The best recourse is decisiveness and preparation. For that, we need information."

"Rory, go get Mr. Smith and Brown," Joseph said. "Tell 'em we've got something important to talk about."

"This could get very ugly," Forrester said. "There's only the six of us."

"If what Preacher Smith told me is true, they all

know how to shoot at paper targets," Joseph said. "Brown said even the women learned how to fire their rifles before embarking on the journey. Remember, I just picked 'em up in Montana, so they ain't had their metal tested with me watching. So, until we see what they can do, we best figure them into a minimum. Only if we see we can't avoid it. There's nothing I hate more than working with amateurs. That's why I came to the Rendezvous to get a few mountain men for my scouts."

"Now we're going to see how brave they are," the captain said. Unlike the rest, he didn't seem at all rattled. It was like he was on a Sunday stroll. "We're going to get out in front of this before it gets in front of us," he added, determined.

"What could get ugly?" Betty asked as she walked up to the crew, whispering. She knew enough to know if they were keeping something from them, it was probably bad. She looked at the captain, but he already had that thousand-yard stare in his eyes. He didn't even break off his stare into the distance. "Whatcha lookin' at, Will?"

"I'm looking for Indians." Will smiled, blinking his eyes like he just noticed Betty.

"You don't sound very worried." Then she looked at Levi and instantly knew it was bad.

"Levi and the captain can come with me," Dahteste said. "I will know how to approach them better than you. Just follow me as I go. You step where I step, and they won't see or hear you."

"All right then," Levi said. "Joseph, Virgil, and Rory will take care of ya, ma'am. We'll be back as soon as we've had a look at the Shoshoni."

"Shoshoni?" Betty asked. "What is a Shoshone?"

"The Indian tribe who burned the Army soldier," Dahteste replied.

"We'll be back as soon as possible," Will said.

Levi went for his horse, but Dahteste said, "No horses. We must go on foot. Maybe we can have a peek and sneak away without them seeing us." She looked at her massive husband and shook her head. "Then again, maybe not."

Dahteste's English got better each day, listening to people talk a strange-sounding language. At first, it sounded like mumbling to her. Not the sharp guttural noises of her native language. Sometimes she would ask her husband to speak to her in Crow, so she didn't feel so homesick. He had learned her language from Rusty and living in Chief Hachta's stronghold in the Rockies.

As Rusty called it, the Words of Webster were stuffed inside Levi's saddle. At night, he picked names randomly and would say them several times, giving his wife their meaning. She remembered everything. Her mind was like a steel trap, and she craved for more information. She wanted to know what made her husband tick and couldn't do it until she understood everything about him. Of course, learning each other's languages was imperative. Still, they both struggled daily due to their vast cultural differences.

"Don't worry, Betty," Levi said. "The captain has gotten us through everything thrown at us so far, so I don't see why he won't do the same this time."

Dahteste had already disappeared down a small arroyo. The captain was right behind her. Levi grabbed his rifle and pulled his hat down to shade his eyes, and he, too, disappeared in minutes. All that was left was the constant wind blowing from morning to night. Virgil looked at Joesph questioningly.

"I know about as much as you do, pard," Joseph said to Virgil. "Whatcha think, Rory? You've fought your fair share of Cheyenne and Comanche back in Kansas."

"There ain't a man alive that knows what's goin' on in the mind of a hostile Indian," Rory replied. He fished his quid from his cheek with his finger and spat in the dirt. "I agree with the captain. We best get ready for the worst. It always seems to be worse than we expect anyway. Hell, arm the preachers and their wives. Times a wastin'."

Ministers Smith and Brown walked toward the huddled men, and the boss cleared his throat.

"What is this I hear about trouble?" Smith asked. "Is there something that you experts can't handle? And what were you up to the last time we stopped and rode over there? Don't think I didn't have an eye on you. I carefully watch my employees all the time, even if it doesn't look like it. We have a dozen back home, so get on with it. What's the problem now?"

"Shoshoni," Rory replied.

"Shasha, what?" Smith asked.

"Shoshoni Indians, fool," Rory spat. He was still angry about how they treated him when Joseph had to run down to the Rendezvous to find more trackers.

"Watch your mouth, young man," Smith retorted. "Remember who you're talking to."

"Mister Breaker is just a tad wound up," Sheriff Walker said. "We have hostile Indians in the way of our progress, and we must determine their strength before continuing."

"Nonsense," Brown said. "You are moving entirely too slow anyway."

They didn't notice when Rory rolled his eyes nor when Joseph frowned. The scouts had been complaining daily about the snail's pace they traveled at. If they continued, it would take them twice the time planned to reach Oregon City.

"That's no way for Christian folks to be talkin' to each other," Virgil growled, surprising everybody. "Rory deserves the same respect that you do, Preacher Smith. You should be ashamed of yourselves." Lovejoy reached into his buckskin shirt and pulled out his tattered Bible. "There ain't a thing here that says you can go about bein' mean to each other. All I read is goodwill toward your fellow man."

"Thank you, Virgil," the sheriff said. "Can I try to tell you what we want you to do? We might have to defend our lives, sir. Back there, when we rode off, we found a man burned to death. They hung him from a spit like a leg of beef. Now our Crow scout says they're some of the same Indians on our point. That'll be over that way. I want you to get your guns out, loaded, and primed for something unexpected. It'll come hard and fast if it comes, so be forewarned. This ain't no joke."

"How good are you with them English firearms?" Rory asked, but now his voice was calm without a sign of sarcasm.

Minister Smith seemed to take a second before he spoke. He looked at Virgil with his perpetual Bible in his hand and nodded. "Fair enough. At least the men are proficient with their rifles, although the women know how to fire and reload to the last one. We prepared ourselves back home before our departure.

We expected to run into trouble somewhere on the trail. We do have the news of distant places like Kansas and St. Louis in the big cities back East."

"It's one thing to read about it and another to experience it firsthand," Joseph said. "Miss Betty here will be in charge of the women. She's fought off Blackfeet Indians and lost seventy of her friends getting this far. She'll show y'all where to shoot."

"And you are going to be where?" Smith asked with a raised eyebrow.

"We're gonna be between you folks and the hostiles," the sheriff said. "Levi, Dahteste, and the captain have already gone to see how many of them there are."

"Hopefully, they'll come back and not with half the Shoshoni Nation with 'em," Rory said.

"Do you know how to shoot too, Mr. Virgil?" Brown asked.

"I'm a buffalo hunter." Lovejoy smiled. "I can shoot the wings off a fly way over yonder with my eyes closed." He laughed, but it was a nervous laugh.

It was contagious, too, and in seconds, they were all chuckling, knowing there wasn't anything funny, but they laughed just the same. They couldn't help themselves.

"Well, go on then," Joseph said. "Get your guns loaded. Five or ten minutes might make a difference. You just never know with angry Indians. We're trespassing on their land, after all."

"If you'd had seen what they've done to that poor soldier, you'd be runnin' right about now," Rusty said, still chuckling nervously.

Breaker, Joseph's scout, began to load the four pistols

in his belt. The sheriff carried four on his belly and another hidden behind his back. Even Virgil was armed to the teeth. Nobody said the wilderness wasn't dangerous. Once a man traveled west of St. Louis, he better be prepared to use his weapons, too. It would be a miracle to cross even a couple hundred miles without an incident. Danger or worse was potentially around every corner.

The bowlegged cowboy pulled out his knife and cut a wedge from his tobacco plug, pushing it into his cheek with his finger. "I'm ready. Now let's see if we can't find some better cover."

Guns & Bullets

They felt like hostile eyes watched as they moved in for the attack. Then, there was silence. The mountain men peered into the inky blackness as they strained their ears. The still night was broken suddenly with sounds of rustling vegetation followed by a muffled groan. They waited for twenty minutes before continuing.

They again moved forward, following the crushed grass, and found a blanket, black boots, and a canteen. All were US Army issues. The ground was bloody and trampled. Grotesk desert trees and a scatter of boulders limited their vision on a moonless night from the arroyo created by the water runoff in the rainy season.

Dahteste slowed her pace but still held a confidence that hinted she knew what she was doing. More so than even Levi or the captain. The woman war chief moved forward a yard or two, then listened and sniffed the air. The signs of a struggle didn't seem to faze her.

It appeared whoever moaned was dragged away.

They followed the trampled trail downhill into the bushes until they made the discovery. A man with soldier's pants appeared dead. He was barefoot, his neck was at an impossible angle, and his face bled from deep lacerations. Another Army man made two soldiers; they had no idea where they came from. Captain Forrester wondered if there were more. Maybe even still alive. The captain spun on his heels as soon as he heard a sound behind him, but there was nothing there. Small animals scurried in the darkness. There were signs of Indians everywhere.

Dahteste scurried out of the arroyo, diving into a small clump of bushes, and she disappeared. In a moment, her head reappeared, and Levi and the captain followed one at a time. They crept with extreme caution from one cover to the next. Suddenly, a mournful sound filled the silence. They all stopped simultaneously and waited for minutes—nobody so much as blinked. Levi had to remind himself to breathe. His heart beat so loud he was sure the nearby enemy could hear it.

Dahteste wiped her brow with her sleeve and sighed deeply. "Nightbirds," she said. "That was the noise we heard, not Shoshone."

"I can't ever remember being so jumpy," Levi whispered. "I wasn't this nervous when the Comanche attacked us back in Kansa."

Dahteste gave her husband a dirty look and mouthed, "Shush."

She put a finger to her lips and whispered something. Levi and the captain nodded, frowning. They began to slowly crawl up the rocks above them. At least then, they would have cover and be on a little higher ground. Every little bit helped if they got attacked. Hopefully, they would get sight of their numbers and not be discovered. They had no idea how far they were away—whoever it was that scared the quail. Maybe they would get lucky, and it would be a small hunting party. Time would tell if their faces were painted for war.

Despite the fact it was night, millions of stars pulsated light years away, illuminating the prairie. They continued to crawl until they heard a horse sneeze. Dahteste and Levi's eyes locked, spread wide. Again, they stopped dead in their tracks. Shoshone Indians would be very close now, but a good tracker knew patience was a virtue and impatience was a death sentence. Now more than ever, they had to tread lightly and ensure they weren't seen.

They slowed down even more, wiggling like worms one foot at a time, always heading for the sound of the pony. Every few yards, they pressed themselves into the ground and waited, listened, and smelled. More ponies nickered. They even heard humans talking in the distance, but they, too, talked in whispers. Everybody had enemies in the wilderness. Some you didn't even know existed until you encountered them. A bear claw necklace hung from Levi's neck, and his wife had eagle feathers woven into her hair. Both were serious warriors. Would their lucky charms help them evade the hostiles?

The flesh on the back of the captain's neck tingled. He hunched his shoulders and tried to make himself as small as possible. If only they could disappear like Rusty and Angus, but that came with decades of training. Thoughts raced through all their minds. The captain worried about the safety of his friends. Never once did he think about his own mortality.

When they got the Shoshoni in sight, they were all stripped to their waist and danced around a fire. Their faces and bodies were painted in bold red, white, and yellow, and in the corner sat yet another White soldier. His hands were bound behind his back, but the Shoshone weren't worried he'd escape. They had already beaten the fight out of him, and he looked nearly dead.

"Thank God," Levi whispered. "This one's still alive." They parted the dry brush before them to have a better look, being careful none of the brittle branches broke. Only his white eyes were visible in the darkness.

"How many do you count?" Levi asked the captain.

"Too many," the captain frowned. "Maybe thirty warriors. Way too many."

The captive was so bruised and dirty that it was hard to tell his color, but the uniform was still mostly intact. This one had sergeant's stripes. Again, the captain wondered what the Army was doing so far west. Or maybe so far east if they came from the other side of the United States. Perhaps they were doing what he had planned on doing and were looking for locations to build more forts to secure the soon-to-come settlers. Still, three men wouldn't have been sent alone. It was far too dangerous, and the Army was aware of the fact.

Three musket shots screamed through the night. Simultaneously, there was movement on the other side of the arroyo. It was the Shoshone warriors. Three lay dead on the ground. Chaos ensued through the Indian camp; women screamed, and men angrily shouted.

Suddenly, the captain heard the loose earth crumble

behind him under the foot of a moccasin. He spun on his heels, locking eyes with a Shoshone warrior. Somehow, he had crept up behind them, but it was too late. The blade of the captain's saber sliced through the neck of the attacker. His head thudded when it hit the ground and rolled down the arroyo. The last thing he saw before he died was the unexpected flash of steel.

"Four down and too many to count to go," the captain said. "We'll have to do better than this, or they'll overrun us."

Levi's heart hammered between his ears as the urge to run made his knees tremble. As he pulled two more pistols, his boots moved with a spasmodic scrape, kicking up puffs of dust before him as he backed away.

"We've got to get back to the others, lickety-split," the captain said. "There are too many. If Virgil and Rory are ready and Joseph has the missionaries prepared, we might be able to lead them into a trap. At this point, I doubt we have a choice."

"What about the soldier?" Dahteste asked. "I can end his misery with an arrow. Once we attack, I doubt they will let him live."

"Yeah, if they don't catch us first," Levi said. "I reckon we're gonna have to let the soldier fend for himself until we thin out our enemy's numbers. He shouldn't have been out here anyway."

Their hearts hammered in their chest, making their knees tremble with the urge to flee. Now, they abandoned hiding. They raced holus-bolus for the safety of their camp, their arms pumping with their heads down and mouths sucking air as they ran a sprint. Hopefully, there would be more than twenty guns waiting. Up to thirty bloodthirsty warrior braves were chasing them and closing in fast. Despite their wild dash for safety, their pace was of scouts who knew what they were doing. Death was on their tails, and there was no room for mistakes.

The three scouts fled for their friends as the Shoshone warriors organized themselves. Hopefully, Joseph would have everybody prepared when they ran into camp. They would have the hostile warriors hot on their tracks. They closed in and saw rifle barrels lined along the hill. Just a little more, and they would be out of their sights. If the missionaries were spooked and shot now, all three would die.

WHEN THE THREE scouts ran past the defensive position made by Joseph, Reverend Smith sighted down his English-made Baker rifle. They were all waiting in formation. Rory Breaker stood beside him. He turned his head and cut a stream of tobacco in the sand. As the captain, Dahteste, and Levi fled, the Shoshone closed in behind them, paving a clean road to hell. Virgil's gun kicked hard as the buffalo gun found its mark and hit the Shoshone leading the charge. He was knocked back ten feet from the impact of the heavy buffalo round.

Brown squinted down his barrel. Despite being terrified, he aimed his rifle with quivering hands, his finger taking out the slack in the trigger. A split second later, twenty-six muskets fired simultaneously. Shoshone warrior braves dropped dead to the ground like bowling pins. Behind them came the second wave. Now, there was no time to reload.

There was a gasp followed by an air-sucking moan.

Rory was shot in the shoulder. Virgil kneeled beside the scout and aimed and pulled the trigger yet again. His heavy tobacco breath brushed against the outer cheeks of the Black man. Virgil turned his head, repelled by the smell of stale tobacco. He plugged the hole with bandages. It was a through-and-through, so no bones were broken. He would be as good as new in a few days. At least he would be if they survived the day. He would have to buck up to the pain and fight on. They couldn't spare the extra rifle and guns, especially with the cowboy's shooting skills.

The Shoshone warriors suddenly vanished just as quickly as they appeared. There seemed to be even more than they had suspected. But they retreated to some unknown location out of sight. Perhaps they had fought enough for one day. Would they return, or had they lost enough men in the first two waves to make them turn back? None of them were sure why they broke off the fight. It was anybody's guess if they would come back or not.

The missionaries had stood their ground with forced bravery and determination. They had helped win the day if it was indeed over. Then again, a man just never knew what was in the mind of an Indian warrior. It was a mystery to one and all. Even Dahteste said each warrior was unique and different in their own ways, and they all had deep secrets and ambitions. None of them were the same. They varied even more depending on their tribe.

"Where did they all go to?" Reverend Smith asked as he reloaded his rifle. His face glistened with sweat. Despite the advice and warnings, they continued wearing heavy frocks that hung to their knees. They still wasted water on things they shouldn't, but when the time came, they did their job without a hitch despite being scared to death, just like the scouts. Everybody but the captain seemed nervous. He was in some angry world he lived in when the violence struck.

Betty Crockett

The first day Betty laid eyes on the captain, she instantly got lost in his stare. Of course, he was the blond-haired, blue-eyed officer who came riding up on a magnificent black stallion to save her life. She should have sensed it then, but she thought her feelings were due to him coming to their rescue. She couldn't have been farther from the truth. Now, she knew she had hopelessly fallen in love with Captain Will Forrester from that moment.

She would lie awake at night, staring at the sky, wondering where he was. He made up his bedroll nightly but seldom slept in it. She stole glances at his blanket all through the night, hoping that he would be there this time. But often as not, it was already taken up when she awoke for breakfast, and he had vanished again. Sometimes, she didn't see him for days. At these times, she felt vulnerable and lonely. She wondered if he loved her too but didn't even realize it.

It suddenly dawned on her that if she wanted to have the captain as her husband, she would have to take the reins and fight for him. He was too wound up in his impossible mission to protect all his friends and those with them. He clearly had no fear of the outcome. He rode into battle like most people dove into a lake. He let it wash over him like water. The captain became one with the enemy and the violence. That was when he wreaked the wrath. Betty had seen him in action back at the Squirrel wagon train against the Indian attack.

It was he and his men who also finished the reign of terror the clan forced on the women. Those who weren't born into the family were often as not stolen from other families or bought and sold like so many horses. They all had to tolerate more than one wife in their husband's bed. It was more than Betty Crockett could take, and that was why she fought so hard that day to survive. Her emotions and adrenaline were at their highest possible level when he came to the rescue, and she became lost in those deep eyes.

When she finally heard the captain walking toward the campsite in the wee hours of the morning, she closed her eyes and feigned sleep. She listened as he lay his heavy rifle beside his bedroll and rested his head on his leather saddle. When she opened her eyes minutes later, he was already snoring softly. She pulled herself up, resting her elbows on his knees and her chin in her hands. She sat like that all night, watching and studying every inch of the man she loved.

Finally, she began to nod off, so she lay down and pulled her blanket to the bottom of her eyes. As they became heavy and began to close, she still stared at the man she yearned to love her back. She tried to stay awake, but in minutes, she was breathing softly and in a deep slumber.

The following morning, Virgil nudged her shoulder with his toe. She looked up into his kind eyes and blinked, then stretched into a yawn. She looked at the captain's sleeping spot, but the bedroll was gone, and there was no sign of Forrester. She felt a frown cross her face, so she checked herself and hid it.

"He got up an hour ago and disappeared again," Virgil said. He gave her a knowing smile. "You've done fallen in love with Will, ain't-cha?"

Betty's face blushed like a rose down to her neck. She asked, "Is it that visible?"

"Not really," Virgil replied as his grin grew. "Not unless you're lookin' for it. I reckon I've become so protective of the captain that I kept an eye on even you."

"Do the others know?" Betty asked nervously.

"Nah, that don't have a clue and cross my heart, it's our secret until you say otherwise," the buffalo hunter whispered like they were partners in a conspiracy.

"And as you're such a close friend, what do you think about that—you know, my being I love and all?" Betty asked.

"I believe it would do Will a world of good to find love," Virgil continued. "At the moment, he's the angriest man I know. Maybe a mature woman like you could settle him down. Neither one of you is a spring chicken. The captain's twenty-eight, just like Levi. Once he's thirty, it may well be too late, but I still think there's still some time to save him from himself."

"I'm thirty years old. Maybe I'm already too old for him." She frowned, and she bravely blinked a tear from her eye.

"What Will don't need is a young woman full of illusions. He needs a woman with her feet planted firmly on the ground. In my opinion, I say that you'd do just fine if you could get his attention. Heck, he may already be in love with ya and simply don't know it yet. But I wouldn't advise you to wait until it dawned on him. His attention span wanes when there's trouble, and I get the feeling we aren't out of the woods yet."

Betty helped Virgil make breakfast. The smell floated across the darkened plains. The morning air was still cool, so she pulled a blanket over her shoulders and used the hot refreshment to warm her hands.

They heard boot heels, and then a hazy figure emerged from the darkness. "Is that coffee made up yet, Virgil?"

"I was just fillin' your cup, Will," Virgil replied.

Levi, Rory, and Dahteste were already sitting around the fire. Each one held a steaming cup—they munched on biscuits with slices of bacon in between. A can of peaches made its way around as they each speared a half. The only place left to sit around the fire was next to Betty.

Have a seat, Will, Betty said as she patted the saddle blanket she sat on. There's only room here unless you don't want my company. She raised her eyebrows.

"Thank ya, ma'am," Will replied.

At first, he was stiff as he fidgeted with his cup. He stared into the dark liquid. A chill shot up his spine, and he involuntarily shivered.

Without a word, Betty used her blanket to cover his shoulders, too. She got an odd look of surprise from Levi and Dahteste. Will didn't budge, but his shoulders relaxed, and he sighed.

"Did you see any sign of trouble out there, Captain?"

Joseph asked. He stood behind Rory, using the toe of his boot to tap him on the back.

"I'm goin', boss," Rory Breaker said. He tossed the rest of his coffee into the fire, stood, and went with the sheriff to get the missionaries moving.

"Nah, everything seems quite enough tonight," the captain answered.

"Maybe we should get the horses ready," Virgil said. "Will you clean up for me here, Betty?"

Betty Crocked smiled and nodded. She gave a knowing look to her friend.

"Maybe you can come and help us, Levi," Lovejoy said. "Or didn't you like my breakfast?"

"Sure thing, pard," Johnson replied and rose to follow. Dahteste ran behind her husband. Suddenly, the captain and Betty were alone. They exchanged looks as she batted her eyes. She snuggled closer and pulled the blanket tighter.

"Isn't this nice and cozy?" Betty whispered. "I bet you don't even know I'm in love with you, do you?"

Will pulled his head back and looked her in the eyes. "I had no idea," he replied.

"That's all right." Betty laughed. "The men are always the last to know."

"No, that's not it," the captain replied. "I doubt I even know what love is. You see, I've never been in love or even close to it as far as I know."

This wasn't what Betty wanted to hear right then, but she persisted. She lay her head on his shoulder and sighed deeply. He didn't even know why, but he wrapped his arm around her, and she melted. It was just an intuition he had. It made her happy and, for some reason, made him feel good, too. Will smiled involuntarily, and Betty saw it out of the corner of her eye. It gave her a tingling feeling inside. She knew she had a long way to go, but there just might be something there. Perhaps the first kindling of Cupid's arrow. She smiled, too, and it reached her eyes.

"Maybe you can teach me what love is," Will said wistfully. "I doubt I have a clue."

This wasn't precisely what Betty wanted to hear, but just the same, it was music to her ears. All she wanted was the littlest sign of what might come to be.

"Maybe we do have a little chance, then don't we," Betty said. "I don't know if I can continue without you now that I've found you."

She hoped for him to fall in love with her just like she did with him, but she knew better. She was lucky to be snuggled up beside him. Tomorrow would be another day.

She didn't know it, but Betty's words burrowed deep into the captain's heart. He wondered what that strange feeling he had in his stomach and why what she said moved him so. His palms became damp, and his back was wet with sweat. It was so new to him that he had no idea what the feeling was.

Rivers Brothers

When Johnny went for his gun and swung it toward the bushes, a shot rang out. When he looked down, he saw a large bullet hole in the palm of his hand. He could see the ground through the wound. He opened his mouth to scream, but nothing came out. Finally, his vocal cords became unfrozen, and a scream screeched out that could be heard for a mile. Angus McFarlin had put a neat round through the center of his hand. His gun lay broken in the dirt.

The two mountain men followed gun barrels into the outlaws' camp. Their pistols were leveled at the leaders of the clan. One was jumping around like his hair was on fire as he held his damaged hand in his good one.

"You shot me, you fool!" Johnny screamed. "I'm gonna kill you for this."

"You best plug that wound with somethin', or you're gonna bleed to death before I get a chance to hang ya," Rusty said.

Neither brother reacted to what the grizzly frontiersman said, but the blood drained from the faces of the four gang members. They knew they were all going to die in the next minutes.

Jimmy growled like a wounded animal when he saw what the old mountain men had done to his brother. His eyes flashed red and were full of violence. He turned to Rusty Steel and snarled like a rabid dog.

"I'm gonna teach you a lesson, old man," Jimmy threatened. "I'm gonna kill you old fools with my bare hands. You have no idea who you've messed with."

In three steps, Rusty was in reach of the angry outlaw. Suddenly, Jimmy saw a fork in his hand, which he swiftly shoved into his right eye. A howl went up like a wounded banshee. He pawed and clawed the fork. He grasped for the piece of metal sticking out of his face. When he pulled it out, the eyeball came with it with a pop, and he howled in an even higher pitch. He was lost in his own world of pain. His gunshot brother stood glaring at the mountain men with pistols in their hands, but they seemed as calm as the day was long.

"I reckon we've got some hangin' to do," Rusty said. "You were gonna hang my friend there to find out where his gold was, weren't ya? Now I'm gonna do the same to you bunch."

Suddenly, Rusty heard a branch crack behind him. He spun around on his heels and shoved a pistol into the guard's belly. By then, Angus was behind him with another barrel poking into his back. The blood drained from the lookout's face. His eyes bounced about like marbles in a tin can, looking for a way to get out. He knew he should have stayed hidden. Now, he was caught like a rat with the rest of the gang.

"I should have known better," Rusty said. "They only

have five horses, so I figured there'd only be five men. One must have died or come up lame. I should have been more careful. It's a good thing they're a noisy bunch, or he would have got the drop on us."

"Either that or they stole the five horses they have," Angus said. "They look like they'll steal just about anything. Did you see that ball of hair? I bet they be Indian scalps."

"Stealin' horses is a hangin' offense, too, where I come from. Go cut the mountain man loose," Rusty told the man who was standing guard. Now, he was as white as a ghost.

Angus shoved his gun barrel in his back, pushing him forward. "And be careful what you do with that knife. My guns pointin' at your head."

Guy Grizzel coughed and spat as he pulled the noose from his neck and got up out of the dirt. He mouthed the words, "Hang these fools," but nothing came out. His face was almost purple, but he'd live, although he would have a hoarse voice for months to come.

"Bring that noose over here and that rope on the horse, too," Rusty said. "We'll hang 'em two at a time to speed things up. We don't have all day to mess around here. We only stopped to save you to morons' lives. How'd they catch two skilled men like you anyway?"

"We was drunk, is why," Gus huffed. "We planned to tie one on right after we sold our furs, so we traded at the Rocky Mountain Trading Company on the first day. That way, we could get drunk all week, pick up our cash on the last day, and head home the next as sober as a judge. But we got so drunk that when we woke up, we were still drunk when the time came around to leave.

And you know how Fred is when he gets a date in his head, so we left anyway. If we hadn't been inebriated, we'd have never been caught by a bunch of amateurs like these."

"There ain't a tree tall enough to hang 'em, Rusty," Angus said. "Then again, I reckon they already knew that when they tried to hang Gus. Are you all right, Fred?"

Fred Barns stiffly got to his feet. He had been tied for two days. It took a few minutes for the blood to begin to flow again. His face was a dark red, and he was as angry as hell.

"I heard those two braggin' about the killin' they've done, but I reckon the rest were just too stupid to leave," Fred said as he rubbed his wrists where the rope cut into his skin. "I doubt men that young would have had the time to do much killin'. The two bad men are the Rivers Brothers there. They're the leaders of the gang. I heard the other fools actin' all brave like around the campfire, but I just figure they were talking to try to impress the brothers. They ain't done nothin' I've seen to hang for."

"We're gonna hang you just like you planned to hang our friend Gus," Rusty said. He made a noose on one end of the rope and a slipknot on the other.

"Get two of those horses over here," Rusty growled. "I don't wanna waste any more time on these fools than we have to."

He quickly threw a loop over Jimmy's head because he was in another world. Now, he had one hand over his bleeding eye socket and was using his good eye to look for the fork. Maybe he believed he could stick it back in if he found it intact. He didn't even notice when Rusty tied the other end of the noose to the saddle horn. The horse shifted its feet nervously. The tension was high. The gang members were scared to death. They knew they were next. Rusty tied the ball of scalps to the lead horse for good measure so that if the Indians found them, they would know what they did.

Johnny didn't want to go so easily. He kicked and bit until Rusty used the barrel of his pistol to thump him in the temple, and he went down like a rock. He wasn't unconscious but dazed enough for Rusty to get the rope around his neck and tied it to the other horse. Angus shot a round off into the air before anybody could protest or work their way loose. One horse bolted like wolves were after it. Jimmy was jerked clean off his feet as the horse thundered forward. He bounded down the trail for a few hundred yards before his head popped right off. It bounced down the trail like it was chasing after its body. It finally came to a stop with the dead eyes staring into the sun.

Johnny began to shake his head and resist. Rusty used the side of his rifle to slap the other horse's rump, and he, too, shot off like a bullet. The horse raced with the outlaw, flip-flopping and bouncing down the trail until they disappeared over a rise in the land. The elder brother's head didn't come off. Eventually, the tired horse stopped. Behind it was a battered, broken body full of cuts and scratches. A large dent could be seen in his skull just before his eyes crawled back into his head.

When they turned to the four remaining outlaws, their eyes bulged, and their hearts thundered between their ears. They had carefully watched as Jimmy's head popped off and rolled down the mountain. It seemed never to stop until it tumbled out of sight.

"Now, what are we gonna do with these four morons?" Rusty asked. "We've only got three horses left."

"I reckon we can string two of 'em to the same saddle," Angus replied. "I ain't never seen it done, but I don't see why it wouldn't work."

"I didn't see them kill anybody, and I think the brothers took the scalps," Gus said. "I heard 'em talkin' around the campfire of a night about how they killed women and children for their hair. They were gonna kill us too, but we wouldn't tell 'em where we hid the gold. If they weren't so stupid, they would have found it."

The four outlaws looked at the mountain man with questioning eyes. They blinked in unison with frowns on their faces. All four seemed puzzled. They had searched the mountain men themselves and hadn't found any gold.

"That's right, stupid," Gus spat. "Your two bosses never thought to look inside our books. One's a Bible, and the other's the Words of Webster. I doubt even one of y'all knows how to read. We hollowed 'em both out to stash the coins in."

Gus went over to their things scattered on the ground. Near a rock was the sack with the two books inside. He pulled them out, and sure enough, both had a hole cut into the center about halfway through the pages. Inside that were the gold coins.

"You best get the other three horses over here. We'll have to tie the two to the same horse. I hope you're right, Angus. I hate to mess up a hangin'. It ain't usually a pretty sight."

"I don't think these boys deserve such harsh treatment," Fred Barns said. "I didn't hear 'em say they killed or scalped anybody."

"Well, if we ain't gonna hang 'em, what are we gonna do with 'em?" Rusty asked. "It's your call, boys. They were gonna kill you two when they were done."

"I know, but still, I don't think they should hang Texan style," Gus said. "It was enough seein' Jimmy's head pull off. I don't wanna see that again."

"How about if we take their guns, horses, and boots," Rusty said. "I don't want 'em followin' us trying to steal the gold all over again. At least they won't be goin' anywhere fast."

"Why, you can't run us off into the desert with no boots on or a single gun," the guard said. "What will we do if a bear comes after us and we're unarmed? We can't be expected to walk on the hot trail. It'll burn our feet."

"You should have thought of that before you tied my friends up and tried to hang one," Rusty spat. "I'm gonna be nice and give y'all some water. That way, you can't say I didn't give y'all a chance."

Finally, the men's boots were all in the fire. They had added a handful of buffalo chips to make it burn hotter. Soon, leather boots slowly burned and melted. Angus and Fred collected their guns and horses. The men stood before the mountain men, scared senseless.

"Well, whatcha waitin' on, you bunch of morons?" Rusty said. He pulled his pistols, aimed at the dirt before the outlaws, and fired off a round. As soon as the bullet hit the dirt, kicking up gravel, they turned and ran. Despite the thorns and stickers, they raced for their lives as Rusty Steel ran behind them, yelling a Crow war cry with a pistol in each hand. Soon, four tiny dots disappeared on the horizon.

"I hate to let such men get away," Rusty said. "If they are killers and they murder again, it'll be our fault. But y'all felt sorry for 'em. We'll have to wait to see how that pans out, won't we."

"What are we gonna do with the horses?" Gus asked.

"I reckon you earned 'em when they put that noose around your neck," Rusty replied. "That mark on your throat is gonna there be for life. At least you'll get paid two horses for your bother. Get your thing together so we can get out of here. I'd imagine there be more of the same out there with all the trappers trying to make it home with their earnings."

Gypsies

The following day, the four mountain men raced for the foothills. Gus and Fred struggled to keep up. They were fast travelers and longtime frontiersmen, but few could keep up the pace that the famous men from the three cabins in the compound high in the Rockies. They trotted through the day until the sun was over head bearing down on the men with oppressive heat. Still, they continued, and the blistering sun didn't seem to slow them down at all. Sweat glistened on their faces, and their buckskin shirts stuck to their backs as they rushed down gullies and arroyos in an attempt to stay out of sight.

Around noon, in the distance, they saw two dust clouds. Rusty and Angus exchanged looks, and they clutched at their rifles with white-knuckled fists and slowed down. Gus and Fred followed suite. The metal sound of hammers clicked. Even though they slowed down their pace, they still moved swiftly. They had to go faster than whoever was out there in front of them.

They could only suspect it would be more of the same —it probably meant more trouble.

When they got close enough for them to see they were wagons, Rusty pulled out his spyglass. As he focused in on the wavering image, it suddenly became sharp. It looked so close he felt he could reach out and touch it.

"Gypsies," Rusty whispered.

"What?" Fred asked.

"Gypsies like there were at the Rendezvous," Rusty said. He read the sign on the top of the side. "It says, Fortune Teller."

"I saw a tent that said the same thing back at the meet," Fred said. "I wonder if they're related."

"No wonder you got robbed." Rusty chuckled. "You're thick as mud, Fred. They're the same Gypsies as were at the meet. What would other folks from Romania be doin' out here?"

When they got close enough to have a good look, the wagons had the sides intricately painted with shades of green leaves and colorful flowers. Painted pink birds with long legs and necks stood in the background. It had four wheels that angled out at the top. The front two were to steer. Intricate carvings surrounded the door at the back. A set of steps on hinges were pulled up for travel. The large wheels were set outside the body, and the sides sloped outward considerably as they rose to the eaves. The roof had a bow-top and canvas stretched tight over the curved wooden frames. A tin pipe from a potbellied stove protruded from the side with a bend like an elbow.

When they nearly reached the wagons at a trot, they both suddenly pulled up, and a blond-haired man dropped down from the spring-loaded bench seat of the trailing wagon. He looked like a Viking. It was not what they expected to see in a small Gypsy caravan. He smiled and walked toward the grizzly-looking frontiersmen without hesitation, proffering his hand.

"Howdy, gentlemen. My name is Tor Solberg from Norway."

"Ain't you a little too white to be a Gypsy?" Rusty asked.

"My wife is a Gypsy," Tor replied. "I married into the clan."

A dark-faced man dropped down from the first wagon but didn't speak a word. His black hair and sharp feathers included a large, hooked nose. He had a three-day growth of beard and wore a colorful shirt and britches but was barefoot like the Scandinavian. The handle of a large knife protruded from a sheath on his belt, but no guns were visible. The men let down their defenses and uncocked the long guns' hammers. They knew they would be there, although they didn't see any guns. Nobody traveled this country unarmed.

"That's my father-in-law, Luca." Tor smiled. "His three daughters travel with us. One is my wife. You might have seen us back at the fur meet. We were there telling fortunes."

"You claim you can tell fortunes?" Angus asked suspiciously.

"Oh no, not me," Tor replied. "You have to be born with the gift. It's not something you can learn. Esmeralda is the one who tells fortunes. She's sort of the leader of the clan."

As if on cue, the wagon door opened. A dark-featured woman pulled a rope, and the steps dropped to the ground. She stood for a moment in the safety of the shadows. When she stepped down, and they saw her face, they were mesmerized. The men could be heard taking a deep breath. Her beauty was something they had never seen before. Maybe it was because she was so exotic.

Her skin was the color of olive oil, and her eyes were as green as a cat's. She blinked long eyelashes as a sensuous mouth formed curls at the edges. Her hair was so black it appeared to have a blue tint and hung to her waist. Her bare feet stepped down the ladder into the dust as she closed the distance between her and the rugged men.

"Welcome, gentlemen. I am Esmeralda. Papá, we will have lunch here, so you and Tor make camp."

As if by magic, a tarp was unwound from the roof of the second wagon in a matter of minutes, and a carpet was laid out to sit on. Fluffy pillows were placed around the rug. In minutes, the smell of fresh, perking coffee and the exotic aroma of tea filled the air.

They sat around in the shade sipping their coffees while Esmeralda and her family drank Romano Cajo or Gypsy tea with lots of sugar. The smell of some exotic incense floated through the air. The foreigners didn't seem to be in a hurry. They all silently enjoyed their refreshments. When their cups were empty, the charming woman looked deeply into each mountain man's eyes as if she was silently challenging them.

"Have you gentlemen ever had your fortune read?" Esmeralda asked. "What could be more exciting than having a peek into what is to come? All you have to do is lay your hand in mine, and I will read the lines."

All four men were mesmerized, even Rusty. Not at

the prospect of having their fortune told but more of having such a beautiful lady hold their hands. Steel didn't believe in fortune readers, and Angus had his doubts but still wanted to touch the beautiful lady.

"The sign on the side of the wagon says it costs ten bucks," Gus said. "I can afford ten dollars to hear you tell me what's in my future. Why, it's a bargain. Whatcha say, Fred? So far, all we've wasted our money on has been whiskey. Maybe we can spend some money for some good for a change."

Rusty frowned at his friend and gave him a look like he was calling him stupid. Some people wanted to believe in every superstition they ran across. But not Mister Steel. Still, he grinned as he watched his fellow mountaineers play along.

"Yeah, the good of your ten bucks into her pocket." Rusty chuckled. "Now, don't get me wrong. I think they can spend their money any way they want. It's just that I don't believe in fortune tellin'. That's my personal opinion, and I don't intend to insult anybody."

"You have every right to be suspicious," Esmeralda replied, smiling. "Especially for so much money. Why don't you just watch and see of you don't have a change of heart? I'm sure you'll find it interesting."

Fred pushed his way to the pillow in front of the fortune teller. She sat cross-legged and rested her guest's hand on the cushion as she studied his palm. She used a long red fingernail to trace the lifeline to the end. The trapper was so happy to have her holding his hand he didn't even hear what she said.

"You have a long future before you, and I see a woman somewhere in there, too," Esmeralda said. "Perhaps a friend or even a wife. You will live to be a wise old man."

"You don't know Fred like we do." Rusty laughed. "There ain't a thing wise about the man."

The Gypsy lady ignored the intrusion. She seemed very focused on her job. Still, none of the men really believed she could tell them what was to come. Maybe Fred, but nobody else. Gus pushed his partner aside and opened his massive hand. Esmeralda fingered an emerald stone she wore on a golden necklace. The lady took his hand and smiled.

There was something about the way she moved, and what she didn't say was what made her so alluring. They all sat leaning forward so they didn't miss a movement or a word of said. Even Rusty was giving in to the urge to have her hold his hand. He and Angus both could afford ten dollars. Still, Rusty refused for some reason.

When Gus and Angus were done, Esmeralda again turned her eyes to the trapper, who didn't want to know his fortune. Or was it the ten dollars that held him back? Of course, just like Rusty suspected, their futures were full of long lives and good fortune. He knew better for the men living in the wilderness. Death could come knocking on your door at any moment.

"If you're that danged stingy, I'll pay for your fortune." Gus laughed. "You did save our skins, so I reckon we owe ya."

Gus handed Tor the money. The lady never touched their cash. She only touched their hands and read their palms. Her father and Tor were in charge of everything else. She was apparently the one in the family with the supposed gift. Finally, Rusty gave in and sat before the gorgeous woman with the green eyes. She smiled and took his hand.

The emerald on her neck sparkled green in the aging man's eyes. Her touch felt softer than any he had felt before. She peered deep into his eyes and smiled. It relaxed the rough old trapper. Maybe it would be more fun than he thought. She sure was a beautiful woman.

When she turned Rusty's hand palm up, the fortune teller froze. She squeezed his fingers so hard they hurt. Her fingernail dug into the line that started at the bottom of his palm. There was a big gap in the middle. It was a bad sign she hadn't seen before.

Suddenly, she dropped his hand like it was poison and stood. She looked down at Rusty, but he couldn't read her thoughts from her expressionless face. She turned and walked away with a trail of dust in her wake. Before she stepped onto the stairs, she clapped her hands twice; then she disappeared as quickly as she had appeared. It was the same with the campsite.

It vanished even quicker than it was assembled, and in minutes, the men were on the wagon seats with the reins in their hands as they pulled away. They seemed in such a rush that nobody even said goodbye. Dust cork-screwed behind the wagon as they disappeared into the afternoon.

"What in the world was all that about?" Angus asked. "What was she on about, Rusty? She looked mighty upset when she laid her eyes on your hand."

Steel scratched his head with a puzzled look on his face. "I reckon you shouldn't have had to pay the money, Fred. Whatever she saw, she didn't seem to like."

"Maybe your fortune is too bad to tell ya, pard," Fred

said. "It was a waste of money since she didn't tell ya nothin'."

"Ya think?" Angus asked. "They ran away like scalded dogs. She must have seen somethin' mighty bad to react like that. Maybe she wasn't all talk and no hat. I figure she told us plenty in the way she acted. There weren't no need for words."

"Don't be foolish," Rusty said. "You know I don't put no stock in such foolishness." But despite his bravado, his voice didn't sound as convincing as usual. The statement sounded hollow and more like a question.

The Outlaws

Rusty had felt eyes on them all afternoon. He didn't have a doubt in his mind that somebody was out there watching. He tapped Angus on the shoulder. They both suddenly vanished into either side of the bushes. It happened so quickly that Gus and Fred didn't even see them disappear. They kept walking without even noticing their two friends weren't behind them. Several minutes later, Fred looked back to speak, but their companions were gone. A worried look crossed his face. Then again, Rusty and Angus often made themselves hard to see, but why now?

Rusty and Angus backtracked around whoever was following. They quickly got behind them and slowed down to see what they were up to. The tracks they found were bare feet, so they would be Indians, although they didn't go to the standard trouble of hiding their tracks. There were footprints all over the place. There were four men in all. Rusty and Angus pulled their pistols but didn't draw the hammers back. Hostile natives could hear the metallic click of guns.

They crawled into the bushes on the intruders' flanks as they continued to follow Gus and Fred. They were totally surprised when they saw four White men. They were the same thieves they let free after giving their bosses Texan hangings. Rusty had been against letting them go but folded to his friends' desires. Now, they saw it had been a mistake.

"Where did them fools get guns?" Angus whispered in Rusty's ear. "When we sent 'em packin', they didn't have nothin'. Now they got four horses trailing behind, and they've got rifles and pistols. But they're still barefoot. I don't understand."

The mountain men locked eyes as Rusty frowned. He nodded his head, and they pulled back the hammers. Four metal clicks seemed so loud they couldn't help but be heard by the outlaws, but they were such amateurs they never noticed the warning. All their attention was on the men before them with the gold.

It appeared when the mountain men friends of Rusty Steel disclosed where they had their gold; it made the remaining thieves crazy enough to take another chance after the deaths of their two gang leaders. They obviously weren't the smartest outlaws on the Great Plains. The Rivers Brothers were the brains of the outfit, and neither one of them could fight their way out of a paper bag.

Rusty and Angus stood and closed in on the sneaky fools.

"Drop them guns and get down on the ground," Rusty yelled as he waived his pistols in the faces of the surprised outlaws. They blinked in wonder. How did the two old cobs get behind them and get the drop on them so quickly?

Rifles and pistols dropped to the dirt in puffs of dust, and the men dropped to their knees.

"Hands behind your head, sparky," Rusty spat. "I reckon you didn't learn your lesson the first time. This time, I'm gonna make sure you never steal again."

Rusty put his fingers to his lips and whistled a shrill note advising Gus and Fred to stop and come running. Not two minutes later, they rushed into the clearing with a pistol in each hand. Now, eight flintlock guns were pointing at the supposed thieves.

"So, where did y'all steal the horses and guns?" Rusty asked. "You'd have thought you would have stolen their boots too. I almost thought you were a bunch of Indians, but you fools were too sloppy in your travels, so I was wonderin' why Shoshone would be so reckless."

"Hay, you're the sneaky one," Angus growled. "That's right, I'm talkin' to you, the one that was out on guard and nearly got the drop on us. Your problem is you're as noisy as a bull in a china shop. What's that shiny stone you've got hangin' around your neck?" He looked over at Rusty Steel.

Rusty took two steps to the man and put his pistol to his temple as he grabbed the emerald and gold necklace in his fist and yanked it off the highwayman.

"So, you got all this from the Gypsies, did ya?" Steel asked as he pushed the barrel into the side of his head, making an indentation in the soft skin of his face.

When the old mountain man pulled the trigger in one whoosh, the night guard's brains spewed out his head and all over the bandit kneeling beside him. He immediately hurled his lunch and began to cry.

"And here I though Fred and Gus said you boys weren't killers," Angus said. "You killed that pretty woman and her kin too, didn't cha? I told you two they would kill again, didn't I? Now you've got that on your conscience. Did y'all rape the women too?"

Nobody dared look into Rusty's eyes. They were blazing with fire and were full of restitution. They all knew they would hang, but nobody wanted to be first.

"I thought that big Sweed would be a hard man to kill, not to mention the old fella with dark skin," Gus said. "I saw that big knife he carried."

Fred's chin sat on his chest, and his mouth hung wide open. "They both looked dangerous enough to take you fools."

"Look around ya, boys." Rusty smiled. "This time, I've loads of solid trees, and we've even got plenty of rope. We can make short work out of y'all this time. And there ain't a danged thing you can say to change our minds. Just ask mister dead-and-gone here lying beside ya with no brains."

The dead man lay on the ground, staring sightlessly at the blue sky. His friend continued to cry as he scooped a gob of gray brain matter from his face. He was at the point of hysterics. The other two looked on with hang dog faces. They knew they had run their course. It was a short leap from the outlaw life to a noose, and although they had avoided with lies and tales now, their time had come, and they knew they were doomed to swing.

Gus and Fred busied themselves, making nooses. As the completed each one, they slipped it over the neck of one of the outlaws. When they felt the rough and scratchy hemp rope around their necks, they knew they were seconds away from paying for their sins.

"I never intended to kill those folks," the youngest

outlaw cried. He wasn't much over sixteen. "We caught 'em asleep like they didn't have a worry in the world. We wanted to steal what they had and sneak off into the night, but the big blond fella woke up, and we had to club 'im to death with sticks. I admit we stole their guns and horses, but they didn't have no shoes. My feet are so swollen up I can hardly walk."

"And what did you do to the three women?" Rusty spat.

"Leroy and Billy raped the pretty one, and we took turns on her sisters. We had to kill 'em too, our they could have talked if they got to the law."

"Where you're goin', you won't need no shoes 'cause you won't be walking; you'll be swingin' from a tree," Rusty growled. "Get 'em on the Gypsies' horses, and let's get this over with. I don't want 'em to start to cry on us. I prefer swift justice once I've decided what they deserve. You lot sure are a lazy bunch to make a career as thieves and murders. I knew I should have hung you four when my friends wanted to let you free. That cost those Gypsy folks their lives." He stared hard at Fred and Gus. They cringed at their friend's comment and stern glare.

In minutes, all three of the living were sitting on horses. Gus hung the guard with no brains alongside his three sidekicks for good measure. When they were done, Rusty pulled out a parchment, scribbled a note, and then pinned it to the lookout's chest.

It said, WOMAN KILLERS, RAPIST AND THIEVES. CAUGHT AND HUNG BY RUSTY STEEL. "Maybe that'll give pause to the next villains that come after us."

Soon, rifles slapped against horses' rumps, and they bolted off and left the riders horseless as the swung from ropes on the same thick limb of an oak tree. In the following silence, the only sound was the hemp grinding against the bark. The last of the Rivers Brothers Gans were dead.

Rusty looked at the necklace in the palm of his hand. He couldn't help but wonder what Esmeralda saw in his palm that day when she read his fortune. Maybe what she saw was her future instead. Maybe that was why they ran off like they did. Five more lives were lost to the wilderness and the wicked men who traveled it.

ARMY STRAGGLERS

FOUR MEN WAVERED IN THE DISTANCE. LEVI AND Dahteste sat in a blind taking turns looking through the spyglass. The strangers seemed to stagger and stumble as they moved forward. They were on a heading that would cross their paths.

"They look like soldiers," Dahteste said. "What in the world could they be doing out here all alone?"

"They must be from the other soldiers we found dead," Levi replied. "The last boy we found died before we could save him. That makes three, and four more make a patrol. Still, I have no idea what a small unit of men is doing all the way out here on the South Pass. This is Indian territory. Seven men are shooting ducks for a group of Shoshone warriors."

"Shooting ducks?" Dahteste asked.

"It's an expression. It means easy to shoot."

The Crow war chief nodded and smiled. "I like that expression, but what will we do with the soldiers?"

"Will won't let us leave 'em out here. I'm surprised he hasn't shown up yet.

"Where is the captain?" Dahteste asked.

"Your guess is as good as mine, but I knew he'll be out there close by waitin' for more trouble. That's just how the captain is."

When he appeared, he startled both Levi and his wife. One minute, they were sitting there alone, and the next, Forrester was kneeling behind them with a worried look on his face.

"Is that the rest of the patrol out there?" the captain asked. "We better ride out there and save them before they join their friends. There is no need to mention how the man burned to death. If they were friends, they wouldn't take it kindly."

He ran back to his horse, swung astride, wheeled it toward the men, and nudged his flanks. The stallion burst forward. Levi and Dahteste rushed to keep up. By the time they were near the soldiers, they were all three together. When the Army men saw the Crow Indian woman, it made them pause. They reached for their guns.

"Don't be alarmed," the captain said. "The Crow Indian is our scout. Who are you four, and what in the world are you doing wandering around in such a dangerous country?"

"I'm Lieutenant Brad Holster out of Fort Leavenworth, Kansas. These are my two privates and my corporal. We were sent on a rescue party to find an expedition. But we haven't had any luck. As a matter of fact, we've had three men disappear at night and have no idea what happened to them. It's a mystery, is what it is."

"We found your sergeant and two more privates," the captain said sadly. "They were all three dead, I'm afraid. Shoshone Indians probably killed them. We've already run into a large war party and had to fight them off."

"But we haven't seen a single Indian on our entire trip," Lieutenant Holster said.

"Yeah, but I'd say they've been watching you ever since you arrived on the plains," Will replied. "There isn't much that escapes the local natives unless you're smarter than them at being sneaky."

"Your men were probably captured when they went out to do their personals at night," Levi said. "That's when the hostiles find us easiest prey when we're most vulnerable. It's a common practice for most of the Plains Indians. They even catch Indians from other tribes like that."

"I hope they didn't suffer," Holster said. "Do you know how they died?"

"I wouldn't say it was too pleasant, but hearin' all the gory details won't do any of you any good, son," the captain said. "All three are dead, though, so God rest their souls."

The blood drained from the four soldiers' faces. They suspected they were dead but didn't know if wild animals or Indians snatched them up. They hadn't seen either so far. Now, the man in front of them was telling them they were gone.

That was when the lieutenant noticed that the man before him was a soldier too. He wore black Army-issue boots and blue pants with stripes down the legs. A US Cavalry hat slapped up on the side and said he was an officer. The saber on his belt told the lieutenant he was a captain.

"Attention!" Holster suddenly shouted. His men wearily came to attention.

"At ease, men." The captain smiled. "Formalities aren't necessary out here."

"Tell me what you were doing out here again," Levi said. "I didn't quite catch what you said."

"We're looking for an expedition that disappeared about eighteen months ago. They left Fort Scott, not far from Fort Leavenworth, to search for places to build new forts. There was a captain, a famous geologist, and a scientist. They were to help select solid ground with good cover to build small Army forts to protect the coming overlanders. They all disappeared without a trace, and we never heard anything about what happened to the expedition. Not even a rumor got back to the fort. I was sent to find the bodies or the graves if they were locatable. So far, we haven't found a trace."

Will Forrester listened to what the lieutenant said, silently wheeled his horse around, and trotted off without a word. The soldiers' eyes curiously followed the captain on the black horse.

"You must forgive the captain. He's been through a lot out here fighting the hostile Indians." Levi knew who they were, too, but he wouldn't betray his best friend. If Will wanted them to know who he was, he could tell them himself. None of his friends would betray his secret. Levi was part of the expedition, too. He sat nervously in his saddle before the soldiers on foot.

"We better get you men fed and rested," Levi said. "You look like you're on your last legs." He exchanged looks with Dahteste. She nodded and rode back to the travelers to warn Vigil and Joseph. They both knew what happened too, but they wouldn't talk if warned in time.

Rainfall

Rain drizzled in the morning dawn. They rode in single file, drenched to the skin. The travelers huddled their chins into the folds of their collars under ponchos, but still, the rain got in.

"It is good to travel when it's raining." Dahteste smiled as she let the water wash the dust from her face. "It washes away our sign, so we are more difficult to follow."

The Crow woman didn't shun the shower. She turned her face toward the clouds, closed her eyes, and smiled. The missionary's heads were down, shoulders bunched, shielding their faces from the peppering raindrops with their floppy black hats.

The sky turned a dismal gray—it was dark and depressing. The semi-desert surroundings were in vivid contrast to what the missionaries were used to seeing back East. Garish yellow lay below the steady climb, making the hill look bleak, never-ending, and even ghastly. Dust turned to mud; covered mesquite stretched as far as the eye could see. The sun disappeared behind cloud cover, and suddenly, a penetrating chill crossed the plains.

Then, finally, they were at the summit, and they began to go downhill after days of climbing the never-ending grade. Water ran along the arroyos, making small rivers across the stretch of the mountain. Gravity took the water down the hill and into the valley below as the streams grew.

Joseph's gaze dropped to his horse's hooves as he spat a stream of juice into the mud. He studied the gradual slope before him. Now, the climb was behind them, and the rain cooled the day. Dust and dirt ran off the horses' heads and necks as hooves splashed in puddles.

The captain used his knuckle along the bottom of his blond mustache to brush the water off. He still hadn't given the soldiers the time to discuss who they were looking for. None of his friends said a word. Betty didn't even know. Only Levi knew every painful piece of the story. Maybe they were the only ones left alive from the entire project.

It wasn't that long ago when Captain Will Forrester set out on an expedition from Fort Scott, Kansas, just 117 miles from Fort Leavenworth. He went with Levi Johnson as his Army scout. Eighteen months ago, he had been assigned to escort scientists and a famous geologist, and the captain was to locate new locations for Army forts farther west. A small detachment was attached to his orders. Forrester studied mapmaking and geography at West Point back in New York from where he came. He graduated with honors and was expected to be a formidable officer like his family before him.

Still, when two Comanche war parties attacked their expedition, most members, including a famous geologist and scientist, were killed and scalped. Sometime after that, the captain lost his arm. Something he refused to accept till that very day. He chose to ignore it instead. That was one of the reasons he rode off to fight ahead of all the rest. He held some profound dark violence that, when unleashed, wreaked havoc on all those in his way. How did he explain all this to Lieutenant Brad Holster and the few men he had left? How would he explain it to Betty?

Will wondered what happened to the few men who had survived, and he sent back to deliver his resignation. That was when he side-kicked up with Levi Johnson, and they headed for their first Rendezvous, eventually meeting Rusty Steel, and climbing the Rocky Mountains. They began their journey to become mountain men together. The presence of the soldiers was the last thing he expected for his future, which was something he apparently had no control over.

It appeared the soldiers he had sent back with his order, too, abandoned their objectives or maybe even perished the same way the rest of the expedition had—at the hands of hostile Indians.

The captain didn't know where to start. He hadn't even asked who invited them to ride along with the missionaries. Hopefully, they would be on their way before he confronted the inevitable. The rain helped put off their attempts to communicate. The soldiers were also wary of his rank. They figured him for more than just an ordinary captain. It was obvious he had skills and a superior education. You could hear it in his form of speech.

If the lieutenant only knew he had accidentally found the very man, they were searching for. He was surprised they hadn't suspected it, but the lieutenant acted like he believed all the expedition's members to be dead and in their graves. That just showed you how little he knew about his present environment. Most men didn't receive the luxury of a decent burial in the wilderness. The vast majority were left for the coyotes and vultures. Only the bones remained to bleach in the sun.

It gnawed at Forrester's belly all night. The revulsion of a bitter urge rose inside. It was something he couldn't push aside or fight back by grinding his teeth. It was the bitter taste of defeat. The same taste he had when the Comanche killed the men in his charge.

Levi pulled his horse up shoulder-to-shoulder with the captain's stallion. The black horse bucked and snorted. He didn't want the company. The massive fourteen-hundred-pound Mustang dwarfed him.

The captain looked at Levi funny and whispered, "Sometimes I envy the finality of death—its certainty. I have to push the thoughts from my mind lest I lose my way. I've felt lost at sea since I fell and busted my head."

"I know, but sometimes you haunt me, Will," Levi replied. Lines bunched at his brow, and concern filled his eyes.

"You're all jammed up with anger," Virgil said. "Until you rid yourself of all that aggression penned up inside, you won't be free from your demons."

"I never thought of myself as an angry man," Will replied.

"You're the angriest man I've ever known," Virgil huffed. A sad look befell the captain. "And maybe the most honest too. Your problem is the cross you bear is just too big."

"I didn't know I bore a cross!" Will replied, surprised.

"We all have some sort of cross to bear, my friend," Virgil replied. There was a deep wisdom in his eyes. "Everybody has problems, and this ain't a perfect world. There are lots of rocks and stones in the way to make it bumpy. You have to believe that before you'll stop trying to right every wrong."

"What am I to do with the soldiers?" Will asked. His eyes looked tired. "Brad Holster won't wait forever. Who invited them to ride along anyway?"

"I was the one who told them they should ride with us, or they would probably perish," Virgil said. It was apparent it pained him to say. "We couldn't leave them out there alone. They looked like they were on their last legs as it is. They've already lost three men on their wild goose chase. I figure the lieutenant is too tired and confused to put the puzzle together, but it's only a question of time."

"How you wanna handle this, Will?" Levi asked. "I'll do whatever you want. We can shun 'em and not tell 'em nothin' if ya wanna. Remember, I was there with ya from the beginning. There's no way we can explain what happened, so they'll understand. It's that or hit it head-on like you do with most things. I don't know what you're worried about. I saw you send your resignation in, and I'll testify to it if I must. Even if we have to go back to Kansas to settle things."

"Why would you ever go back to Kansas?" Will asked. "You have a life here."

"Uh-huh." Levi smiled. "But I never got paid. I figure

the Army still owes me my wages. You know you can't shake me. We're in this all the way, just like the day we started our wild adventure. I reckon we'll see it to the end together, too. And I ain't askin' ya 'cause it ain't up to you to decide."

Joseph rode with the soldiers. He was keeping his ears sharp to hear any comments about the captain. The lieutenant and his men seemed too tired to think and didn't talk much either. They were listless and so weary they tilted in their saddles, rocking themselves to sleep. Betty Crockett rode beside the sheriff. She knew something was cooking the way the old friends rode off talking among themselves. She noticed the change in Will's face, too. It was more drawn and tense. She inconspicuously stole a glance at the three.

Lightning cracked across the prairie as the rain slanted with the wind and descended in torrents. Their visibility was reduced to a hundred yards. Beyond that lay a blanket of water spilling from the heavens. The angry sky roared with thunder. Giant black clouds gathered as one and nearly blocked out the light. The temperatures continued to drop.

The soldiers were so tired they began to shiver. Their defenses were bottomed out, making the going difficult for already worn-out men. The missionaries continued despite the discomfort. After the fight with the Shoshone, Pastor Smith had become a good leader, and they followed his rules and instructions from Brown down. Of course, his were relayed from Sheriff Walker. There could only be one head of such a group of travelers, and Joseph had claimed that position and had proven he was worthy.

Walker had organized the journey from Montana

and would see it through to Oregon City or bust. But the sheriff lived for challenges. He had been a trapper, buffalo hunter, Indian fighter, and sheriff, so he had skills enough to be a leader in such an unforgiving land. With the combined forces excluding the weary soldiers, they presented a serious threat. The problem was whether the local Indians realized it before it was too late. That remained to be seen.

Levi and Dahteste disappeared for long spells. Long enough to make the sheriff worry, but they always returned. With his Crow wife at his side, he went on lengthy jogs out ahead to ensure they were unaccompanied, and the trail was safe. When the rain began to pour, they headed back to Joseph and the others. A man could easily get lost or turned around with such low visibility. They could walk two hundred yards to their flanks and miss each other altogether.

Joseph led the line of riders down the now slippery trail. Nobody was in a hurry, but Joseph knew all he had to do was keep his bearings and go downhill. Despite the weather, he hunkered down and carried on. Rain ran off his Texan-style hat like a drainpipe. Any variation in angle would let him know he was going the wrong way. The captain rode just far enough out front so they could see his silhouette. His horse sidestepped and snorted as they lumbered their way down the never-ending grade.

Sometimes, the lightning lit up the prairie, and they could see him out there alone. Some of the horses spooked and nearly threw their riders. Captain Forrester seemed to be arguing with or shouting at the weather. Up close, his eyes were rivered by tiny red lines, but behind that was the fire that burned in the man so hot it was nearly all-consuming. At the same time, he had a nobility that nobody could deny. It flowed out of him like waves of heat.

The next time the lightning lit the plains, a dozen painted faces looked back from three hundred yards away. The rain had all but stopped as everybody froze. It appeared that the travelers and the Shoshone had inadvertently run into each other or maybe they were waiting for them to seek revenge for the braves they killed. The clouds began to part, and the sun once again began to shine in isolated rays of light.

As soon as they caught sight of the warriors, their insides turned to jelly. They could hear the insects talk. Sweat and water glistened on their faces. Only the missionaries were oblivious to what could happen. They looked on with almost curious faces, just relieved that the rain had stopped.

Other than the few Blackfeet that tried to starve them out when the sheriff was at the Rendezvous, they hadn't seen anything like the stories they read in the nickel novels from back East. Even when the Shoshone struck only the scout Rory Breaker was winged in the shoulder. It had all seemed almost too easy.

Now they had seen the war paint up close, and they were all as scared as they had ever been. Red, yellow, and white slashes covered the braves' cheeks and foreheads. Their horses were painted, but the rain had made the dye run down, staining their legs.

Suddenly, the captain wheeled his horse around and gigged its flanks, lunging down the trail to intercept the possible threat. Nervous riders spooked the horses loaned to the soldiers. They could sense the human's fear. The lieutenant had lost three men to hostile Indians, but they had yet to come face-to-face.

The Shoshone reined in as the White soldier turned the black horse sideways on the trail, blocking their way. He used the inside of his arm to feel the gun hidden under his coat. Wild, fiery eyes flashed at the unexpected visitors.

"Maybe they're peaceful," Reverend Brown whispered behind the sheriff and Betty.

"That paint they're wearin' on their faces ain't for the county fair," Joseph replied. "Them's fightin' colors is what they are."

The sheriff pulled a half-chewed tobacco plug from his pocket and popped it into his mouth. The quid bulged in his cheek. The sheriff leaned over and spat into the dirt. Spit splatter stain covered the right hove of his horse. Suddenly, they were all so rattled that the earth beneath their feet felt as if it was gone. A dozen more painted faces appeared on their other flank. They were set up for a crossfire. Joseph shifted the chew to his other cheek.

When the Army men saw the captain in the light, they prayed to God the seasoned officer wasn't a glory seeker. Their eyes were ever watchful as they were glued to the captain and the Shoshone warriors beyond. The sergeant wore red suspenders crisscrossed over his faded long-john underwear with no shirt. An Indian had snuck into the camp late at night and stole it without being detected. This left them puzzled and scared of the unknown. They were just about to get to know what they didn't before.

Virgil dropped down, his boots splashing in water puddles. He rested his buffalo rifle on a squat boulder and pointed in the general direction of the Shoshone Indians. As the clouds began to disappear and rays once again bleached the land, his eyes were slits against the glare. Small, bullet-like pupils stared at the riders with reserved caution. Lovejoy wasn't a violent man unless someone forced his hand. But if you did and he got you in his sights, you would be singing with the devil before you realized you were dead.

Joseph and Rory wrapped their hands around their pistol grips. They were ready to pull at any second. All they needed was a sign from the captain or the Shoshone Indians. One wrong move, and all hell would break loose.

The Captain

Everybody froze—on both sides. The captain's horse shifted its hooves nervously. His eyes blazed with violence. They all saw it when he drew his saber. Rays of sun glared off the blade. The Shoshone braves exchanged looks. Some shook their heads, and a few even turned and walked their horses away. An argument ensued between the warriors. As voices raised, the eastern travelers continued to stare. Glances shot over shoulders.

The warriors kept an eye on the famous soldier. They had heard what happened at the Rendezvous while fighting other White men and Blackfeet Indians. They imagined what he might do to them if they crossed him. With some men, it was better to walk away and fight another day. Still, a reckless Indian brave was always ready to risk his life for fame and the honor of being in the elders' songs. He might even be ready to risk the other braves' lives.

Levi wheeled his horse around and rode toward his friend. His size caused the Indians to pause. The metallic click of a hammer behind Johnson as Virgil took a bead on the nearest target. Levi swallowed hard, trying to remain calm and impassive. He could feel the energy come off the captain like hot shots of electricity. To Johnson's surprise, Forrester nudged his horse toward the painted Shoshone. His face was an impassive mask. He gently flicked the rein against the stallion's mane, easing him even nearer to the painted faces.

The warriors had heard rumors of the bluecoat soldier. At first sight, he was unmistakable, with his saber hanging from his belt, missing arm, and long yellow hair. They knew when it was drawn, even though they might stop him, he would lob off heads before he fell. None of the warriors wanted to have their spirits denied entry to the next world because of a missing face. None of them wanted to have their heads roll in the dirt, either. It would be the ultimate insult. Yet the war chief was ready to test fate and all for hopeful fame.

Sunlight flashed off the shiny steel and the captain's ice-cold blue eyes. The medicine men of the tribe had already left. They said the yellow-haired captain was bad medicine and was to be avoided. But warriors didn't always follow what their spiritual leaders told them. Sometimes, they didn't even listen to their chiefs. Warriors often went off the rails, but it was ignored and taken with a grain of salt. The war party leader thought today could mean a great victory. His braves weren't so sure it wouldn't end in a blood bath and many of their lives.

Indians were different than White men when it came to losses of life in battle. Warriors were greatly valued, as were their wives. What an Army general considered necessary costs the Indian warriors believed to be a massive and unnecessary loss of life. Most battles involved numerous fighters, but they usually turned for home after one, two, or maybe three braves were killed. Nobody wanted to depopulate their tribe and return to tell the wives their husbands were dead.

This was why the medicine men and chief's orders conflicted with Dark Dog, the Shoshone war chief. They knew more men would die than acceptable. These were part of the ten men who killed their twenty-armed enemies faster than a man could smoke a pipe. The elders were the wise Shoshone who turned their horses and calmly walked away. Today was not a good day to die. Perhaps tomorrow.

Forrester pulled his black horse to a stop. He fished in his shirt pocket for a tobacco twist and a handful of matches. He passed it to the Shoshone Indian Will, thought to be in charge. Nobody knew why the captain took such a chance. He was so close to the Indians that he could touch them, smell their body odor, and even their breath and what they ate. It was obvious he wasn't afraid. His gaze was calm and steady, but his flashing eyes didn't miss a thing.

The chief carefully took the twist and passed the matches around. While they filled their bowls, the captain scratched a match to life on the skull cracker of his sword and puffed his ceramic pipe. The smell of sulfur hung in the air. Levi loomed behind him, but he didn't dare twitch a muscle. His eyes were glued on the colorful faces. What had looked like tense, angry men now seemed strangely relaxed.

Still, nobody said a word as they all smoked in silence. The captain lay his saber across his lap. They could all see it and knew it would be in hand in the blink of an eye, but he didn't seem interested. They all continued to enjoy the fresh tobacco—everybody but Levi Johnson. He felt his guns under his shirt as beads of sweat popped up on his brow and neck.

Joseph sat beside Betty and said, "Well, I'll be. I ain't ever seen nothin' like it. The captain done tamed the hostiles."

"Do you really think it's over?" Betty asked. "It didn't even start yet. I've seen firsthand what Indian warriors can do. Especially when they wear war paint."

Sheriff Walker locked worried eyes with Betty's and shrugged his shoulders. He turned back to the Shoshone. Virgil still had a bead on the leader sitting on his horse right beside the captain. It was the strangest thing he had ever seen, and he had no idea how it would pan out.

"Please, God, don't let anything happen to Will," Betty prayed. She didn't notice she said it out loud.

Miss Crockett hadn't seen the stares either. Rory and Joseph both wore puzzled faces. Virgil didn't have to look. He wore a knowing smile. Betty had confided in him, and it was their secret. He wondered if it was a secret to Will, too.

Dahteste walked her Appaloosa slowly toward her husband. She acted like she was strolling in a park. Her eyes stared at nothing, and she made no indication she even noticed the Shoshone warriors. The woman war chief looked right through them. She smiled when she pulled up beside the horse and rider towering over her. Despite her petite size, she had a presence about her that made her seem bigger than life.

The Shoshone Indians ignored Dahteste, too, but they felt she was also dangerous. Nor had they missed the two men waiting on horses with their hands resting on their pistols or the man with the buffalo gun. The leader stared at Lovejoy like he was challenging him to dare fire. Virgil looked back and smiled, which unnerved the war chief as he struggled not to show it. His face turned red with anger, and he looked away. Unlike other White and Black men, they had encountered, they didn't appear afraid.

Their confidence began to melt the brave facade of Dark Dog and his warriors. But he knew another opportunity to be sung in the songs of his elders would never come again. If he missed his chance now, he would probably never be given another. So, he chose to defy orders, but he hoped to save the lives of his men regardless of the outcome. He also hoped he didn't lose his head.

Murmurs ran through the group of Easterners like wildfire. Still, the missionaries had little idea of the potential danger. It looked like a powwow or the sharing of a peace pipe as far as they could see. But the sheriff was from Kansas, and they had their share of the most dangerous, hostile Indians of them all—the Comanche. So, although he looked on amazed, he didn't let his guard down any more than Beaver Johnson did.

Dahteste appeared uninterested, but her bow was in her hand, and a quiver full of arrows was strapped across her back. The firepower she lay to bare, beat the flintlock rifles and pistols man-to-man. She could fire three arrows in two seconds; they had never seen her miss—even when firing from a racing horse and shooting from under its neck.

Smoke hovered over the group of men as the smell of burning tobacco floated in the air. Dark Dog couldn't take his eyes off the captain. His warriors' gaze shifted from the White man to their leader, and doubt showed in their frowns. One sudden move or the wrong word or etiquette would instantly turn the world upside down. Will returned the stare. It was almost like nobody, but these two men were there. They had mentally blocked out everybody else so they could focus all their attention on their opponent.

Forrester nodded, never letting his stare waver. Dark Dog returned the gesture and nudged his horse, walking away from his men. Captain Forrester followed behind as he struggled with his nervous stallion. Its nostrils flared as he stomped his hooves, kicking up dust clouds. Its neck and rump quivered in nervous anticipation, and the captain ground his jaw.

Will didn't quite know what to do. It looked like some sort of duel. All the Shoshone warriors looked on as the drama played out. Nobody could imagine what would happen next. The enemies forgot each other as their minds were glued to what was unfolding before them. Nobody had ever seen Dark Dog act this way before. He defied their spiritual leaders. The medicine men sat on their horses in the distance, waiting for the inevitable to play out. It wasn't what would happen, but when would it happen? It could be any second now.

One red and one White warrior silently walked their horses to a stop a hundred yards apart, wheeling them around until they came face-to-face. For the captain, the world and all sound vanished in that second before the clash. Once it happened, it would all be a blur, and he often couldn't remember the details. His anger made him see red, and his memory was still foggy in certain situations. It was like the captain's brain had a self-protection mode that erased much of the most violent acts from his memory or shoved it back into the darkest recesses of his brain.

Will's adrenaline surged, and the hair on the back of his neck stood on end. Goose bumps spouted across his forearms. Dark Dog's horse stomped its hooves. The Indian held a large tomahawk in his fist. The black flint blade was honed to a fine edge, and its long handle allowed the wielder an exceptional reach. There was the slightest gleam of a smile on the captain's face and a deepening frown on Dark Dog's.

Horses reared and thundered forward in a sudden burst of energy. Hearts raced a hundred miles an hour as they pounded in their heads. The clash was a fraction of a second away. They closed in and clashed as Forrester used his saber to block a chop on the first pass. A cut at the edge of his scalp seeped as the first blow drew blood. They wheeled their horses around again, and the stallion reared, kicking its feet in the air.

Heels dug into flanks as animals charged again; their lungs heaved, and they snorted. Both men held their weapons over their heads, ready to strike a lethal blow. The impact was imminent as the Shoshone raised his hatchet for the kill. He had drawn first blood and was thirsty for more. He could already hear his name in the tribe's songs. The yellow-haired soldier wasn't as dangerous as the rumors claimed. No White man was a match for a Shoshone warrior.

Dark Dog had blood in his eyes and a bad taste in his mouth. Suddenly, his confidence evaporated like a warm breath on a cold day.

The captain faded and faked a slice but dropped his saber low beside his waist at the last moment. He watched as Dark Dog rode right into the blade. Steel reflected sunlight through the blood on the saber protruding from his back. Nobody's head was taken. The medicine men in the distance turned and nudged their horses into a trot. It was over, and the outcome was just like they had warned. At least the one-armed warrior spared Dark Dog his head. He would pass into the spirit world intact, although he would be seen as foolish.

Dark Dog sat on his pony's back with shock and wonder on his face. He was stunned he wasn't the victor after all. He was convinced he would prevail after the initial pass. He almost got the captain the first time and was sure he would succeed the second. But he had been outmaneuvered and had lost. Just like the medicine men had warned him, he sat astride his pony with a long piece of steel protruding from his stomach.

The sword remained transversing the Shoshone war chief. The captain wheeled his horse around as he slowly approached the dying man. When he wrapped his fist around the grip of his saber and withdrew the blade, a gush of wind escaped the Indian. He teetered on his saddle one last time, then tumbled off and into the dirt face down. Blood pooled beneath his body as the flies gathered, drawn to the smell of a fresh kill.

In the end, forced laughter cut the stillness of the Easterners. A frown eased off the sheriff's face as the slightest hint of a curl touched the corner of his lips. Levi and Dahteste made a long sigh. They were just a few yards away from it all and had seen the surprise in the warrior's face. The captain had done the unexpected and won yet another battle. How many wins did he have left in him?

Lieutenant Holster watched the captain intently. Finally, he put the strange soldier, the West Point captain, and the expedition together. He wondered why he hadn't seen it before. Now, he could see the pain and torment in his face. Brad instantly knew this man had done more for his country than should be asked of a soldier. Right then and there, he decided that he would look no more for a captain that no longer existed. Sometimes, it was better to let things go for a better outcome. Reporting back what he had seen would never do the captain justice, so he believed it was better to claim he had found his grave.

Brad continued to stare at the remarkable fighter. He managed to finish the fight by himself and without further loss of life. As for the warrior, he brought it on himself. They had all seen how the other riders left and didn't even look over their shoulders. They all knew what the outcome would be. No brave could be forced to follow a foolish war chief. He had bitten off more than he could chew. The future had been written in stone, and he could do nothing to change things.

His sergeant looked at the lieutenant with a curious look and raised an eyebrow. "What is it, sir? You've got a funny look in your eye."

"It's nothing, Sergeant." Holster smiled. "I was just in awe with how the officer avoided unnecessary bloodshed and still won the day. I've never seen anything like it; then again, what have I seen when compared to such a man?"

The Compound

When the weary mountain men walked up the last steep stretch of trail right before arriving at the compound, smoke curled from Angus's chimney. They exchanged questioning looks. With a glance, they saw all the horses were in the corral, less one. The big black dog ran ahead, wagging his tail like a broken hinge. He immediately began to bark at the animals in the pen and run around the compound, happy to be home.

"I bet Pine Needle is here getting things ready for our return." Angus smiled as he looked at the string of smoke. A little worry seemed to accompany the grin. He glanced around, but his Crow wife wasn't in sight. "She must be around here somewhere. I hope she isn't angry. I told her I'd be a couple of weeks."

"Why'd ya tell her that when you knew it takes two weeks to get there and two more to get back," Rusty said. "And we weren't gonna go there and turn right around and return home, were we? If you told her the truth in the first place, you wouldn't find yourself in this position now. Every time you leave her for a spell, you tell her a lie."

"If I don't, she gets angry, and they ain't lies; they're little fibs," Angus grumbled. "You know what she's like when riled up. I figure she gets angry for less time if I come home late. If I tell her before, there's no end to it."

"The things you put up with to keep that woman." Rusty smiled.

"You know how I am with the Crow women," Angus said. "They like a man who knows how to dance and cut up a rug. I make good company of a winter in the teepee, too."

"It feels strange returning without the boys," Rusty said.

When they walked into the compound, they felt the ghosts of Yosemite Bob, Syracuse Sam, and Portland Pete. All three had fallen victim to wicked men. If only they had stayed back in the mountains and not gone to the Rendezvous. Or would someone else have lost their lives just the same? It was impossible to say. Anyone of them could have been shot when they rushed the Squirrel Clan. It was just bad luck or destiny, whichever label a man preferred. Still, nothing could change the outcome.

Rusty's cheek bulged. When he sucked on his quid, it accentuated his rugged face. He spat into the green grass. His eyes were full of life.

"Yesterday's gone, and ya can't get it back," Rusty said. "I reckon it's better to have been a has-been than never-was. They were all three fine men. At least they all lived to ripe old ages. What'll we do with their things? I guess now Levi, Dahteste, and the captain can live in one cabin and Virgil in the other with Dennis."

"That gives you, me, and Pine Needle a little room to move," Angus said. "It was getting cramped with all of us in one room of a winter."

Pine Needle came riding across the compound yard, bumping her horse down from a canter to a walk, and pulled up by Angus. Her eyes were full of fire—her mouth a hard line. She kicked her leg over her horse's head and slipped to the ground. She took two steps to Angus, hauled off, and hit him in the jaw so hard he staggered. She turned on her heels, led the horse to the stables, and finally stormed back to the cabin. She didn't even say hello.

"Pine Needle, darlin," Angus said. After his wife hit him with a haymaker, he shook his head, rubbed his jaw, and spat out a glob of blood. "Wow, did she wallop me good that time!" He shook his head and blinked.

"She's a mite riled up, ain't she, you old fool." Rusty laughed. "Sometimes silence is the best answer. You better bow down to that woman before she takes a mind to kill ya. You ain't no match for her anymore. You're gettin' older, and she just seems to be gettin' younger."

Angus ignored the sarcasm, then laughed. "Yeah, and one day you'll see a monkey fly out of my butt." Finally, he felt the heat of embarrassment drain from his face. It was replaced with anger, and he, too, stormed for the cabin. Seconds later, metal pans banged against the walls, and muffled sounds came from behind the door. Then, there was finally quiet.

But Rusty had seen it happen time and time again when Angus was away for long enough that Pine Needle got angry. When his crow wife got her hackles up, staying out of her way was best. Steel also knew that now he would have to give them a spell alone until they made up and his wife was appeased. After three Crow wives, Angus learned that Indian women weren't like ladies from back East. When they got angry, you were going to find out and quickly. He wondered how it was going with Dahteste. At least they had more in common than old Angus.

It was true; for some reason, the Crow women of the nearby tribe thought Angus was quite a catch. He was a good provider and was available when Pine Needle needed him, but he was also gone enough to make her love him more. It was true; the Crow women fancied him for his clever dancing moves. Indians put a lot of stock in a good dance. Most of their ceremonies were based around them.

Rusty checked the two vacant cabins while he waited for his friend to make up with his wife. When he walked through the homes, he noticed things of Bob, Pete, and Sam. But the empty feeling he expected to have, wasn't there. It almost felt like it was their time, and it was all right. The three of them had had a good run and lived life to the fullest in a place where only a few were allowed to remain. They could thank their lucky stars; they had lived the lives they had.

Rusty had expected to have died long ago. He started out his life as an orphan on the St. Luis River. At that time, he was no more than a common thief. Lucky for him, a riverboat captain had taken him in and taught him the ways of a seafaring man. He eventually became a captain until French outlaws captured his boat, which he burned to the ground. If he couldn't have it, nobody was going to.

As sunset neared, the sun hovered over the horizon, lighting clouds to the west in a spectacular blue glow. It appeared immobile at the end of the world, then slipped behind the horizon in what seemed like seconds. A blanket of stars rolled across the sky from horizon to horizon. Twinkling entities that came from light years away.

That night, the three sat in a comfortable silence on the cabin porch. Smoke squired out of their pipes as orange bowls reflected in their eyes. Lightning bugs lit up here and there, making the night appear magic. A carpet of stars lay across the sky. Pine Needle's face was iridescent in the moonglow. The anger had passed, and she lay her head on her husband's shoulder. Now he was back safe and sound.

Angus and his wife smiled in the dark, but you could only see their teeth. The porch sat in the shade of the moonlight. Crickets began their nightly racket as coyotes sang a choir in the night. They sat in the dark for hours, contemplating their future and their mortality. Only Pine Needle was free of ugly thoughts and worry. Then again, Indians lived for the moment, not the future like most White men did.

The Crow Indians were just happy they could walk the earth free, men and women. They never took the life they lived for granted. They realized how delicate balance they lived in, and soon it would become even more of a tightrope act. As more White men trespassed, the game became more and more scarce, and killings were on the rise.

The following morning, Mountain Dennis came riding into the compound with a string of mules and horse trailing. Three Crow warriors escorted him home. They had just covered the porch table with breakfast. Steam rose from cups of hot coffee. Green grass and trees surrounded the three homes and stables. A zigzag post fence enclosed the property.

Of course, the land didn't belong to the mountain men. Like the Indians always said, they belonged to the land, and it had no owners. Yet they all had a territory carved out. In many cases, by bloodshed. As tribes grew or others depopulated, the power and possession of hunting rights shifted.

Unlike White men who divide the land up like it was a giant cake, butting it into squares of land. They often offered what wasn't theirs either. If what Joseph said was true, soon, there would be an exodus of travelers of all colors from one side of the country to the other.

"Well look what the cat drug in." Rusty smiled. "Thank God, you made it. I see Hachta was lookin' out for you, too."

"I'd have never made it on my own," Dennis grinned. His gold tooth shone in the morning sunlight. "It was a stretch gettin' from the Green River to the foothills. But once I got there, I ran into these Crow braves, and they were lookin' for me. The chief sent 'em. I've never been so happy to see an Indian in my life."

"Lucky for you, all the real thieves were out lookin' for gold." Rusty chuckled. "Most folks ain't interested in stealin' a few mules anymore anyway. Not with the Rendezvous just ending. Not even the Indians steal mules anymore. Now, the horses are another matter."

Rusty and Angus made more food, and in half an hour, the animals were in the corral, and Dennis and three braves came to eat breakfast. The conversation shifted from English to Crow. Angus had been the first to master the language. Of course, he was on his Indian third Indian wife, and they all came from the same tribe. He spent long stretches in the winter in the teepee in Hachta's stronghold with his wife, Pine Needle.

Rust Steel learned his Crow from his years of friendship with the chief. They had been blood brothers for many years, and it was known across this side of the mountains. The Crow warriors preferred to eat sitting on the edge of the porch. Dennis took his place at the familiar table. Even though they had separate cabins, they spent many winter days and nights inside and many more outside on the porch. It was where they all gravitated to summer and winter.

Now, there were three less, and their absence was noticed. Everything they did made them feel their missing friends even more. That and their personal items lay scattered from the first cabin to the last.

"What is this about Sheriff Walker wantin' to bring two hundred wagons across the plains by way of the South Pass?" Dennis asked. "It sounds foolhardy to me."

"You know the White folks back in Washington, DC want the Indians to stop huntin' and trappin' and become farmers," Angus grumbled. The braves frowned. "How they can figure out what's goin' on from two thousand miles is beyond my comprehension. Why, there ain't a person one from Washington that knows anything about the wilderness now that Davy Crockett's dead."

"Why don't you go and tell 'em to be good little Indians and turn their long guns into plows?" Dennis laughed. "Make 'em grow corn and potatoes. Why, I've never met a Plains Indian one that was a farmer."

"I can't believe them fools back East are trying to plan a powder keg situation from across the country,"

Rusty said. "If Joseph is right and hundreds of wagons begin to cross just north of here, the local Indians may well become anxious. I reckon there will be trouble for sure. Especially with tribes like the Blackfeet and Shoshone."

The braves exchanged puzzled looks. They weren't quite sure how far a mile was. It could be from there to Canada, for all they knew. They measured their time in days and distanced in sleeps. Four sleeps meant a four-day walk.

"Don't you boys worry." Rusty smiled. "There's no way trains with two hundred wagons are gonna hold up along that trail even if the Indians were invitin' and friendly, which they ain't."

"I hope Joseph takes good care of our boys and Dahteste, too," Angus said. "I'd take it poorly if somethin' were to happen to them too."

"Stop it with the negative thoughts," Rusty retorted. "Have you ever noticed how dangerous the captain has become? I think we best worry about the folks they run into and not about them. He's a good Samaritan with a gun in his hand." He laughed until he got a stitch.

It was contagious like it often was. It echoed across the mountain and down into the nearest valley bouncing off the canyon walls.

Trail to Oregon

Betty rode a bay quietly beside Capt. Forrester, her eyes straight ahead. After the clash with Dark Dog, Will's energy seemed drained. She had expected something similar when the Blackfeet warriors attacked their wagon train. But this time, they were spared the extended violence. The captain had contained and defused the situation and only had to take one life. That was because the Shoshone war chief was a foolish glory seeker. Lucky for his warriors, they chose not to follow his path.

Of course, if Dark Dog had won, he would now be a famous war chief. That was what he had bet his life on. Now, he would never be in the songs of the elders. He would be used as a lesson of what not to do. He would be an example of a warrior gone astray who disregarded the chief and medicine men's orders. Now, he would have to face the spirits with a stain on his soul. He wasn't the first reckless warrior to bite off more than he could chew. He would have plenty of company in the Shoshone spirit world.

More like him would follow, too. Especially when the dam was just about to break, and European Americans would come in a great flood of humanity. When he saw the captain's blood, he was sure he had won. He had felt elated. The medicine man had talked like he was some spirit impossible to slay. After the first pass, he knew they were wrong. Now, he lay on the ground gutted. He wondered how long it would take for him to die. His fellow Shoshone warriors had left him to his foolish dream. Nobody even looked back to watch him pass into the spirit world.

Lucky for Betty, Will allowed her to whisper sweet nothings in his ear. He was exhausted from battle, even though it was just a small skirmish compared to the Squirrel Clan. The other had been out and out war. Still, it affected the officer despite only one life lost. He continued to wonder when the lieutenant would discover he and the expedition leader were one and the same. The captain was the man he was searching for all over the wilderness.

It was his own fury the captain had to tame. It was a fast and clumsy rage that made it a short leap to revenge. He took a deep breath and forced his heart rate down. The fiery ball of electricity in his stomach began to wane. He brushed his mustache with his knuckles and sat tall in his saddle. His eyes dared anyone to challenge him. Once his blood was up after a fight, it took the captain time to settle down. Usually, Levi was the one who brought him back to earth when he ran off the rails. It was beginning to become a full-time job.

Levi and Dahteste rode right behind Will. Johnson kept a close eye on his friend. He had seen the man undergo a world of changes in just under two years from when they first met. The Crow woman watched her man with a furrowed brow. She was worried too, but not about the captain. Her concern was her husband and his close bond to such a dangerous soldier. His reputation alone would bring more warriors like Dark Dog.

There was usually a warrior or two in most tribes with a vision of fame and honor or illusions of grandeur. Indian warriors put a lot of stock in the name they made for themselves during their lifetime. It would also be important to them in the afterlife. If the feat was remarkable enough, the chief might even change their name for something more favorable or suitable depending on their achievement. This would make them a man of honor. The downside was that you would die if you lost, and nobody would sing over your grave.

Levi's wife knew how Indian braves thought. She had fought side-by-side with them through many battles with the Blackfeet Indians. Soon, the captain would become a target to many reckless Indians of any of the six tribes living there. Maybe even a few women warriors, too. The more famous he got, the more men would wish to take a chance and test fate to win the big prize. She remembered when she was still a warrior and not a war chief. There was little she wouldn't do to advance her standing in the tribe. Few women qualified to be war chiefs, but still some famous ones were sung in the songs of the tribes.

Unbeknownst to them, Captain Forrester was already being sung about in the elders' songs of the Shoshone tribe. The head medicine man began to formulate a rhyme in his mind as soon as they saw the one-armed captain with the long knife in all his fury. He hoped if he sang about his bravery, the officer might spare him and the warriors' lives and not chase them down and take their heads. Lobbing off the enemies' heads rang a bell that couldn't be unrung. The news raced through the Indian population like wildfire in both the mountains and the plains.

Virgil pulled the brim of his floppy black hat over his eyes as he squinted into the light. He looked at Reverend Smith from the shadows of his brim. "How are you and your people holding up, sir?"

Smith appeared surprised but smiled and replied, "This is our church—this is our chapel," the preacher said with outstretched arms before the vastness of the plains. Spirals of light came down like in a cathedral. "No matter where we go, we are in God's hands. Wherever we go, he is in our hearts. Here is just as good a place to worship as any. Maybe with all this wonder and gloryful scenery, it is even better."

"It's hard to believe God would create such an unforgiving land, ain't it." Virgil chuckled. "We always talk about all the good the Lord has done, but he's been up to a passel of mischief too."

"I thought you were a religious man, Mr. Lovejoy," Smith said, surprised.

"I doubt you'll find many who worship more than me, but I still find some things puzzling. Maybe instead of worship, I should say study. That's it; I study the Bible. In most cases, the words are clear and easy to understand. Other times, some words have a double meaning, and phrases contradict each other. Then again, it depends on who was the writer and creators. I, probably like you, read the King James Version translated in 1611."

"You seem to know a great deal about many things, Mr. Lovejoy," Reverend Smith said, staring into his deep brown eyes. "I'm afraid I have been indoctrinated into the Boston Presbyterian Church, so I stopped studying the Good Book and began to practice and preach."

"It's a long read which requires much contemplation." Virgil smiled. "After you read it a few times, some phrases take on a different meaning than at first sight. That is what puzzles me. I wish it were more direct. Perhaps I'm not as clever a man as I sometimes think. I know it's vain, but it happens just the same."

Brad Holster pulled up on the other side of the captain. He looked at him in a new light. Before today, he had been a mystery and even a little foreboding. His manner of speech set him apart from the other mountain men, although he was apparently one of them now, too. His dress was halfway between an officer and a pioneer. He was obviously an Indian fighter, although it was apparent, he didn't relish the fact. He had spared a number of painted faces today. Something that was obviously no small feat.

At first, Forrester ignored him—or at least that was how it seemed. But then he appeared startled when he realized Lieutenant Holster was beside him. It seemed to come as a shock. Will locked eyes with the lieutenant. Brad saw a thousand-yard stare. He couldn't hold eye contact and broke off and stared at the ground.

"I don't know who you are, sir," Lieutenant Holster started. He dared look into those blue eyes again. He saw a puzzled face. "I thought I did, but in the end, I didn't. The man I was sent to look for is obviously dead and buried. At least, that's what I will say if I ever make it back to Kansas and report to my superiors in Fort Leavenworth."

Brad paused for a moment. He swallowed hard. He couldn't take his eyes off the saber the captain wielded so well.

"Your secret is secure with me, Captain Forrester," Holster said. "I reckon Mr. Johnson was your scout, wasn't he? I was told I might find him with you. Now I remember they told me he was a big man. That was an understatement. I guess I took quite a while to put the pieces of the puzzle together. To be honest, I wasn't looking for a giant or one-armed man; beg your pardon, sir. We've been through hell and back trying to find you. Before I came out west, I had another image of what I would find. I never expected it to be such a hostile and unforgiving land. Now that I've seen how difficult it can be, I see my orders in a new light. I know I will return a different man like my men if they, too, survive."

"In such a country, you can never take survival for granted," the captain said. "You don't have to call me captain. Will's fine."

A trace of a curl appeared at the edges of Forrester's mouth. He gave the young aspiring officer a look of understanding and gratitude. The captain made a long and drawn-out sigh like a heavy weight had just been removed from his back. The muscles in his face and shoulders relaxed. He looked five years younger. He brushed his empty sleeve with the back of his hand.

"To be honest, like it or not, you are our captain," Lieutenant Holster said. "You hold the highest rank. Plus, if I started calling you by name, it would confuse my men—at least what's left of them. None of my soldiers call me Brad, but you can, although never in front of my soldiers." Now, he smiled. "Even though we're in the middle of the wilderness, I believe in following protocol, sir. I would have thought a West Point graduate would too."

"After you live here a year, you come back and say the same thing and mean it," Forrester dared. "It might not be as easy as you think."

The horses walked on listlessly, and some missionaries nodded off in their saddles. The only shade was the brims of their hats. They all had chapped and cracked lips from the constant dry wind. Still, Dahteste acted like she was on vacation. Her never-ending curiosity was sparked with the slightest provocation. She smiled most of the day. Levi wasn't so sure that the Shoshone were gone for good. In his experience, hostile Indians usually did precisely what you didn't expect.

"I'm glad you discovered what happened to the expedition," the captain said. "How could a man explain such a thing? Especially to a bunch of superiors who have no idea what it's like in the wilderness. You still don't know exactly what happened, and I'm not the man to tell you. I've put all that dark past aside, although it seemed never-ending. Maybe your experiences out here in the wilderness will give you a glimpse of how difficult it is to survive. Do your men know?" he raised an eyebrow.

"No sir, they don't, and I don't intend to tell them either." Brad shook his head. "If they say something, I'll just brush it off. I know how it is to lose part of the men in my patrol. I've nearly lost half. I can't imagine what it must be like to lose them all."

"Just for the record, a few of my soldiers did

survive," the captain replied thoughtfully. "I even sent one back with my resignation. He was supposed to report to Fort Leavenworth. I had had enough fighting. But as you can see, violence still follows me around like the plague. I wonder if they, too, perished or were filled with the same living hell I was and walked away."

"I don't think it's you, sir," Holster said. "This country is deceiving. Oh, sure, it looks bleak enough, but the real dangers lay just under its skin. I lost my men and didn't even know what happened to them. They simply vanished in the night without as much as a squeak. Had I run into a bunch of painted faces like those Shoshone, I might have shot myself to avoid capture. Back East, that's what they tell us is the best course of action. Before being tortured to death by hostile Indians, it's better to steal your life away so they can't make you suffer."

"I've never found myself in such a situation nor had such thoughts," the captain said. "Maybe you should forget everything you were told back in Washington and study what you see out here. There's not a single man in the capital who knows what it's really like west of the Missouri River. They just think that since they are bigshots in the capital, they can make the best decisions for people who live out here."

The whole time, Betty Crockett sat tensely in her saddle. She knew the Army lieutenant was looking for the captain and scout of a famous expedition but never imagined it would be Will and Levi. She wondered who else knew. Worry washed over her like an ocean wave, but after quietly listening, trying not to be noticed, she heard more of the story and began to understand why the captain was who he was. Now, she felt he needed her more than ever. Maybe it was women's intuition. Or was it just a hunch? But she was hardheaded and determined to help him save himself. He needed a rock, and that was what she planned to be for him.

As though he could read her mind, the captain turned his head and looked deep into Betty's eyes. She felt the blood flush her face and got a little lightheaded. She wondered what was going on inside that brilliant but troubled mind of his. Now, it was clear that she, too, knew his secret. Now, the pieces of her puzzle began to fall into place, too. She began to plan how to win the captain's heart. She knew he was at least half-willing, and she was as strong a willed woman as she knew, so it was right up her alley. She had to believe that determination would win the day.

Levi looked around at his harsh surroundings and liked what he saw. It was going to be another challenge. With just a glimpse at his wife, he knew she felt the same. The atmosphere was still and oppressive under the withering rays of prairie sun. Still, they enjoyed the heat on their brown faces. Levi was so dark; if it wasn't for his size, he could pass for an Indian at a distance. Besides the captain, they appeared as different as night and day, but their ways were now becoming more and more similar. As were their desires and aspirations.

They both sought a simple life. Levi was happy trapping the streams for beaver and hunting elk and buffalo. It wasn't that different from his childhood back in Southeastern Indiana. Yet, the idea of an adventure made them throw caution to the wind. Then again, it wasn't all that safe in the Rocky Mountains either. No matter what the type of terrain, the wilderness was always full of potential danger.

They continued to travel at a steady pace all through the day. Although tired now, the missionaries didn't lag behind like in the beginning. They all understood if they didn't do as they were told, they too could perish from one day to another. And they had yet to see any wild animals. They hopped against all odds they wouldn't run into a grizzly bear. Lucky for them, it was too arid and dry. But then again, it depended on what they smelled in the distance with their powerful nose. They can follow a scent for miles.

Dark clouds began to form on the western horizon. The sun broke through with rays of light on patches of ground. From one moment to the next, they were caught unawares as the sun disappeared, and they were cast into the night. The wind dropped to nothing, and the air became heavy and thick. Lightning struck silently across the distance, lighting up the end of the prairie. There wasn't a thing standing in sight other than the travelers.

"We must have all been asleep in the saddle." Rory Breaker snickered nervously. "Night's nearly on us. Somebody come along with me to look for buffalo chips. I don't fancy wanderin' out in the dark alone. You heard what the lieutenant said. His men vanished at night when they were probably tending to their personals."

"I'll go with ya, Rory," Virgil said. He pulled one pistol out of the four he carried in his belt. "Put a gun in your hand, son. That leaves us one arm free. I've got the polk-sack, and you pick up the chips."

The metallic sound of metal as two hammers clicked. In half an hour, several fires were burning a light blue flame. Under that lay red-hot coals. Buffalo chips gave off more heat and burned cleaner than wood. Across the stretches of land, they lay in the thousands, already dried and baked in the sun. It was also the only propellant available.

By the time they had finished dinner, they were too tired even to talk. Everybody went to bed except the captain, who had disappeared at dusk, not to be seen again all evening. Then again, that wasn't strange behavior for Forrester. At least with him wandering out there in the dark, they could rest easy and have a good and much-needed sleep. They didn't even bother to put out a guard.

Late that night, the scouts were all asleep. Virgil lay in his bedroll. He was staring at the sky through slits. If you looked, he appeared to be asleep, too. A solitary man tiptoed across the campsite. He wore a US Army uniform. His heavy boots scuffed the ground. Lovejoy froze, closed his eyes, and focused on his hearing. A pistol lay under his saddle. His hand was hidden under his blanket as it crept toward the grip. Soon, it was in his fist.

Virgil suddenly sat up with wide eyes and pointed his pistol at the supposed thief. "One move, and you'll be shot dead, boy."

"I don't trust a man with curly hair," the private said. "I can't help but imagine small birds laying eggs in there. I've been watchin' you read your Bible. You ain't gonna do nothin'. What are you doin' with so much money anyway? And point that gun somewhere else before I get angry."

"You best get your hand out of my pocketbook, thief," Virgil warned. "I don't know how you got into the

Army, but if you think you're gonna steal from me, you won't live to see tomorrow."

"There ain't a place in America where a Black man can shoot a White man, fool," the private spat. He reached into Virgil's money pouch, feeling for the gold coins.

Lovejoy pulled back the hammer and shot him in the chest. He stepped over and leaned in close to watch the life leave his eyes. "That'll teach cha not to steal from me. And I don't take kindly to sass. There was a time I'd put up with such a mouth, but not anymore. Too bad for you." He looked up and saw the lieutenant. "Sorry, sir, but I don't suffer folks who steal. I'm surprised you didn't know what kind of man he was."

"Officers usually don't have the luxury of selecting the soldiers attached to their command. I've had more than one rotten apple in my ranks, yet I am surprised at Pvt. Stills. His brother is back at the fort. I wonder if the siblings are alike. Soon, nobody won't be left to return to Fort Leavenworth. You, too, should be more careful who you talk in front of about all that gold you made from your buffalo hides. Gold brings out the worst in a man."

As soon as Forrester heard the gunshot, he wheeled his horse around and gigged its flanks. The captain rode into sight, beating his black stallion to a whirlwind pace. When he pulled up, his back teeth locked as his muscles tensed. He felt his face flush with anger. He swung down from his horse and leaned over the body. He nudged it with his boot. He used his toe to flick his hand over. Hidden in his palm was a knife. Will used his toe to kick the weapon out of reach. You just never knew, so it was best to be safe even though he looked like he was dead or dying.

"I guess it did with Stills," Virgil huffed. He began to reload his pistol. "He didn't seem the type."

Sheriff Walker took two steps to the dead man and peered down. "He looks dead enough to me." He spat a stream of brown juice and hit him between the eyes. "Good call, Virgil. I reckon that'll be the last time you run that big mouth of yours, though, won't it? It ain't wise to let folks know you've got money."

"There seems to be more thieves, bandits, and murderers than normal folk about with the Rendezvous," Levi said. "And the sheriff plans to bring hundreds of people along this same trail. You'll have your work cut out for you, Joseph."

Lieutenant Holster was appalled. Not only was he harboring a dishonest man, but he had also lost another patrol member. If this trend continued, soon, he would be the only one left. That is if he survived himself. Life was in a delicate balance in the wilderness. He never believed Virgil to be such a hard man. Then again, he ran with some of the ruggedest men he had ever known. He wondered if he would offend one of them and get shot, too. The food in his stomach climbed to his throat as he staggered from the body, fell to his hands and knees in the dirt, and retched.

Snake River

Vultures made lazy circles in the sky overhead as they walked their horses along the riverbank, searching for the most accessible place to cross. In the shallowest spots, the other bank was only yards away, but a network of islets made several short crossings necessary.

Four by four, they waded and swam across the Snake River, hanging onto their saddles while watching for Shoshone Indians. River crossings were notorious for hostile attacks. In the water, the travelers would be their most vulnerable. That's why Joseph ordered them to go in fours rather than all at once, risking the entire expedition. Sure, it would take ten times longer, but safety would be on their side. The cool but still morning showed no sign of the blistering heat to come. The water in the river was cold.

Of course, Captain Forrester was the first of the group to cross to the other bank to ensure it was safe and there wasn't an ambush waiting. Then he rode up and down the water's edge daring anyone to interfere.

His black horse stomped the ground as he pranced up and down. This was where the Indians crossed, too. All these trails that the European Americans and supposed explorers claimed to have discovered had been made and traveled on by Native Americans for thousands of years.

Once they made the crossing, they stopped to rest and dry their wet clothing and saddle blankets. The horses grazed on thick green grass in the shade of trees as they slid their jaws and flicked their tails at flies. The steady current rippled downstream, making a bubbling sound.

"Don't y'all get too comfortable," Joseph warned. "Fort Hall is too close to camp here. It'll be more comfortable there, not to mention safer." He removed his hat and used it to shade his eyes from the sun as he glanced at the time of day. "We need to be on our way in two hours tops. Just because we're wet don't mean we can't travel."

Four hours later, they had Fort Hall in sight. It wasn't quite what the missionaries expected. When they were told the next stop would be a fort, the images brought up in their minds were massive structures full of soldiers.

Unfortunately, Fort Hall couldn't be farther than the pictures in their memories, but still, it was some semblance of real civilization. The elation on the faces of the missionaries was almost comical. Even the scouts were happy to see some semblance of order after the chaos at the Rendezvous. At least, that was what they expected.

All of them except Dahteste. She had never been in a fort where White men lived and didn't want to stay inside those walls for the next few days. She would rather take her chances with the hostel Shoshone outside of Fort Hall. Four cannons decorated the front of the building. They were chained to the outer walls and were a clear and present threat. She pulled her horse up beside her husband and clutched at his arm.

There was nothing dead in sight, but still, the buzzards continued their search. Most of them were no more than black dots on a blue sky, but the occasional curious vulture swooped down to have a closer look. They were massive, with a two-yard wingspan with long dangling talons. Maybe they were waiting for more of the travelers to die. The last soldier had been buried too deep for the coyotes and raccoons to dig up. Private Sill's burial had little to no ceremony. He was treated like a common thief. As the lieutenant hammered the cross into the ground with the flat of a shovel, Reverend Smith read from the Bible and said a prayer.

Then, they all turned their backs and walked away. He had betrayed the Army, his superior officer, his fellow soldiers, and above all, the very people who rescued him and his companions and virtually saved their lives. If that was how he showed gratitude, he wasn't worth the dirt they covered him with.

Joseph had wanted to leave him to the vultures, but Rev. Smith refused to continue until he had a proper burial. He assumed the private was a Christian and demanded he be buried as such. But that, of course, didn't entail eulogies or speeches on how he lived. There was nothing good to say about the man. Virgil read something from his Bible as he ran a brown finger under the lines. Joseph waited until they were done, then walked over to the fresh grave, spat a yard of brown juice on the pile of dirt, and grumbled. They wasted two hours on a man that wasn't worth a minute in the sheriff's mind.

Lieutenant Holster was embarrassed—or better said, mortified. The fact that one of his soldiers even considered stealing from the mountain men appalled him, so had Virgil not shot him, he would have ordered him to stand before a firing squad. The lieutenant just hoped the captain's attitude toward him, and his two remaining men didn't waver with the knowledge that Holster didn't have a handle on his command, especially after showing how noble the mountain men were. Then again, gold would do that to some people. They became obsessed with the idea of owning the precious yellow mineral and metal. Being both was what made it so precious. Men have chased after gold for as long as time itself. All the way back to the Egyptians.

Still, the lieutenant felt he should have seen it coming. His weariness had made him less observant. Also, the loss of his men had shaken him to the core. It was quite a shock to awake one morning and find men missing from the camp without any sign of a struggle. Then again, gold was the most potent drug of all. Even stronger than opium. Some who appeared to be good men all their lives were poisoned by the mere thought that it was near.

"Fort Hall?" Dahteste asked. "Is it like our stronghold where we have our teepee back home?"

"Joseph says this one is much smaller than Chief Hachta's camp." Levi smiled. "From what he says, I reckon it's even small for a fort. You know just about as much as I do, girl. Don't worry, darlin'. Nobody's gonna bother you with me and Will around. I won't tolerate any poor manners in your presence. They can think what they want of Indians, but they best respect my wife."

"Won't there be soldiers in the fort?" Dahteste asked. "What will the captain do?"

"I reckon the captain is smart enough to figure out what to do when the time comes," Levi replied. "There'll be a few soldiers but mostly traders and folks; a fort needs to make it work. Sure, the government provides money to keep it open, but that's not the only thing needed to stay alive—especially a target like an army fort.

"This ain't gonna be like a real fort back in Kansas," Sheriff Walker said. "A trapper by the name of Nathaniel Wyeth built a trading post here, and he later sold it to the Army to be used as a fort. If I'm not mistaken, he had several such establishments across this stretch of frontier."

"At least we can forget about the Shoshone warriors for a while." Dahteste smiled, but her eyes told another story. Levi had never seen her so nervous. There was something about the fort she felt too confining. Maybe it seemed like a large jail cell or a prison to a person who had lived their life in the wilderness with no confines at all. "I guess I'll have to walk into the lion's den, won't I."

Levi nodded as he stared at the whitewashed walls standing over thirty feet high. A square turret rose out of the front corner. It had windows at the very top with heavy timber shutters and gun slats. Joseph had been there before. The original building had been enlarged but was still not much more than a trading post like its origins. Still, it was a perfect place to rest for a few days, both for the people and the horses.

Outside the walls, there were a half dozen teepees. Smoke squirreled toward the sky from several campfires. Indian men and women moved about leisurely in the safety of the shadows of Fort Hall. The missionaries were shocked to see their presence. Levi and Dahteste shot looks over their shoulders and chuckled. The Bostoners were getting shy of Indians since they saw the Shoshone warrior attack the captain.

There hadn't been the expected battle, but they had seen the fiercely painted faces and the violence in the eyes of the war chief. Lucky for them, the captain took it all in stride and managed to contain the danger to himself. Smith stole a glance at the captain and wondered what made him tick. He had never met a man like him. He seemed so full of something mysterious, but it was foggy and elusive, so he couldn't quite put his finger on it.

Captain Forrester led the way into the fort in the wilderness. Miss Crockett rode directly behind him. Thirty mounted horses filed in. They walked their animals under the thick double door wooden gate. To their right, horses nickered and neighed from a string of stables. In the back of the small compound were two large buildings. They were built of heavy, hewed logs. Chickens ran across the yard, fleeing from the intruders. Somewhere behind a building, a rooster crowed. Donkeys in the last stable hee-hawed, protesting the disturbance of their silence. The fort appeared to be lazy as the midday sun that blazed down. Long shadows stood before empty porches. The only sign of life was the horses that moved listlessly in the corral. A tarp spread over their heads to ward off the rays.

Captain Forrester rode up to what he believed to be the Army's official quarters and stepped down from his stallion. Boot heels walked across a wooden porch. He knocked on an ajar door, but nobody answered. He pushed it in with the toe of his boot. It squeaked as it swung open. The captain craned his neck to see inside. At a desk sat a man with his feet crossed on an open door. His head hung precariously from the back of the chair. He suddenly snored loudly, then sighed and swallowed. Captain Forrester cleared his throat, but the man under the large hat didn't move. Out of patience, he grabbed his boots and swung them to the floor, awakening the man with a start.

"Who the hell do you think you are?" The words escaped the duty officer's mouth before he realized who he was talking to. The first sign of danger was in the captain's eyes. From there, he took note of the battle scars and mix of clothing. Everything he saw said this was an Indian fighter and, therefore, a dangerous man. Besides that, he wore his hat slapped up like the Seventh Cavalry and believed him to be a captain because of the saber. He hardly noticed the missing arm. Just like the captain went through life like he'd never lost an appendage.

The duty officer jumped to his feet and stood at attention. "Sergeant Wilco, Sir!" He saluted properly. The captain figured he was probably a soldier, although he hardly looked it.

"Are you the duty officer, Sergeant?" the captain asked. "And where, may I ask, is your uniform? If you were out on the plains, I could understand the lack of formality, but here in a fort, I just don't understand. Who's the commanding officer here, Sergeant Wilco?"

"Why aren't you the commanding officer, sir?" Sergeant Wilco replied. "I've been here for six months now, and all I hear is that somebody is comin' to take charge, but they never arrive. As soon as I saw you, I figured you to be our new officer."

"There are a lot of hostile Shoshone warriors out there, mister," Forrester said. He didn't answer Wilco's question. "We just ran into a couple of dozen, and they were all painted for war."

"We have an outhouse right here in the fort," Wilco replied, "so we hardly go out but to hunt for game, and most of the time, we buy from friendly Indians that live outside the walls. You must have seen 'em when you rode in."

"Do you know these Indians who bring you elk and deer?" the captain asked. "Do you know any of the people that live around the fort? Is there more than one tribe living here, and who are their enemies?"

"That's a lot of questions. No, not really, but they seem to be pretty friendly to me," Wilco replied, but now he felt he had missed something. "Now that you mention it, most of the time, it's different Indians that come and go. To be honest, I can't tell one tribe from another. But here in the fort, you've got nothin' to worry about, Captain. Nobody could get in here if I don't want 'em to."

"Are you always so full of yourself, mister?" the captain asked. "I just walked thirty mounted horses right into the courtyard and didn't see a single guard or anybody for that matter. Remember, sir, I had to wake you up. You didn't even have the headquarters door locked. Now you tell me how hard it would be for thirty or forty Shoshone warriors to do the same. This place is wide open. I'm surprised the hostiles haven't ridden right in and taken what they wanted. How would you know? You would be asleep."

"I was just havin' what the Mexicans call a little siesta," Wilco said. "Did you see them cannons out front?" The sergeant asked, refusing to own his mistakes.

"If there's nobody there to load and prime the cannon and then light the fuse, what good are they? I doubt they would be very useful unless the enemy advised you before they came. Otherwise, hostile Indians would be sitting at your dinner table waiting for you to wake up. Those cannons are at too close a range unless you used a small shot anyway. Then, it would kill anybody in front of the fort, including your friendly Indians. Do you even know what kind of loads you've got in those cannons?"

"Why, we've never had to use them before," Wilco replied.

The sergeant's face blushed a deep red as he realized he had failed miserably as the fort's duty officer—at least in the eyes of this veteran captain. He suddenly noticed he had one sleeve pinned at the elbow. He wondered who was brave enough to take such a man's arm.

Rocky Mountains

Like many mornings, the men were up an hour before the first hint of dawn. Crickets chirped their chorus, indicating that no intruders were nearby. Occasionally, they would stop their chatter, and Rusty, Angus, and Dennis would stop and stare. Then, they would resume until the first traces of light showed on the eastern peaks. In the morning glow, the mountains looked blue, just a few shades darker than the sky. White clouds passed between the compound and the stars. Like a carpet, the sparkling dots rolled back toward the west until they disappeared.

Rustling noises and banging metal echoed through the still morning. The aroma of coffee floated in the air. It mixed with the smell of pine trees, breathing life into a new day. By the time the sun peeked its eye over the world's end, the mountain men were sitting with their breakfast before them. Steam rose from the hot coffee, contrasting with the mountain's cool air.

"It seems like the cleanest place on earth after being in the Rendezvous," Dennis said. "Look at how green the grass it. Why, it's almost blue like they have in Kentucky."

The corral was full of mules and horses. The Crow Indians had yet to come down and collect part of the small herd and the chief's profits from the trade meet. Either that or Rusty would send up some smoke signals and have a chat with the chief. Maybe they would want them to come to them. If that were the case, a few days wouldn't make any difference. Now, they had to grieve. It was the first opportunity they had. From the time of their friends' deaths, they hadn't stopped long enough to ponder on their old pards.

They rummaged through Pete, Bob, and Sam's things and set aside anything special they wanted as a personal keepsake. Other items they packed into bundles to give the Crow tribe that lives half a day farther up the mountain. Of course, many of the cabin's items were everyday necessities that Levi and Will would inherit. Now, they would have their own home in the compound deep in the wilderness where men seldom came and fewer left.

"Maybe we can start building that extra room on the cabin for Levi and Dahteste," Angus said. "That would be a nice surprise. Of course, we'll leave the teepee where it is, so Dahteste has a place to get away from us White folks." He snickered.

Rusty closed his eyes for a second and took a deep breath. "It sure does smell better than the trappers meet. I've never smelled so many unbathed bodies in my life. Some of 'em had such an odor I'd have sworn they were polecats in human suits."

"You ain't the best smellin' critter yourself come a winter," Angus said.

"Any fool knows if you take a bath in the winter, you'll catch pneumonia," Rusty growled. "It's best just to wash up lightly. Plus, in the winter, it ain't me that smells; it's them furs you poorly cured. Why they stink worse than some of them fellas at the meet."

The table was covered in cast-iron frying pan biscuits, gravy, bacon, boiled eggs, and a gallon pot of coffee. Steam rose off freshly baked cornbread as bubbles spewed from the spout. As they wolfed the food down, the only sound was forks and knives scraping against tin pans. During the meal, nobody uttered a word like always. The silence continued into another cup of coffee and a pipe of tobacco each.

When Angus was finished, he burped and said, "Mighty fine eatin'." He looked at the sky and used the flat of his hand to block the sun low in the sky. "Thems smoke signals, Rusty. You best take a peek. It might be Chief Hachta sendin' us a message."

Rusty didn't move and replied, "And one of his braves will keep sendin' 'em until I reply, and I ain't in a hurry right now. We just got home, so let me enjoy my breakfast and a smoke. Then we need to look at what we need to add a room onto the boys' new cabin."

"It ain't a new cabin," Dennis said.

"It is for them," Rusty replied. "Especially if we add on a room to give the new couple some privacy."

"I'll be glad to get rid of the chief's part of the money," Angus said. "A thousand dollars will go a long way in an Indian stronghold. It'll buy medicine, blankets, gunpowder to hunt, along with a hundred other things. We made it this far without losing what we earned, so I ain't in a hurry to go out and risk our luck again. Maybe it'll be better if the Crow chief comes to us and brings a bunch of warriors. There still may be some thieves out there who know about our jackpot at the fur Rendezvous. Some men will do most anything for a pouch full of gold."

"Did ya see all the garbage everybody left once Rendezvous was over?" Angus asked. "Why rubbish was scattered across hell and half an acre."

"One man's garbage is another man's treasure." Rusty chuckled. "Three days after the meet, I bet you there wasn't a trace of our presence. Indians ain't like White folks. They don't throw anything of any use at all away. They'll find some good use for what you might think is worthless, and it might be the most unlikely thing. So, I figure they went through everything left behind. What they didn't take on the first pass, they'd have taken on the second, third, or fourth pass."

"I'm glad I went, and I was glad when we left," Mountain Dennis said. "Maybe mostly when we left. If it weren't for the Squirrel Clan, I figure we'd have had a fine time. I know we had some fun, too, but the losses outweighed it all in the end. My cabin is so quiet it's the loudest it's ever been. Anyway, it doesn't matter what a man thinks or wants; life is gonna give him a dose of good or bad fortune or, more than likely, a little of both. Right now, I'm happy where I am and don't see travel in the future."

"Just like that fortune teller said?" Angus asked.

"I reckon she was a fraud," Rusty said, even though he wasn't wholly convinced. He still remembered how she looked at the lines in his palm and the shock on her face. "If she were any good, she would have seen her future too. You saw those thieves had her emerald necklace."

"I doubt she gave it up without a fight," Angus said. "I guess her luck ran out just like it does for normal folks."

Once Rusty finished his pipe, he stood, and his moccasins silently crossed the wood plank floor, making them groan. Steel stepped into the yard. When he looked up, it was just like he had said. A brave continued to send him smoke signals. The dark puffs of smoke contrasted against the cloudless blue sky. He sat on the edge of the porch, picked up a stick, and drew in the dirt to the side. The Indians communicated differently than the White and Black men from back East. Some signals represented animals, so he had to translate the story as he went. Finally, he looked back at his notes in the dust.

"Well, I'll be," Rusty said. Both Dennis and Angus were sitting on the edges of their seats.

"What's the smoke signals say, pard?" Angus asked. "I couldn't make heads or tails of nothin', and I've lived off and on with the Crow Indians for over a decade now. At least I spend the winters in the stronghold."

"Chief Hachta is going to make a powwow in our honor," Rusty said, surprised. "I've been to pow-wows before, and it's a big deal. I've never heard of Indians making one in a White man's honor. I reckon it's a first."

"So, what's so special about that?" Angus asked. "I've been to a dozen myself, if not more."

"That's my point." Rusty chuckled. "This one ain't gonna be like a normal powwow. It's gonna be held here in the compound. It looks like a bunch from the tribe are coming down to visit. We've had the odd visit from Chief Hachta, but we've never been honored. I don't even know what we did that made it special, but I like it just the same."

"I like that we're being honored," Angus said. "We all know you're the chief's favorite, so he never pays us much mind. When I stay with Pine Needle, it's like I wasn't there. My wife says it's best not to attract attention when a chief is involved. Now, he's gonna come down here and thank us for bringing back his gold."

"Many a man would have kept all the money and walked away," Dennis said. "And there wouldn't be a danged thing the chief could do about it. Maybe he's just surprised we stayed honest."

"He knows I'm honest," Rusty growled. "Him and me be blood brothers."

"That's why he don't worry about you." Angus laughed. "We don't have the same relationship, so we always worry a little about us. You know how Indian warriors are. There's not a man alive that can say what's in their minds."

We better get the place spruced up a bit. We have three-gallon kettles, so we best start more coffee on all of 'em. The signals said the chief and his escort left their camp about an hour ago."

Full Moon

Betty Crockett sat on the top of the alure high on the fort walls. From the square turret, a door opened onto a small platform designed for the soldiers to return fire from the safety of the fortress if they were attacked. From the *chemin de ronde,* she looked across the wilderness as the moon glowed, casting silver shadows across the country.

She heard a sound behind her and saw the shadows of boots under the door. It squeaked as it slowly opened, casting light from a kerosene lantern. Will's silhouette appeared. He closed the door behind him, shutting out the artificial light. He was shy and uncertain of what he was doing, but he clumsily blundered forward, taking a chance.

"Sit down, Captain," Betty said. "There's plenty of room here." She patted the box she sat on. "Don't be shy, I won't bite. Really, Will, why don't you give me a chance at least?"

She smiled a reassuring smile, setting the captain at ease. Maybe it would be easier than he thought. When it came to women, Will actually didn't have that much experience—in relationships, at least. He had gone from one school to another, and although he did court a couple of women briefly, he hardly had the time an ordinary man his age would have. Being accepted into West Point to study was a hurdle all the alumni struggled with. Then, if your dream did come true and you reached the bar set by your peers, then you had to study day and night to keep up. It wasn't considered the best military school in America for nothing.

The school had produced some of the finest soldiers and officers in the country since 1802. He was fortunate to be among the ranks, have survived the pressure, and have graduated with honors. Then, to have it all fall to pieces after so much preparation. It was a miracle it didn't break the young officer. It certainly did leave its scars. Most men wouldn't be able to live with such a failure. He would remember the doomed expedition for the rest of his life.

But, still, the captain pushed on almost like he was obsessed. He felt an inherent need to protect all his friends. He couldn't remember if he felt this before the accident, or maybe it was produced by the amnesia. He was no longer sure. Levi, Rusty, Angus, and now Virgil were really the first friends he had ever had. His fellow students back at college were all snobs from wealthy families. But even back then, Will was so focused he ignored the way they looked down at him because he chose to be different and ignored them. Even though he came from as prestigious a family as most, he wasn't like them.

The captain never showed interest in their outside activities. His studies didn't allow him the time. He was a born loner, just like when he was back in Southeastern, Indiana. Of course, then, he had no choice, as his parents had no neighbors. There, too, he lived in the wilderness but without the dangers of hostile Indians and grizzly bears.

He leaned against the wall, stretched his legs out before him, and sighed. It was long and deep, like he was letting out years of stress and worry. He suddenly felt like he had gotten a load off his chest. He was startled when Betty scooted over, snuggled up to his side, and lay her head on his shoulder. When she first touched him, she felt his muscles tense up, and he became stiff. He hadn't expected her to be so abrupt and forward. But Betty now knew if she didn't catch her man herself, he would wander away, and she would lose him in the vast wilderness. That was something she had no plans on doing. She was going to stick to him like glue.

She took his hand in hers and held it to her cheek, then pressed her lips to his palm. Her eyes pooled with the simplest touch. She swooned over him so all he could see was her. She locked her eyes with his and pulled him closer, daring him to kiss her. She had abandoned all her plans of being proper and letting the man make the first move. She knew if she did that, Will would never build up the courage to take her hand in his or even kiss her.

"You're not going to ignore me tonight, Will." Betty giggled with mischief in her eyes. "Now that I have you in my grasp, I don't plan to let you get away."

"But...," he went to protest, but she pressed her lips to his before he could stop her. She parted hers and kissed him like he'd never been kissed before.

Of course, Betty was head-over-heels in love with

the captain. Now, all she had to do was convince him he was in love with her, too. She believed it was with all her heart, but he obviously was ignorant of the fact. She hoped if anything would work, it would be their emotions and feelings. If she could get Will Forrester to stop thinking for just a day, she could woo and careen him until he was like butter in her hands.

Betty just knew she could do it. Everybody in her family was strong headed, just like her uncle, Davy Crockett. They weren't made of the same stuff most men and women were made of—they were from the Tennessee forests. She knew what she wanted, and there was nothing that was going to step in her way—not even the captain.

Betty pressed her body against Will's as the kiss deepened, molding herself to his shape. She felt him stir under her as her body smothered his. She kissed his mouth, eyes, cheeks, and forehead. It was as though no matter how often she kissed him, they weren't enough. She hungered for him to need her just like she needed him.

"You know you can't choose who ya fall in love with," Betty whispered. "All ya can do is see how far down the trail you can go together once you're hitched."

"How do you know when you're in love?" Will asked. The little hope things would work out today vanished like a strange smell on a windy way. The question was like a knife piercing Betty's heart. "I feel more mixed up than ever. I guess I've never really been in love, Betty. Maybe I wouldn't know if it bit me in the butt." He smiled despite his confusion about his emotions and feelings toward the woman cuddled up against him.

"If you don't know, I guess you aren't in love with me

after all," Betty huffed. Disappointment flushed her face.

"Maybe the problem is I don't even know what love is," the captain pondered. He drew his head back and looked closely at the blond-haired beauty. She wasn't a young girl any longer. He was sure she was older than his twenty-eight years. Somehow, none of it made any difference. "I come from a military family. My father shakes my hand when we meet. I've never even seen my mother and father hold hands in public. I dated a couple of girls who were daughters of friends of my father's. He was the one who set the meetings up. To his disappointment, neither one could understand me. Then again, that's not odd because often I can't explain myself. Maybe you can teach me to love you. I think I'm willing—no...I know I'm willing if you'll give me a chance."

Betty laughed and said, "In your strange way, you just made me the happiest woman in the world. You sure are an unusual man, Will Forrester. I should have expected love to be different with you, too. Everything else is. I just didn't know how different it was gonna be."

She sighed, lay her head on the captain's shoulder again, and stared at the night sky. She made a wish before the falling star she saw burned out, and it was too late. Will looked at her out of the corner of his eye. He knew she had made a wish and was sure what it was, too.

"Sheriff Walker said it won't be long until we arrive in the Oregon Territory," Betty said.

"Are you going to stay like you said?" Will asked. "I mean when we get to Oregon City. If I remember right, you said you didn't want to travel over trails you've already seen."

It suddenly struck him that maybe she would leave the group once they arrived at their destination. He hadn't done much to encourage Betty. He did know that people fell in and out of love at the drop of a hat. Maybe it was time for him to take some of the initiative. He wasn't getting any younger, nor was she. Levi and Dahteste seemed happy enough, and they must have a more complicated life, with one being a Crow Indian and the other a White man.

If they could do it, maybe he could too. Will had noticed the changes in his friend, Johnson, since he got married, and most of them were good. Of course, at first, there was a twinge of jealousy. He had to share his best friend. But soon, Dahteste became part of the family, too, and everybody seemed happy. Even Chief Hachta, back on the mountain, seemed pleased. She was one of his war chiefs, after all.

Betty seemed to be made of the same stuff her Uncle Davy was made of; may he rest in peace. Maybe she was just the perfect complement for a man accustomed to running around life anchorless. He needed something to ground him, so he didn't run off the rails whenever he saw an evil deed. Maybe he didn't have to stick his nose in other people's business so much.

"How about another kiss?" Will asked, but now his eyes twinkled and were full of confidence. "I liked the first one just fine."

Leaving Safety

The compound in Fort Hall was chaotic. With no officer present for half a year, the place had succumbed to laziness and lack of discipline. Soldiers were what they were because they weren't expected to make decisions. The officers were supposed to be there to do that. That was why the Army attached educated officers to show the often rough and rugged privates, corporals, and sergeants what to do.

The problem was that the man in charge didn't make it across the wilderness and to Fort Hall. Forrester didn't even know if the replacement officer was coming from the east or the west, nor did the duty officer. Like many soldiers who ventured into Indian territory, they perished on the way to their destination, just like the captain's men in the expedition had. He knew he couldn't stay and take command but couldn't leave a handful of soldiers as they were, either.

Full of determination, like always, the captain confronted the duty officer. Sergeant Wilco was asleep at his desk as usual. The rest of the soldiers didn't even come outdoors until the sun went down. Then, they spent the evenings in the trading post in the corner of the fort's courtyard. They had all the travelers' needs, including whiskey, which the fort soldiers used to drink their boredom away.

This time when Captain Forrester entered the duty officer's office, he slammed the door hard behind him. He startled Sergeant Wilco so badly he fell off his tilted chair. His hat dropped over his face. He lay on the ground and couldn't see who had entered so abruptly. Again, he growled and snapped out before he realized who had woke him up.

"Get up off the floor, man," the captain growled. "You're making a fool of yourself."

Wilco grabbed his hat, struggled to his feet, and stood as erect as he could with a heavy hangover from the previous night. The arrival of travelers and even an officer didn't seem to have bothered the soldiers' routine in the least. They ignored the officer's suggestions and continued as they had for months. For them, it was fine to live in a comanderless fort. Of course, this way, nothing was expected of them.

"When I arrived, you said I was the commanding officer, so I'm going to make some changes here," Forrester growled. "I'm promoting you to lieutenant, Wilco. With you in charge, if and when the actual commander comes, if the fort remains in the same conditions as I found them in, you will be court-martialed and possibly stand before a firing squad. Do you understand me, sir?"

"But I never asked to be an officer in charge of the fort," Wilco cried. He looked like he was nearly in tears.

"Are you in the Army or not?" Forrester yelled. "Come on, man, give me an answer."

"Why, of course, I'm in the Army," Wilco replied, cringing under the hard stare of the one-armed captain.

The duty officer suddenly saw the violence in his eyes, and he nearly wet himself. He just realized he was looking at a man who had killed at the drop of a hat. He believed he might just put him in front of a firing squad if he didn't do his job. But the last thing he wanted to do was be an officer. Then he would have to tell his friends the bad news. But the alternative was a few slugs of lead. He preferred the former.

"Then you'll do as I say, and I don't want to hear another word about it. I'll be coming back through here shortly on my way back to the South Pass, and I better not find everybody drunk and the fort a mess when I return. Do you understand your orders, Lieutenant Wilco?"

Suddenly when he heard his name used with an officer's title, he found he liked the sound. But, like it or not, he couldn't disobey an order. Especially when it came from such a scary captain, he made a note not to cross this man, or it may be his first and last act as an officer.

"Yes, sir, I understand perfectly," Wilco said in a shaky voice.

"So, what is your first job?" the captain asked. "I mean, right now, what can I expect you to do?"

"Go and fetch the men from the saloon?" Wilco asked, not quite sure what the captain wanted to hear.

"That's a good start, Lieutenant," the captain replied. "I would suggest that you sober them up and get this fort spotless before some officer arrives who isn't quite as nice as me." Forrester smiled at the irony. "That also means you are to get to know the Indians that are living outside the fort. Make sure they aren't the enemy, and they don't poison the food they sell you. I also expect a special patrol every month, and you will take notes so that when I get back, you can show me the results. The Army doesn't pay you to sleep off hangovers all day. As the fort lieutenant, I expect you to keep a strict log of all activities. Get me a pen and paper so I can write out your commission, mister." The captain sat at the duty officer's desk and began to write. "Are you still here?"

Wilco literally ran for the door. He even forgot to salute, but the captain didn't mind. He even chuckled after the new officer left. It was the only way he could see that might work. Apparently, Wilco still had some semblance of a soldier in him. Now his grit would be tested by not only his men but maybe even by the Indians.

It wasn't what the captain would have wanted if the new officer of Fort Hall arrived soon, but maybe by the time they sent another replacement, Wilco would have risen to the task. All he could do was hope. Like Betty kept telling him, he couldn't put out every fire he ran across. Three hours later, they were back on the trail nearing the Oregon Territory. They were less than five hundred miles away now, so it was just a matter of days.

After the run-in with the painted Shoshone warriors, they saw no more Indians. They knew they were there because Dahteste assured them they were. At times, she said she could smell them. But apparently, they had seen the captain continue to ride with the travelers, and they clearly didn't want any of the dark magic the one-armed officer possessed. They had already lost one foolish brave, and he paid with his life for his indiscretions.

The warriors were told to allow the Easterners to leave in peace just as long as they left their land and didn't kill any more Shoshone Indians. They would suffer the trespassers to avoid an incident that could cost a leader his position as chief. As it turned out, the chief and medicine men were right, and the renegade warrior was wrong.

One day, they would be wrong, and then they would be the ones to pay the price. No position was permanent in the Indian Nations unless the leader was a famous and respected war chief across the board. But few such leaders existed, and many Indian males wanted to take the places of the lesser-known leaders, so they were always up to a challenge. Being a tribal chief was often a double-edged sword.

They traveled the south banks of the Snake River. Then they navigated the Snake River Canyon until they came to the steep and dangerous climb over the Blue Mountains before riding along the Columbia River to the settlement of Dalles and finally on to Oregon City. It was only four hundred fifty miles compared to the endless cross of the South Pass, the weather began to cool, and the vegetation became richer and denser. When they crossed into Oregon, they all saw the riches the people back East talked about. It was truly a promised land.

The missionaries were all fidgety, knowing their journey was finally coming to an end. The light at the end of the tunnel wasn't a train, after all, and it looked like they would all survive. No small feat after what they had seen the crossing was like. Of course, the last few hundred miles seemed like nothing to the men and women who came all the way from Boston. Now in a few days, they would be at their destination after a hard, arduous journey.

Levi, Will, Dahteste, and Virgil were ready to turn around and head back home. Especially Levi longed for the deep forest like his childhood birthplace. It was the same for Dahteste and her family. The captain went wherever his friends went, and Betty and Virgil followed him. Johnson and his wife had seen enough people to last them a year at least. Betty was just happy to be riding along. Will had asked her to come. It had come to her as a shock right before it was time to leave. She thought he was going to leave her. Betty was ready to follow him anywhere.

Soon Reverend Smith and his flock were tiny dots on the horizon as they headed off to meet with the other missionaries who had come before them. Their job was done, and Joseph was already anxious to leave. It was Levi who convinced him that he was in a hurry to go nowhere as the winter was nearly on them, and he could spend the winter with them in the Rockies. They had plenty of space now that Bob, Sam, and Pete were gone.

Traveling alone, they moved three times as fast as they had with the inexperienced missionaries. All of them were mountain men, trappers, and buffalo hunters and had experience with hostile Indians too. As they moved back across what would become The Oregon Trail, they kept a low profile, so if anyone was out there watching, they would probably not detect them. Above all, they were master trackers and scouts. They knew they would be home in a few short weeks.

Rory Breaker left them at the bottom of the South Pass. He was from Kansas, so he wanted to at least get back East before the cold set in. If he was lucky, he might even make it home. He would meet the sheriff in Montana the following season, ready to organize the longest wagon train in history.

The six remaining travelers raced across the countryside. They were all strong and healthy, and none of them were old enough to slow them down. In two weeks, they would arrive back in the compound with the three cabins and one teepee.

Three Cabins

The first light snow had fallen. Rusty, Angus, and Mountain Dennis sat with their coffees on the porch, but now they wore their bear skin coats to ward off the early evening mountain chill. Dirty pie pans cluttered the table. They had just finished off a light dinner. They passed a ceramic jug between them as they added a splash of whiskey to their hot refreshments.

The room extension of the cabin had gone so quickly they were surprised when it was done well before Levi and Dahteste returned. Every day, Rusty looked out the front window to see if there were any new tracks in the yard. The only signs were the footprints of raccoons and the occasional brown bear.

As they sat in a comfortable silence, sipping on their last cup of java for the day and a nightly smoke, the woods were unusually silent. Not even the coyote and vultures were heard or seen. Rusty wondered if someone was out there watching. Could it be Crow warriors have returned? It wasn't like them to make unnecessary trips, especially after the winter snows had started.

Of course, the powwow was not only unexpected, but it was also huge. Hundreds of Crow Indians gathered in the compound yard to dance and sing, and it was all in honor of Rusty Steel, the chief's blood brother. He had sold their furs, and like the honorable man he was, he had returned with the money. Something that most White men wouldn't do. Especially when trading with Indians.

Chief Hachata never doubted Rusty would honor his word, but as usual, there were always disgruntled warriors who felt different. Part of the reason for such a big powwow was to show those same braves where this small group of White men stood in relation to the Crow stronghold a half day's ride from their homes. There were always young braves too full of testosterone for their own good. They demanded the trespassers be run off the mountain. Most of them were afraid of what they didn't know. White men were still quite a mystery for some of the men in the Crow camp.

At the celebration held by the Crow tribe, even Angus came out of his shell and performed his dancing skills to the delight of the widows and single women of the tribe. It was still a mystery to all how he charmed the Crow women, even at his age. But they stood in line to have the opportunity to cut the rug with the old trapper. His wife, Pine Needle, stood nearby as proud as she could be.

It also helped that he knew the Indian's language like he knew his own and their customs too. Few men had lived so long with an Indian tribe. Even Rusty, who had lived with the Flathead Indians, but he too nearly mastered the Crow language as well as Angus. It was considered essential in their coexistence in the Rockies.

The powwow had lasted so late into the night, even after the aging mountain men had called it a day and turned in, the party continued until the wee hours of the morning. Tobacco flowed as buffalo steaks were devoured, and the singing and dancing continued.

Rusty didn't know when they left, but in the morning, when they awoke, all the Indians were gone. There wasn't even a trace that they were there other than the warm coals of the cook fires.

As the three men and a black dog sat with their thoughts, they puffed on pipes silently. So much had happened in the months prior they only wanted quiet. Nobody shared their thoughts, but all of them were thinking about Levi and the captain. They wondered if they would ever make it back or would the wilderness swallow them whole like it had so many before them. Maybe not killed or wounded but distracted with some new discovery that seemed more inviting than returning to the isolation of the mountains. Still, all three hoped against all odds they would return soon.

Enough time had passed for them to make the long trek. Had they been held up or injured? Rusty nor Angus saw Dahteste not returning to her tribe and family there. That was their best hope for their return. But maybe something happened, or Sheriff Walker had talked them into heading back to Montana to organize a two-hundred-wagon train to cross the wilderness and to the Pacific coast of the country.

Horses crushed fresh snow as bushes rustled at the edge of the compound. One horse at a time filed into the large yard inside a zigzag fence. The first one they saw was Dahteste. As she was a Crow war chief, she led the way in case they ran into any young warriors who looked to run off the rails and take the trespassing situation into their own hands, even if it was with their friendly neighbors.

Rusty was already on his feet, shifting his weight nervously from one foot to the other. A smile spread across his face that stretched from ear to ear.

Angus jumped up and did a jig. Even lazy Dennis walked to the edge of the porch to see the rest of the family return home. Virgil followed, and then they were surprised to see Kansas Sheriff Walker. Rusty rushed to the other side of the yard and stretched his neck to see. Sure enough, Captain Forrester rode drag with a rifle across his lap.

"Hotdog!" Rusty yelled. "They made it back just like I said."

They were even more surprised when a White woman with yellow hair followed Will into the compound. It was Betty Crockett in the flesh. The three aging mountain men wondered what that meant as they looked from her to the captain.

"State your business, sparky." Rusty smiled. "Why it's Levi and the captain come back home," he mocked, acting like he was never worried.

Levi surprised Rusty when he dropped down off his massive Mustang and grabbed his old friend in a bear hug that lifted him off the ground.

Whoa, whoa, whoa there, son." Rusty laughed as Johnson dropped him to the ground.

Levi inhaled a deep breath and smiled. "There ain't nothin' like mountain air. It's the cleanest in the world."

Dahteste gracefully slipped off her Appaloosa and

hugged Rusty. Angus eventually lumbered over to the arriving group, and he got a few hugs too. It was just like old times. They even had a special guest. The sheriff had told them one great story after another, and he promised many more over the coming winter in the Rocky Mountains.

Hell on High Water

Levi Johnson Mountain Man Scout 14

I dedicate this book to the great Rocky Mountains and the Native American Tribes who have populated it in the past and live there today.

"Never be discouraged. If I were sunk in the lowest pits of Nova Scotia, with the Rocky Mountains piled on me, I would hang on, exercise faith, and keep up good courage, and I would come out on top."

Joseph Smith Jr.

Wild Horses

Captain Forrester, Levi Johnson, and Virgil Lovejoy rode through the forest with Sheriff Joseph Walker riding drag. Rory Breaker was on point somewhere, way out front. He was an able-bodied man for a cowboy lost in the Rockies, so nobody gave it a second thought. They all rotated, riding both point and drag to even out the risks. No man there would ask another to do something they wouldn't do themselves.

They only spared Virgil the scouting job because he had other qualities, just as valuable. His keen shot with a buffalo gun kept him in the middle, ready to down any distant threat before they got into the range of pistols or most long guns. His skills came from long days, weeks and months shooting buffalo from a half-mile away.

They weren't expecting trouble since the Rendezvous was over and the buffalo herds vanished. This year, more men than ever came to the mountains and the plains. A surprising number of hunters sought the valuable prize. They far exceeded their expectations and by the season's end had killed hundreds of thousands of buffalo. Carcasses and bleached-out bones were left to scar the countryside. At the same time, they were taking food out of the local Native Americans' mouths and denying them valuable skins to cover their homes and make blankets.

These actions created yet another uproar, making it harder for those who desired to peacefully live in this wilderness paradise. But sometimes one man's paradise was another man's hell. In the mountains, a change in the wind could bring doom and destruction. Every single man knew to live for today because tomorrow might never come.

They all knew from experience that, while lost in the forest when you least expected it, danger could be waiting around the corner. Flintlock pistols filled their belts. Each man carried four, five, or even six weapons, besides their knives. Every shot had to count when dealing with the enemy in numbers. Rifles lay across their laps as they threaded their way down the mountainside on horseback.

A single mule followed behind the riders with large slabs of freshly killed elk piled on its back. Salt glistened on the recently killed meat. Tracks in the snow followed them like a long snail, winding and wrapping its way down the steep grade. Levi used his memory to follow the powder-covered trail. Only a few mountain men and the local Indians traveled there.

Suddenly, the horses balked and nervously shifted their hooves. Virgil's mare screamed. It wasn't the steep angle the riders were guiding their animals down, but the horses sensed something dangerous just out of sight. The men struggled to keep from being thrown and finally dismounted. Levi stroked his mustang's snout and whispered into his ear. Johnson visibly calmed the animal, but Forrester's stallion was ready to charge regardless of what the threat was. It seemed to have been bred for battle much like its owner, so it pulled at its reins and continued to stomp its hooves and kick its hind legs.

Still, nobody had any idea what was spooking the horses. Sheriff Walker came trotting up to the mountain men. He had been riding drag a few hundred meters behind. Worry etched his face as a wake of dust followed.

"Where's Rory Breaker?" Walker frowned. He could feel the dangerous energy in the air. Even though they didn't know what it was, they knew something was wrong. They just couldn't put a finger on it—at least not yet.

"He's somewhere out there on point," Levi whispered. His eyes narrowed as his brow furrowed. "Hopefully the threat is between us and your cowboy, but I don't think it's Indians. The horses usually don't get riled up by veteran braves unless they're reckless. They know to ride wide around us downwind. I wish Rusty was here. With little more than a sniff he'd know what's out there just like Dahteste. We seem to only value a person's sense of smell when we need it, now that somebody ain't here that has it. There're more skills than meets the eye required to live safely in the Rocky Mountains. I wonder what else we're missin'?"

They walked their horses carefully forward, each man with a rifle in his fists. They hoped and prayed that Rory Breaker, Sheriff Walker's right-hand man, was all right. The buckaroo was fast with his guns, an excellent shot, and could ride better than any of them. He had spent his youth as a cowboy on a ranch somewhere in Kansas. Still, he didn't have the skills the mountain men had, not even the sheriff who was once a trapper and buffalo hunter a long time ago. Rory had worked for Sheriff Joseph Walker for years before they set out to cross the South Pass and on to Oregon. He had been the one who held off the Blackfeet Indians when they sieged him and a bunch of greenhorn missionaries. They didn't even know the danger they were in, but Rory suspected.

They crept down a few feet at a time, careful not to snap a twig or kick loose gravel. Every minute or two they stopped to listen, but there wasn't a sound. The hair stood up on the backs of their necks. Everybody was as tense as a primed trigger. It just needed someone to caress it and the powder keg would explode. They held their breaths as they took another step.

What came tumbling into their field of vision on the trail right in front of them was a massive ball of tan and brown fur amid a flurry of growls. It appeared so suddenly, even though they expected something, it caught them by surprise. A grizzly bear had latched on to a massive mountain lion and they were tearing each other to pieces. Virgil tried to take a bead, but they moved too quickly in their struggle for life and death. The animals didn't even notice the humans.

The massive feline's jaw latched firmly onto the enormous bear's neck, and the grizzly's yellow teeth sunk deep into the cat's back. It was just a question of time before the nervous system of the mountain lion snapped from the pressure on its spine or the bear suffocated. Still, the observers stood with their mouths open so wide their chins hit their chests.

High in a tree, well behind the fighting animals, yelled Rory Breaker as the tip waved to and fro. "Up here! In this scraggly pine!" His green eyes were spread wide. He was so scared his hair stood on end and the blood drained from his face.

The Kansas cowboy held a pistol in his shaking fist as he wrapped his other arm tightly around the thin trunk at the top. It looked weak and brittle, like it could break with the next sway produced by never-ending gusts of wind. He was clearly out of his depth.

Rusty waved his hands and put his finger to his lips. He didn't breathe a word. As long as the two wild animals were busy in their struggle to survive, the mountain men stood a chance of creeping around the danger. Rusty motioned for them to swing wide. Virgil had finally caught the rhythm of the fight and believed he could kill one, but that would leave the other alive, with all its attention focused on them. If the bear survived, which was the one they bet on, they would look like dinner.

As they crept around the danger, the struggling animals began to tire. They fought sporadically as they huffed, trying to gobble much-needed air. They stopped to rest and catch their panting breaths before beginning their combat again. As they came even with the beasts, they were close enough to smell the intense fear—both theirs and that of the angry animals.

Suddenly, the grizzly's and the mountain lion's eyes shot up toward the White man in the tree. Rory had ignored Rusty's instructions and began to yell and scream again. He was too frightened to think straight. It was his first encounter with a grizzly, not to mention the most enormous mountain lion he had ever seen.

"Don't leave me up here, fellas!" Rory cried.

Those few words full of fear snapped the animals out of their trances, and their attention went to an easy meal. The mountain men froze in their tracks. Rusty didn't dare wave his hands again. With them so close to the wild beast, he would draw their attention, and they were far too close for comfort. The beast focused on a meal up in a pine he could quickly scale in seconds.

The cat's eyes flitted back and forth. It wasn't as interested in eating a man as it was getting the bear's teeth out of his back. He clamped his jaws tighter and tried to snap the grizzly's neck, but it was just too thick. They were at a virtual standoff, and the cat saw no possible victory, so its thoughts turned to flight. It was like a spontaneous switch that flicked on in its head, and its intentions instantly changed direction one hundred eighty degrees.

The grizzly suddenly let go of the cat, which released its own death bite and raced away as fast as it could. Blood ran down its back from four thumb-sized holes. Still, it didn't appear to register the pain as it looked for a way to flee, dodging both the bear and the trappers to one side. The cat had no interest in more confrontations. It wasn't even interested in the White man high in a tree anymore. It would rather flee for its home and lick its wounds in the safety of its mountain cave.

The bear turned for the fragile pine and broke into a run as Rory's voice yelled, raising in pitch until it was just under a scream. The mountain men calmly took beads on the attacking animal. When it hit the tree with all its power, they heard a loud crack, but still, it didn't go down. Breaker swayed from side to side as the tree threatened to split in two, dropping him within reach of the massive paws of the bear.

Four shots rang out nearly simultaneously. At first, they thought they had all missed—something that had never happened before. Soon, four bullet holes bubbled blood, so they knew they had hit their marks, but still, the giant bear didn't go down. It didn't even slow. The grizzly's interest was still on the easy meal in the top of the tree. Adrenaline had it so pumped up that it hardly felt the gunshot wounds.

It surprised everybody when Captain Forrester drew his sword and calmly walked up to the menacing beast. He acted like he was on a Sunday stroll. He was standing right behind it when it realized he was there. Spittle spewed from its mouth as it roared again. Then, it suddenly went silent.

The hilt of a saber stuck from its eye socket with the tip poking out the back of its massive head. How the captain found the strength to drive the saber through its brain and skull, nobody knew. He was so pumped up with energy that he felt like he had superhuman strength. He stood before the dead beast, huffing and panting like a wild animal.

Just as quickly as it began, it was over. They only heard the huffs of the dying bear's lungs over a breeze singing through the pines. They looked up, and Rory was still there, clutching the tree for dear life.

"You can come down now, Rory," Sheriff Walker called out. "The lion's ran off, and the bear's dead. Just don't break your neck on the way. That pine looks like it could snap at any minute."

Breaker blinked and frowned as he looked under him, still unconvinced that the danger was over.

"You do know that both grizzly bears and mountain lions can climb trees, don't cha?" Levi asked, smiling.

For him, it was just another day living in the wilderness. He wouldn't even call this day a close call. Nobody had even been injured. Only Rory's pride was damaged, but Johnson knew he would get over that.

White Ghost

The sun glared overhead, reflecting off the bright crystals. Something moved in the bushes, but not a trace of man nor beast could be seen or heard. Crickets suddenly chirped their synchronized choir, stopping momentarily and resuming their chatter. Lazy white clouds floated between the earth and the sun, forming cotton-like figures. A blue sky stretched from mountaintop to mountaintop high in the Rockies.

Long shadows cast by massive pines stood all around him, leaving an overpowering odor. The tops swayed in the early fall breeze. The first snow had fallen, and everything was white, blotting out tracks of all living things. Lumps of snow fell from bough to bough and finally plopped to the ground. Small flurries like white dust devils ran across the countryside, kicking up white powder.

Ants crawled into his eyes and nose as he lay motionless, oblivious of the pesky insects. The flies located him in the first five minutes and had been buzzing in his ears ever since. Even though his legs were bare, he didn't feel the cold, or maybe he ignored it. The alpha predator patiently waited. Hours had passed before he finally blinked his eyes. He wore an albino wolfskin coat that was hard to see with the fresh white powder. His face was painted white like a mask, making him blend in with his surroundings. Only his black eyes made him all but invisible. Mud mixed with gray ashes matted his hair, making him appear more like a ghost than a meager mortal.

The large Blackfoot war chief's gaze appeared cold and deadly under a massive brow. His face had an unhealthy yellow tint, but the monster inside the bag of bones disregarded all pain and welcomed the suffering because it kept him sharp. The blanket of snow rolled brightly for as far as he could see.

White Ghost was a renegade Blackfoot Indian. Years previously, he and three members of his tribe rode off against their tribal chief and medicine men's orders. They decided to take their futures into their own hands and start a war with the trespassers, killing their buffalo and stealing their hides. Long ago, his father was murdered by French trappers. Now, he sought revenge on them all. Their color and language mattered little. He planned at least to try to run every European-American off their land or die trying. He thought to start with killing as many as he could then and there. He had already killed so many Indians he had lost count, and that included warriors from his own tribe.

Many *other Indian* tribes were among his targets. All of them were enemies of the Blackfoot Nation. Or if they crossed him or tried to stop what he was doing, then even the Blackfeet Tribe from where he came would become targets. He was on a mission and intended to allow nobody to interfere or hinder his success. Anyone or anything that stepped in the way died at his hands. He would show no mercy.

Thud...thud...thud. His heartbeat slowly throbbed. His eyes were fixed and expressionless. Nobody knew what happened inside that evil mind, not even the men he rode with. His breathing nearly stopped as he slowed his metabolism and voluntarily began to shut down his body. Only the breeze pushed tall grass and bushes as it came in light gusts. Woodpeckers hammered on tree trunks as crows cawed from branches. Another snow would fall in the night just in time to erase the footprints with a new blanket of powder, making it difficult to track White Ghost and his braves.

Streaks of white paint ran down the front and back of his legs and arms, making him look like a skeleton. His brow cast a shadow on his hypnotizing stare. His men waited back three hundred yards deep in the bushes. They were all skilled at creeping up on the enemy, but White Ghost was the Blackfoot master. Beside him laid a long bow and on his back a leather quiver of arrows. A brace of flintlock pistols was shoved into his pants.

A single bead of sweat popped up on his brow and threaded its way over the wrinkles and around his ruddy complexion, into his deep, dark eyes. Even the salty water didn't make him blink or flinch. A dozen whiskers populated the chin of an otherwise smooth face. His long black hair hung past his shoulders. Sheathed knives hung on either side.

White Ghost's unwavering stare traced across the distance. Before he made a move, he had to ensure nobody else was there. He closed his eyes briefly and listened intently, but there were no out-of-place sounds. A log cabin surrounded by a zigzag wooden post fence stood less than seventy yards away. Smoke drifted from a stone chimney as empty chairs dotted the porch around a table. Still, nobody was visible. Maybe they were asleep.

Sun slanted through the trees like rain, making dark shadows grow under the gable roof. Finally, he saw movement behind the single window next to the heavy timber door. It was closed to keep out the weather. Beside the cabin was a neatly stacked cord of wood. A tall, wooded structure was at the edge of the fence, not much broader or deeper than the door. It emitted a rank, overpowering odor that strangled the fresh air.

When the grizzly-looking mountain man stepped outside, his breath disappeared with the breeze. He wore a bearskin coat, knee-high moccasins, and buckskin britches. A gray beard and shoulder-length hair framed a rugged face. He held a steaming coffee in one hand and a long gun in his other.

He leaned the rifle against the wall and sat at the table as he stuffed his ceramic pipe from a twist of tobacco. His eyes followed his finger under the line of print on the newspaper. A second image moved behind the four wavy glass panes. The smell of sulfur momentarily filled the air as the wooden stick produced a blue flame. The mountain man puffed the pipe to life, leaving his head in a haze of smoke as his eyes quickly returned to the newspaper.

The war chief's eyes slowly narrowed as he breathed deeply through his nose. He could smell the ripeness of his victim. He was close, and the time had nearly come. Still, he waited for a second White trapper to come out.

He knew there were at least two, and it was said that there were maybe even more. A patient man wouldn't get caught off guard. White Ghost wasn't in a hurry, nor was he afraid. He had all the time in the world to do what he had come to do, and he planned to do it right. For him, fear was a feeling that had long ago vanished.

Three mature warriors sat silently in the bushes, awaiting their chief's return. There were no other objectives left in their lives but to follow White Ghost wherever he went and do whatever he wanted. They no longer had an opinion of their own as they blindly followed their war chief no matter where it led. For them it was enough to simply follow him to their demise.

They all knew they were on a one-way journey. Still, they waited for the leader's signal impassibly. These warrior braves no longer had any expectations in life. They knew they were on their last voyage and were heading for Hell. All they asked was that, on their way to doom, they could keep their leader safe from all the dangers that surrounded him.

The war chief's drawn face pulled into tight, sunken cheeks. No smile lines creased his face, indicating a grin rarely crossed his lips. Door hinges creaked as the cabin's front door opened, and a second mountain man stepped onto the porch. He wrapped his hands around the warm porcelain cup and kicked the door shut. Another folded newspaper was under his arm. He took a seat beside the first man. White Ghost smiled as he looked through the window and saw no more movement. Perhaps the others were gone.

The bushes rustled when he grabbed his bow and drew two arrows from his quiver. One lay cradled in the bowline, and the other protruded from his fingers. It looked like a smile tried to grace his lips, but it turned out to be more like a gruesome gash. Suddenly, White Ghost stood, but still, they didn't notice. Both men were busy with their morning drinks and tobacco while reading the newspapers they had acquired at the Rendezvous.

The war chief finally whistled to get the mountain men's attention. The first one startled and then lunged for the rifle leaning against the wall. He responded much quicker than the Indian expected. An arrow with white feathers traversed his lung and pinned him to the wall. It was over in less than a second.

The second mountain man turned to run off the porch and dive for cover. A long arrow with a heavy flint-stone head pierced the side of his knee, slicing through tendon, ligaments, and cartilage, nearly taking off his leg at the joint. It folded under his weight, and he dropped to the ground like a sack of potatoes. It all happened so suddenly that nobody was ready. The rifle remained leaning against the wall. Steam rolled off hot cups of coffee. Everything went silent. The same silence that usually followed death.

The frontiersman nailed to the log cabin wall sagged as his heart stopped, and he drew his last breath. A thin arrow held up all his weight, but the dogwood didn't break. The second pioneer howled like a gutted wolf as his vocal cords strained and the muscles in his neck stretched tight. After several minutes, his voice gave out, becoming a silent scream on a distorted face.

White Ghost stood at the edge of the tree line, watching with curious eyes. His gaze was intense, as if he were memorizing each detail so he could later recall

all that happened, watching it in his mind's eye. Killing White men was the only thing that gave him a good feeling, maybe something like pleasure, and even though it was fleeting, he was still addicted. He seemed to crave more and more all the time. With each death, he seemed to want the next even more.

Of course, at first, it was about revenge for losing a family life. But as time passed and his fame grew, something evil invaded his being, like a poison vine strangling a plant. So, it was no longer about honor or restitution but instead a habit—both the death of an inferior race and watching the life go out in their eyes. Especially when he had the time to torture his victims for a few days, it would be the most prolonged death they could have ever imagined. He was a master at drawing it out, making it very slow and terribly painful.

He turned on his heels and jogged back toward his waiting men. He knew he should have called them, but he felt like pushing things to the limit. It made him feel more alive. Despite the reputation of the mountain men from the compound, they were just as easy to kill as a couple of old women. The widows in his tribe would have given them more trouble. His eyes smiled at how easily he defeated them. One was surely dead, and the other wouldn't last long if he weren't rescued. But even if they did save him, he would be back again to finish the job before it was all over.

He slowly walked back to his braves with an arrogance few men dared. He stopped halfway and whistled. He wanted his warriors to see what he did, so they sang about him in elders' songs and even more men would fear his wrath. He heard footsteps on soft morning snow. The frosted cover crunched under their feet.

Gossip ran rampant through all the Indian nations, just like every other race. It was also one of the only means of communication besides smoke signals. Rumors would become facts, and they would become songs that would serve like newspapers from back east when sung. The Indians' information tree was much more effective than Easterners' newspapers and posters. Both carried tainted information, though one was distant and hard to acquire, but the Indian gossip came and went whether you wanted it to or not.

Hook Scar was the first Blackfoot warrior to come running. He was as faithful as an old dog. His Indian name was so long that even the members of the tribe shortened it to Scar. The ancient wound ran across his high forehead and onto his cheek, twisting to his jaw. Beyond that was a missing ear. He wore his battle scars proudly. Usually only a look from him was enough to tame an enemy or make them turn and run for fear of their lives.

"Black Crow, make sure you have a good look, but whatever you three do, don't kill the old man," White Ghost warned. He sounded satisfied. "I want to watch him suffer for a while. The scavengers will arrive as soon as we leave, and they'll probably finish the job. Maybe he'll still be barely alive enough to tell the rest of the White men what happened. I know there's more of them living up here. I heard it from some Crow Indians. They told me right before I killed them. They disclosed all their secrets in exchange for a quick death."

Black Crow, a short Indian with bowed legs, nodded to his war chief. He was the best rider of the little war party. A Comanche war party had captured him when he was young and he was forced to live with them for several years. But he did become as good a rider as his kidnappers. He flicked his braids over his shoulders. They hung halfway down his back.

"Why didn't you call us?" their best tracker, Nuka, asked.

His name meant younger brother. He was White Ghost's youngest sibling. From a child, he followed him blindly wherever he went despite the fact the man-ghost usually ignored him. White Ghost treated him like a pesky insect. Nuka pulled back his hair into a ponytail. It made his sharp features stand out. He had a longbow strapped to his back and a rifle in each fist. He passed one to the war chief. "You take too many needless risks, big brother."

The Discovery

They could see vultures circling overhead as soon as they got a mile from the compound. The sight of the scavengers gave them a sense of urgency. Hopefully, they weren't too late. When they got nearer, they heard coyotes racing through the forest, heading for the smell of death. One hungry pack disregarded their presence as they raced right past them down the same trail. They didn't appear to notice they were even there.

They ran forward. When they jumped the fence, the yard was void of footprints. They stopped and looked all around. They wondered if this could be a trap, but they neither saw nor heard anything. They carefully cocked their pistols and snuck around to have a peek at the porch.

Moments later, screams echoed through the mountains and bounced off canyon walls. He couldn't hold back his suffering when they cut off his leg. The agony was too much to bear in silence. Again came howls much like wolves, but it was a human's cries of pain dragged from the deepest depths of his being. It was excruciating suffering caused by Levi sawing through flesh and bone. Virgil stirred hot coals in the roaring fire. He used a shovel to fill a metal bucket. The tin glowed orange from the heat of the cinders. Waves of warmth and steam rolled off the surface.

All this brought back dark memories to the one-armed captain. He, too, remembered the pain and the smell of burning flesh above all. That and seeing his arm laying in the dirt. Ever since that day, he had refused to fully acknowledge that he was missing an arm. It certainly didn't seem to slow him down. If anything, it made him more determined and more dangerous. He never hid his pinned sleeve, even to his most desperate enemies. From a stranger's perspective, he looked proud to have sacrificed a limb. Nobody knew exactly what the captain thought.

"Hang in there; I'm just about done, pard." Levi huffed as sweat drained from every pore of his body.

His hands were slippery with blood and perspiration. Claret covered every nearby surface and pooled beneath the wounded mountain man's leg.

Johnson blinked his eyes to wash away the salt. His breathing was fast, and his heart pounded painfully between his ears. "Hold 'im now, boys. This is gonna hurt like the dickens. Bite on that wood like ya mean it, dag-gum-it!" His eyes narrowed and his mouth was no more than a slash. He ground his jaws as he contemplated the task before him.

"I can do this." Levi clenched his jaws. He knew in one quick motion it would be over. "Come on, old pard, hang on," Levi prayed. He closed his eyes briefly as he prepared to finish the job. He was covered in a cold sweat and had to focus to keep from trembling. He felt a dark cloud overhead as though shadows of ghosts were biting at his heels.

The born tracker raised the large Bowie knife, and the sun flashed off the blade as he brought it down, chopping through the last bit of knee. He grabbed a jug of spirits and generously dosed the stump. Then he put it to his lips and gulped, then gulped some more. His friend's eyes rolled back into his head, and he passed out.

"Quick now, let's get this done before he comes around," the captain said. "If he wakes up, it's just gonna be that much worse. If we're lucky, he'll be out until it's over."

They picked him up under his arms, dragging the good leg behind them, and shoved the stump deep into the hot coals. Foul-smelling smoke rolled off the burning skin and out of the bucket, but it sealed the wound. Then it was over. They were all winded and exhausted. It had been a nerve-racking experience. Virgil carefully covered the raw stump with some brown powder from a can, and then he wrapped it in bandages. He clicked his tongue as he shook his head.

"That's a mighty bad lookin' wound for an arrow," Virgil said. He picked up the arrowhead and inspected it. "Just look at the size of this thing."

They all had been wholly focused on the task, but now exhaustion had taken over. They didn't even see the two men walk up to the porch. Each had a heavy rifle in their hands. Even when they were standing beside the building, they still didn't notice them.

The grizzly-looking mountain man cleared his throat and asked, "Is that there Gus Grizzel missin' a leg? What in the world happened to him? He looks like he's on death's door. And where's Fred? Usually, those two are like peas in a pod. Where you find one, you'll always find the other." Rusty Steel shook his head and spat a stream of brown juice into the dirt. He blinked his eyes and looked around the yard.

Will stood, brushing dust off his empty sleeve. He pulled off his hat and nodded toward a freshly covered grave at the edge of the fence. Wood planks groaned as Rusty walked to the table. An empty glass sat beside another jug of corn liquor. He poured half a glass and drained it in one gulp.

"And all that work we did to save these two from the Rivers Brothers, and now look at what happens," Angus whispered in awe. "How'd it go down, Levi?"

Gus was still unconscious. His breathing was fast and shallow. It was anybody's guess right then if he would make it or not. Time would tell the story. His face was the color of cool ashes from a burned-out fire. His skin was cold and clammy, but he was covered in sweat just the same. At least it was a sign he was still alive and might have enough in him to survive, despite the loss.

"Did ya find these in Gus and Fred?" Rusty asked as he picked up and studied the arrows. Then, he focused on the feathers. "These arrows belong to White Ghost. This ain't the first time I've seen these, so the owner's close." His gaze went past the compound and across the distance. This far down the mountain, the land was more stretched out and manageable, and a man could see much farther.

"Who's this White Ghost?" the captain asked. "I don't believe in ghosts, and I've never heard you mention the name before, either. So why all the mystery?"

"Of course, he ain't a real ghost, Will." Rusty frowned. "Whatcha take me for, a fool? He likes to dress up like a phantom, is all. See how long these arrows are? He makes 'em special himself, just like he does his bows, and they're longer too. It makes 'em go farther, faster. And the feathers are all from albino hawks. He's a Blackfoot, but he's so bad even his own tribe don't want him around. I doubt he likes them much, either. There's four of 'em in all. At least, that was the last I heard. The other three would be Black Crow, Scar, and Nuka. He ain't the kind of war chief that draws big crowds. The men who ride with him have vowed their lives to their leader. Like Gus here, anybody else who runs into them usually dies or at least gets badly wounded. The man is so evil, he's famous. I'm sure he left Gus just alive enough for us to see what happened. Still, I'd recognize those arrows anywhere."

"I've never heard of a Blackfoot Indian by that name," the captain said. "If he's so dangerous, why haven't we heard either of you talk about him? Especially somebody so feared, and you say he's famous? From how you talk, you'd think it was the boogie man."

"We don't talk about 'im because we thought he was dead," Angus replied in a whisper. It was as if he talked too loudly, the ghost would hear. "He was such an evil man that once he died, nobody wanted to remember 'im. Folks got angry if ya talked about 'im. I ain't seen the man personally, but Rusty has. Once I heard he was dead, I pushed all the nightmarish stories out of my mind and can't even remember thinkin' about 'im since. Ain't it strange how your brain will do that? Then again, the stories about that wicked man were hair-raising."

"I never believed he was dead for a minute." Rusty

finally broke his silence. "During my lifetime, he's died four or five times, at least. The first couple of times, I believed it all right. But by the third time, I knew he was playin' games. He must be getting on in years by now. I reckon he might be about my age. Whatcha say, Angus?"

"There on abouts," Angus replied. "Then again, how old is a ghost really?"

"Don't start talkin' nonsense on me, now," Rusty warned. "I don't kin to fools. I imagine I'd have known if I'd seen a ghost. When I saw 'im, he was flesh and blood just like us. If he bleeds, he'll die soon enough."

"Why is this fella so famous?" Joseph asked. "Most famous outlaws are in the newspapers or the nickel novels. This one nobody wants to talk about. I wonder why that is? What makes this renegade so different than the rest? Different enough that people wanna forget he ever existed."

But Rusty was only partly listening to what they said. He was staring into the distance as his fingertip brushed across the pointed tip of the arrow. He cocked his head to one side, and for a second, he thought he heard Indian war drums, but it was only the wind.

"We can't let this go," Rusty said. "We're gonna have to track 'im back to where he came from. Now that he's started again, there'll be more than a couple of victims. The last time, he killed over a hundred, counting men, women, and children, not to mention the horses. The fool is a killing machine, and he has no other purpose in life. At least that's what I seen in his eyes last time I gazed at 'em. They used to say he lived in a cave at the water's edge in a place called Hidden Lake, high up in the mountains. I don't know anybody that's been there but me, but for most folks it's just a speculation."

"You do know what happened here could have just as easily have happened to us, don't cha?" Angus asked as he stared at Rusty. "I reckon the task befalls us in the end. Somebody's gotta stop this madman once and for all. He's a curse to his community and a mortal danger for trappers and hunters, not to mention the people passing through."

"Somebody go to the stable and get me a horse," Levi said. "We're gonna have to rush Gus back up the mountain. Whatcha think, Rusty? Will he make it?"

Gus was still unconscious, but beads of sweat covered his face, neck, and arms. Virgil touched Gus's forehead, and he was burning up. His breathing was becoming shallower by the minute. He was probably in shock. They were all lucky he was out cold. Otherwise, he would be screaming his head off. They didn't have a thing for the pain other than whiskey, so they hoped he remained unconscious for as long as possible.

"He'll have to, I reckon," Rusty replied. He was as angry as Levi had ever seen him. "We've got to get him back to the house where Dennis and Betty can care for 'im. If we leave 'im here, one or two of us will have to stay too, leaving us short if we're gonna chase this outlaw down. He's as dangerous as they come, and it won't be safe on this mountain until he's dead and buried."

"Better killed, burned, and buried," Angus growled. "This man ain't that easy to kill."

"We have to bury Fred first." Virgil huffed as he pulled out his Bible. As he headed to the edge of the compound, he began to pray.

Lovejoy checked his bandage handiwork on Gus's leg and even impressed himself. It would do until Dennis could look at it back home. Dennis Breed was the compound veterinarian, so he cared for the banged-up or sick mountain men, too. He had an array of herbs, powders, and poisons.

An hour later, a teeth-clenched curse followed Lovejoy as he threw the last shovel of dirt on the grave. He would usually still be reading from the Bible, but how their friends died and were wounded made him too angry to read and pray. He rushed through the ceremony, closing his Good Book without reading another line. Everybody was in a hurry to get back home and prepare to track White Ghost to the ends of the earth if necessary.

Above the captain's sun-darkened face was the slapped-up brim of an officer's cavalry hat. Below the bill were angry blue eyes. A week-old beard stubble darkened the captain's face. It added a few years to his appearance; he already looked older than Levi, and they were the same age.

"We're gonna have to make this right for the boys and every other living soul that monster stole the life out of," Rusty growled. "I'm gettin' mighty tired of standing around the graves of our friends."

They slung Gus over a saddle and tied him down so he wouldn't fall off. He was still out cold and looked as pale as death. Doubts filled the minds of his friends and rescuers. They all wondered if they had made it in time or whether they were too late to save Grizzel's life. It was clear it would be touch and go, but they had to try. There was always hope.

If they managed to get him to their compound alive,

at least he would be safe from further attacks. Time would tell when he finally came around, if he regained consciousness at all. They were still waiting to hear the story in detail, but Rusty knew the truth. It would have happened so fast that they hardly knew what was going down. Fred was dead before he even knew death was out there spying on them both.

Back to Safety

Finally, when they all rode into the compound, Gus was just beginning to come around, despite being tied down over the back of his horse. They could all hear him groan and swear. He recovered consciousness as soon as they stepped into their snow-covered yard. In seconds, the word was out, and everybody came running. Dark red blood contrasted with the white bandages on the short stump of Grizzel's leg. He struggled to breathe doubled over a saddle.

"Get me off here, will ya?" he huffed in a barely audible voice.

"Not a word about who did this until I figure it out," Rusty whispered. It was just loud enough for his companions to hear. "I don't want to scare 'em all to death before we know how we'll go at this. We know where that old ghost's goin', and he ain't headed this way. I reckon he wants us to chase him onto his territory and probably up to the lake. Then he'll know the lay of the land like the back of his hand, and I reckon we're gonna oblige, but it won't be what he's expectin'."

As soon as Dennis stepped off his porch and saw his friends' faces, he knew there was trouble. And here, he had expected a tranquil winter without mishaps. It was the same wish he made each fall, but he had never had a mellow winter to date. For some reason, he kept expecting the next one to be the one.

Dog ran around the yard like every time he returned from a trip. He chased the horses a couple of laps, then raced around the fenced boundaries, marking and barking up a storm. Nobody paid him any attention because he always acted the same. Nobody knew the black dog's age, but he still acted like a puppy—another trait his old master, Rusty Steel, had.

Breed walked over, took Gus's horse's reins, and looked at his leg. He shook his head and got close enough to have a whiff. He wrinkled his nose and frowned. The wound was just beginning to smell rotten. He held his hand to Gus's clammy head and nodded. He felt Gus's pulse as he felt his own to compare. It was weak, but it was there. When he touched the stump, Gus groaned as he bit his teeth and tried to resist another scream. His jaws ground as they fought to hold it back.

"Get me off the horse," Gus said with a gravelly, fading voice.

"We've gotta scrub that wound down till it's raw," Mountain Dennis said, now deadly serious. "Who knows how much dirt got in there? Then, we can wrap it with a damp cloth, cover it with canvas, and stick it in a bucket of snow. The cold will reduce the swelling and ease the pain. If we rub the stump with methylated spirits, it'll harden quick. I just hope you didn't nick a bone and some chips are still inside. That'll raise the risk of infection. All in all, I'd say it's a miracle you got 'im here alive."

Gus groaned some more as they untied him and gently lifted him down and onto a large blanket. Then, they each took a corner and carried him into Mountain Dennis's cabin. A small fire glowed in the corner, and a circle of light shone from a kerosene lantern on the dinner table. Three beds were in the very back. A potbellied cookstove stood beside the window. When they got him settled in a bunk, Dennis went to work. Two minutes later, Betty Crockett was standing at his side, working as his nurse. Together, Gus got just about as good attention as could be expected in such a remote location.

Mountain Dennis oversaw caring for sick or wounded livestock, so he naturally gravitated to becoming the compound doctor, too. Sometimes, the Crow medicine men would even stop by and ask for some of his modern medicines, powders, or elixirs he acquired yearly at the Rendezvous. Everything needed was available at the fur trappers' meet held once a year for the last fifteen years. Even the rarest medications were for sale for a price, like everything at the trappers' meet.

Five hundred customers walked down from the mountains to sell their furs and barter and buy goods of every description. He had even bought needles and catgut for stitches, sharp scalpels, and forceps to clamp arteries. Breed had never studied to be a veterinarian, but it came to him naturally since he was born and raised on a farm. He was always surprised at the semi-lattices of barnyard animals and human beings. Once you got past the thick skin, even pigs had similar organs.

Dennis growled at everybody until they left the room. He didn't need the whole compound looking over his shoulder. Still, as focused as he was, he couldn't help but note Betty's perfume. When he breathed in, it made him a little dizzy. Every man in the compound was a smidgen in love with the blond-haired beauty, even if she wasn't a spring chicken. She held a mature grace that they seldom saw in the wilderness. He wondered what the special occasion was for her to wear such alluring perfume. Then he shrugged it off and enjoyed the fresh smell of a healthy woman as he worked on their friend.

"Gus never could stay out of trouble," Dennis growled. "And poor Fred was too dumb for his own good. At least we've got a fighting chance to fix one of 'em up. That is if the Good Lord is willin'."

Outside, Levi caught Dahteste in his arms after she raced across the yard barefoot in the snow. Happiness danced in both their eyes and was visible to anyone paying attention. Reuniting was a special occasion. Still, Dahteste looked at her husband with raised eyebrows. She was one smart cookie and figuring out what was up wouldn't take long. She probably even saw the smoke signals, but chances were, as they were Blackfeet, she couldn't decipher the message.

Captain Forrester rode his horse around the yard like he was checking to ensure everything was secure, but he was confused and trying to hide it. He had been looking forward to seeing Betty upon his arrival, but he'd hardly caught sight of her before she ran off to be a nurse and help Dennis tend to Gus's leg, much like he rode off to put out every fire he saw. Maybe they were more alike than he had suspected. When he saw Dahteste run for Levi, a pang of jealousy stung like little thorns. He wheeled his black stallion for the north exit and rode out of the compound without a word.

His horse's shiny black coat contrasted with the white snow-covered surroundings. It pranced proudly as they trotted out of sight. Soon, they were a black dot in the darkening distance. The captain had the habit of riding off in the early evenings without warning. Usually, it was because he was looking for threats and was worried about what he considered to be his family. This time, it was to hide his jealousy. It was a brand-new feeling for him, and he clearly didn't like it. He felt it was below him to have such sensations. Maybe he was more like other human beings than he had thought.

Both Levi and Dahteste saw him and frowned. He was Johnson's best friend, and Levi knew Will was lonely and confused. Since they lived in a virtual wilderness, having a companion or even a wife was important. But then again, maybe the captain was destined to be a loner. Time would tell if he got up the nerve to confront Miss Crockett.

"You need to have a talk with the captain," Dahteste whispered in her husband's ear. "You are his best friend, you know. It's your job and nobody else's. Who else would he listen to but you or maybe Rusty?"

"Uh-huh, and Rusty thinks it's all a folly anyway," Levi replied. "Tell me exactly what you want me to tell 'im. You know I ain't the captain's boss no more than he's mine. We're partners, not employees. Let 'im be; I'm sure he'll get around to sidlin' up to Miss Betty. Or at least I hope he gives her a chance. I think she feels somethin' for him, but I ain't quite sure. Women have always been pretty much a mystery to me. At least until I met you, darlin'."

"Why are all men alike?" Dahteste grumbled. "It doesn't matter if they're red like me or white like you. Men always leave the romantic advances to the women. Why do we always have to come begging for you to pay attention to us? When they do, they're like a doe in a hunter's gunsights and don't know what to say. All this bravery on the battlefield don't add up once they get home. Lucky for you, I'm a forward woman."

"Those words sound like something you've heard somebody else say," Levi replied, holding back a smile. "I thought you had all the braves chasin' you around when you were a young woman."

"They all wanted me because I'm different and won't let anybody tell me what to do." Dahteste laughed. "That and because I am so beautiful."

"So, why did you fall for me and not for one of them Crow warrior braves if they were so crazy about cha?" Levi laughed. "I hardly made an advance on ya."

"That's the problem I'm talking about. Why I fell for you is still a mystery even to me, Levi." Dahteste had a naughty look on her face when they locked eyes. They hadn't seen each other for several days, and she yearned for his love.

Johnson grabbed her arm and pulled her into the shadows beside the nearest building. He put his lips to hers, and they kissed, and it was just as good as the first time. He could hear her heartbeat race in her chest. She listened to his, and it sounded like a deep bass drum. When their lips touched, she drew in a deep breath and melted in his arms. For just a moment, they completely forgot where they were.

"Help with the chores, you two, then you can go to your cabin if you wanna court and spark." Rusty laughed. "By golly, it sure is grand to be back home. I don't know why we ever venture outside the compound's fence. Every time we do, it spells trouble."

They unsaddled the horses, brushed them down, and saw they were watered and fed. The animals always came first before they cleaned up and had something to eat themselves. By the time they finished, the day was coming to an end, and the sun was no more than an orange sliver at the end of the world. Fire-flies glittered in their silent dance across the yard and to the tree line —an owl called out in the night, waiting for a response from its mate. The reply came from the other side of the forest.

Once they finished the chores and the slabs of elk they had hunted they had their meal. Virgil was allowed to head for the kitchen while the others cared for the animals. Then, they would have hot food and coffee on the table by the time they finished.

Virgil made them all wait impatiently, seated around the table as he said grace. Since he made the food, even those not as religiously inclined as he respected his beliefs as he respected theirs—even the Indians.

As usual, nobody spoke as the famished travelers scoffed down every bit of food served and were wiping down their plates with chunks of fresh white bread.

Rusty stifled a burp and said, "Excuse me, ladies, but men will be men even if women are around." He chuckled like a naughty child. "I reckon we best talk about what happened to Gus. Is he gonna make it, Dennis?"

"Betty and I've done everything we could, so it's out of our hands now. It all depends on how tough an old cob Gus really is. I know Fred would have never made it this far; rest his poor soul. In my opinion, at least Gus has a fightin' chance."

The hinges on the front door groaned as Army boots hammered the wood plank floor. The captain stood behind Levi and across from Betty, but he avoided her eyes, fearing he would give away his secret. He wasn't even quite sure what the secret was.

"Who killed Fred and crippled Gus?" Dahteste asked. She suspected somebody wicked, but she never imagined who it really was. She, like all her tribe, thought the ghost was dead.

"The four wickedest men I've ever run across are responsible for Fred's death and Gus's missing leg. I reckon he crippled Grizzel on purpose, so he'd live long enough to tell us who he was. I doubt he thought I'd recognize his arrows right off like I did."

Dahteste's face froze when Rusty mentioned four men and arrows. "Were they long arrows with white feathers?" she asked as she held her breath. His expression suddenly turned into an unreadable mask. Now, she was a Crow war chief and was as serious as death.

Levi noticed how rigid his wife's body went. He had never seen her afraid, but now he saw just that. Dennis also gasped because he had heard the stories, too. Anybody living in the Rocky Mountains for any time had eventually at least heard about the renegade Blackfoot war party and its leader. The other visitors to the compound were oblivious to the name or the reputation.

The lieutenant, corporal, and private were unaware

that such a dangerous Indian even existed. The same went for Betty. They had all been fortunate enough never to have laid eyes on the evilest man in the Rockies. Only Rusty Steel had seen him in the flesh and would recognize him with a glance. He had been close enough to gaze into his dead eyes, and he knew what they were up against.

"His name is White Ghost," Rusty replied to the Crow woman. "But I reckon you already know that, don't cha?"

Dahteste mouthed the words but was afraid to say his name out loud. Even as a child, they told her if she wasn't good, White Ghost would come to her in the night while she was asleep and steal her away like he had so many young boys, girls, and even women—the men he killed after torturing them within an inch of their lives. Every person in her tribe knew who he and his men were. Their names were whispered around campfires at night by the elderly. The young didn't like to think about him. It reminded them of their childhood nightmares.

"Tomorrow, Levi, the captain, Joseph, Rory, Angus, Virgil, and me will head out to find this character and end his story once and for all. This time, when he dies, it's gonna be for good, and you can mark my words on that."

"I'm gonna have to stay here and take care of Gus," Dennis said. "If not, he's probably gonna die. I can't make no call on 'im in the state he's in now, but he'll need some serious lookin' after."

"Well, we can't leave the compound alone without protection," Rusty said. "The lieutenant, corporal, and private can stay behind. Dahteste can help ya, too. If you have any serious trouble, she can hightail it for the Crow camp and ask Chief Hachta for help. It's only a few hours' ride."

"And what if I don't want to stay behind?" Dahteste asked, clearly offended. She didn't like anybody but Chief Hachta bossing her around. "I don't like people telling me what to do. Remember, I'm a war chief."

"Well, then, act like one," Rusty growled. "I run this compound, like it or not. I have the contacts with your chief and all. I doubt he'll agree if you go against my wishes. Everything I do, I do for the good of us who live in the compound and our friends in the mountains. You're gonna have to learn to do as you're told sometimes, young lady. I'm doing all this for our own good. Here, we need somebody to be in charge if the going gets tough, and you're the only reliable fighter I have to spare."

"I know you Army boys can fight, but with all due respect, all three of ya are in poor shape, so you'd better protect the compound with your rifles and pistols. We've got extras if ya need 'em. That means you're in charge, young lady. Every person we leave behind is your responsibility, and don't take it lightly. I expect them to all be alive when we return, just like I plan to bring all our boys back with me."

Dahteste sat silent momentarily as she ran over what Rusty said in her mind. He even sounded like her chief, so she felt she had better bow down this one time and do what was best for them as a group and not as a few warrior braves.

"All right, I'll make sure everybody stays safe until you get back," Dahteste said. Her mouth was no more than a gash, and her face impossible to read, but there was truth in her words, and Levi knew how serious she was about her responsibilities.

An hour later, horses' hooves hammered the north trail as the men rode out of the compound and toward what was said to be Hidden Lake. Flurries of snow followed the pounding hooves in their wake. None of them had been there except Rusty, and he said that was over fifteen years prior. The red water in the lake was poisonous, so few people ventured to a waterless place so far out of reach and hard to get to. But it did make the perfect place for an outlaw gang or runaway renegade Indians to hide out in plain sight.

Higher Ground

The small war party continued to climb higher into the Rocky Mountains. The trail became so steep they had to lead the horses by the reins. The four Indians traveled silently and never seemed to tire. Even though they were beyond middle age, they continued briskly, like young men. They paced themselves, maintaining a steady rhythm as they trotted for their hideout near Hidden Lake. A place only they dared to inhabit. There they felt like they were at the end of the earth.

If they could lure the famous mountain men to the complex of caves, they would have them in their clutches. All White Ghost had to do was keep them interested. He started to plan a few tricks to play on the fools following them. Once they captured them, he could take their lives slowly, killing them one minute at a time.

Who knew how long a man's body could hold up to extreme torture? In White Ghost's experience, it varied greatly. Some fell dead instantly from fright, their hearts giving out before he had the time to enjoy their deaths.

Then, others suffered as much as the loss of limbs, sight, and hearing before surrendering their spirits. He enjoyed the ones that were terrified the most. He got a particular pleasure knowing he was the reason for their terror. It was one of those few things that made him feel good, and he wanted to experience it again and again.

White Ghost abruptly stopped. He turned to his warriors and said, "Nuka, you and Scar go back and capture the women at the mountain men's big compound. If there are any men left, kill them. We have the most important members of their tribe following us, so they won't have ample defense. I'll run that fool Rusty Steel out of the Rocky Mountains and all his friends with him this time, but first, I will capture and torture him. I'll have him telling me his deepest secrets in an hour. Maybe I'll torture the women first and make the men watch. White men are sensitive like that. We can watch them make fools of themselves. They will say anything to save their women."

No sooner did the war chief give the order than the two Blackfeet warriors shot off like scalded dogs after the women left back at the compound. They lived farther up the mountain near the significant enemy stronghold. White Ghost had said there was a young Crow woman and a tall, blue-eyed White lady with yellow hair. This was one of the few things that Scar liked to do.

When the torturing included women, he was all eyes and ears. If the chief allowed him, he even liked to participate in provoking the women's pain. But he didn't stop at torture. When his chief wasn't looking, he went far beyond that. Then, his sadistic side took over, and his lustful desires got placated. Many women he was told to finish off were a source of pleasure for him just before they died.

Still, he knew better than to damage the goods before they got them back to White Ghost. There would be hell to pay if there was even a scratch on them before their chief could practice his evil skills. Maybe he would skin them alive one slice at a time before the eyes of their men. They could only assume they both belonged to two of the White men. How else could they have gotten so far into the wilderness?

Nuka and Scar stepped up their pace and were now racing through the forest. They passed trees, bushes, and buffalo grass in a blur. They knew how to use nature's shadows to remain unseen. They had a good run ahead of them, but they never doubted or considered defeat or that they would be unsuccessful. They always succeeded when White Ghost planned things. If he said the women would be nearly defenseless, they believed him. He had always led them on a safe path of murder and mayhem in the past, so they felt no need to doubt his reason now.

The sun crawled toward the western horizon, but they continued to rush forward. They hadn't even broken out into a sweat yet and were hardly winded. From how they went, it looked like they could run like that for days. This is why White Ghost chose these men to follow him and saw no need for more. Sometimes, more numbers meant a lesser quality of men. He preferred to work with few and only the best.

Nobody doubted their successes, just like they knew their war chief would capture the mountain man Rusty Steel, which would mark his demise. Perhaps after this, the man-ghost would play out his death again, only to fool everyone. They only believed he was dead because they desperately wanted it to be true. He always marveled that the rumors and stories spread like a forest fire between appearances. He didn't even have to fan the flames any longer. The blaze caught all on its own and spread across the country as fast as smoke signals.

Nuka looked up, and the moon said it was nearly three o'clock. They stretched their necks to gulp down fresh mountain air. They climbed astride their horses and continued to walk into the night. A blanket of twinkling objects rolled across the sky from light years away, producing just enough light to continue.

Nuka waved the gun barrel silently, indicating that they pull up to a stop. He sat and waited with his shoulders bunched as he crept his hand around the grip. He waved the rifle in a short arch again. Scar dropped the right rein as they stepped down. They tied the horses to a tree and continued on foot. All they had to do was follow the smell of burning wood—that and the outhouse at the edge of the compound. Both were clear indications that White people were nearby.

They carefully pushed their way through thick brush and brambles, and then they came to a stop. They strained their ears to listen. Nuka parted the grass with his hands and gazed at three yellow windows on three cabins. They were all occupied, but with how many men? Maybe they could steal the women away without causing a ruckus. It was unlikely, but it didn't matter now anyway. They were committed, and now there was no turning back.

The chief had ordered them to retrieve the women and bring them back; that was precisely what they would do or die trying. Still, they had gotten away with so many murders that they no longer felt even the slightest pangs of fear or paranoia. They had all the confidence in the world because they always killed their targets and got away scot-free. There was no reason that today should be any different.

Nuka's mind returned to the woman with blue eyes and yellow hair. He wondered what it would be like. Soon, he would know.

The shadows of a stand of trees edged out to the end of the large compound. Three houses, an outhouse, and some stables stood inside the boundaries. Strings of smoke came from all three chimneys. This surprised both Nuka and Scar. There wasn't supposed to be an ample defense. They peered through the dense bushes outside the fence and waited patiently to see who appeared and whether there were women. Maybe the chief's information wasn't as good as it should have been.

As the night passed, they didn't see any sign of life in the windows. It wasn't until the last cabin in the row lit up like a lantern, casting yellow light into the night. The kerosene lamp reflected in the foggy window.

By the time morning came, the wide clearing was illuminated by several orange glowing windows. The Blackfoot Indians could see White people around a table inside the closest building. The yellow glow of lanterns reflected in the slightly steamed glass.

As soon as the first vestiges of light crept into the compound, a man appeared in the open door. Again, light spilled onto the yard, but it disappeared when he closed it again. The smallish soldier wore a blue military uniform, black boots, and a funny round blue hat. He raced for the little building at the edge of the fence with his head down. He kicked up puffs of snow as he ran for the outhouse. A spring-loaded door opened and then slammed shut behind him. A groan of relief came from inside.

Private Henry Blinds was utterly unaware that the notorious warrior braves were only feet away. He had been in too much of a hurry to pay attention to his surroundings. He wanted to get back to the table where the two women were. Even if he was too shy to enter into the conversation, he liked just sitting close enough to smell the patchouli oil on Betty and Dahteste, the smell of mint.

Corporal Butch Sorely eyed the women over the brim of his cup. Steam blurred his vision, but that way, the women couldn't see he was staring. Betty's features glowed in the firelight, and her face shone warmly. He knew something was going on between her and the captain, but Forrester wasn't there, and it was clear to everybody that she wasn't married.

Forrester might be a captain, but to the corporal, he was just another West Point snob who had no idea of what he was doing. He figured all Betty could do was shoot him down, and it wouldn't be the first time. At least it was a source of entertainment for the day. Maybe he would get lucky, and all his dreams would come true. He daydreamed about her blond hair and sky-blue eyes. He saw them arm in arm.

Cpl. Sorely noticed Betty's blond hair, thin and delicate features with dark shadows below her blue eyes that belied her past. Under the beauty and good sense of humor lay a serious woman who loved and lived powerfully and simply. She was as uncomplicated and drama-free as a White woman got.

"Why are White men always talking about principles and honor?" Dahteste asked. She acted like the men weren't even there. Nobody even noticed Pvt. Blinds was missing. They hardly even noticed him when he was there.

"Is it the same with your people back at the Crow stronghold?" Betty asked. She couldn't help but notice the uncomfortable faces of the men at the table. "Maybe it's men in general that are foolish and not as smart as they think."

To the dismay of the soldiers, the women continued to speak as though they didn't even exist. Then Dennis came into the cabin. He took off his hat and slapped off the snowflakes. Both women greeted him, something they hadn't done to either Butch or Henry.

The women weren't dumb, and they knew what was on the minds of the young soldiers. It didn't take a brain surgeon to figure it out because the tall and lanky one named Butch was already eyeing them like a hungry animal.

The women grabbed their coffees and stepped onto the porch for privacy from the gawking men. Of course, Lieutenant Brad Holster was the perfect officer and gentleman. They couldn't say the same for the corporal. They saw footprints in the snow leading to the only outhouse in the compound, but it was a double seater, making it a little wider than usual.

"I wonder what happened to the private. He seems so shy and unassuming," Betty said. "He seems so out of place here in the wilderness. I wonder what brought him here."

Betty and Dahteste both heard a voice and immediately stopped talking and turned their attention to the edge of the forest. The Crow woman war chief sniffed the air, and she instantly frowned. Little by little, the Indian unexpectedly came out from the almost-dark stillness. The private banged open the door and ran for the cabin. He didn't know why, but the hair stood up on the back of his neck.

There wasn't even a hint of a breeze. The big Indian almost looked like a ghost. Suddenly, Dahteste realized he was a Blackfoot Indian. He was an enemy of the Crow tribe. When their eyes locked, she saw the evil behind the stare. A gangly Indian with his hair pulled back into a ponytail appeared before their eyes. She instantly knew it was one of White Ghost's warriors, and he had come for them.

Dahteste exchanged looks with Betty. The White woman saw the concern, but she also saw an anger she hadn't noticed before boiling inside the young woman. Without a word, she knew they were in trouble. If the woman Crow war chief was worried, it would be as serious as it gets.

Ambush

A dog barked in the distance, and Rusty's large black canine growled in reply. Or was it the sound of a wild wolf? It was too far away to be sure. Goosebumps sprouted on their arms as they crept forward. They could all feel it, but they couldn't identify the threat. Of course, they knew it had to come from White Ghost, but in what form? From what they heard, he was a master trickster. So, they knew they could expect something different.

As they climbed higher into the mountains, Angus and Rusty related some of the stories of the Blackfoot warrior they called the white ghost. Each one was more hair-raising and horrible than the last. Of course, it was a self-given name, but the rumors were that he had become what he professed to be—a phantom of sorts. He encouraged such beliefs in every way. That was why he painted bones on his arms and legs and his face eggshell white. In the summer, he even painted ribs on his body, so he looked more like a living skeleton and therefore believed to be ghost.

That was precisely what the war chief wanted. The more his life was shrouded in mystery, the more dangerous his enemies would believe he was. The more questions about him, the more he would be feared. He well knew that men feared the unknown the most, so he played on this weakness to acquire his goal.

At least, this was what the local Indians thought. The Blackfeet simply spoke of the spirit of the white ghost. It was a fact for them, and in his birthplace, no one doubted it was true. They had known him when he was still considered mortal, but now, he was more of an evil spirit to the local tribes. Still, he was feared by one and all, regardless of whether they were among those who believed he was a ghost or simply a wicked man.

Levi had taken the lead, but nobody took the chance of riding way out on point. They would confront whatever they were about to encounter as a force of one. That was their best course of action to avoid needless loss of life. So, the man on drag was close to the pack, and the rest rode behind Johnson. Rusty followed his apprentice, using his acute sense of smell to detect any changes in odors. They were all keenly aware of everything around them. If they missed something, it could cost them their lives.

Many Indians had such frontiersman skills but rarely did anyone born outside the wilderness. In the civilized world, people lived on top of each other, floor after floor. There was no privacy or possibility of escaping the rest of the world. Natural odors and aromas mixed with a menagerie of too many stinky people. Then there were the locomotives, which spewed black smoke and soot everywhere they went. The modern cities were a world turned upside down compared to the mountains' beauty and healthy clean air.

A bullet zinged through the air and clipped the leaves on a nearby bush, and immediately after, a crack rang out. They ducked and looked for traces of gun smoke, but the breeze swept it away as soon as the unseen opponent fired. The dog crouched as the hair on his back stood on end. His ears shifted, searching out the enemy he knew was there. Finally, Rusty watched his ears until he saw where Dog sensed the shot came from, and he took a potshot back. They could hear the lead slug slam into a tree trunk, but there was no sound of a wounded person. The only sound was of rustling leaves and whistling pines.

"He's baitin' us," Rusty whispered. "He's tryin' to lead us into a trap. This Indian don't like killin' his enemies right off. He likes to capture 'em and torture 'em to death if he has the chance. That just makes it harder for him to succeed. If he came right at us straight off, he might get a few before he goes down himself. But trying to take us all prisoner is gonna be a trick I wanna see. I wonder what other tricks he has up his sleeve."

"If a Blackfoot war chief thinks he's going to capture one of us, he has another thing coming, and it won't be pretty," Capt. Forrester grumbled. The danger vibrated in his voice. "I don't care if he thinks he's the devil's gift to earth; I'll chop him down to size given the opportunity."

"There's four of 'em, and they're seven of us, but we'll be on their ground," Levi said. "That gives them the edge and makes up the difference in numbers. We'll have to be mighty careful if this fella is as dangerous as y'all say. We can't count on superior numbers being enough if they know the lay of the land and we don't."

"I still don't understand why so much fuss about one man," the captain growled. "I've never met a man yet that couldn't be killed. He can be my guest if he wants to test us out. I'll happily take on the burden. I'll prove once and for all that ghosts don't exist."

Two more shots rang out. This time, they kicked up dirt ten yards away. It was clear the shooters couldn't see the targets. They were baiting them to follow. Just the same, hammers clicked as guns were drawn. They all knew not to trust their usual judgment with this character. He was famous for doing the least expected things. That was why he was so successful. He always seemed to be a few steps ahead of his enemies. Now it was time for the mountain men to catch up.

"Keep sharp, now," Rusty said as they crouched and moved forward, despite the gunfire. "He's up to somethin'. I don't know what it is yet, but I reckon we'll know soon enough."

They had their answer minutes later. All seven men saw the two baby bear cubs as they dropped into the clearing from a low limb of a dense tree above them. They cried for their mother—they all knew it was one of the most dangerous sounds in the forest. Shouts, cries, and laughter came from behind them. The bushes rustled, and a tree broke. Suddenly, a black bear was roaring and slashing its paws as it ran into the clearing and neared its young. It stopped, stood on its hind legs, and sniffed the air, then it roared. Goosebumps sprouted on the men's arms as they all gasped for breath.

Everybody froze, hoping if they didn't move, she

might not notice they were there, but they were upwind, and she smelled them immediately. Before they knew it, the bear was twenty yards away and closing in too fast to swing a rifle barrel into play. So, they pulled their pistols. The lead shot peppered the bear's eyes and nose as it screamed in pain. She slapped her paws at the vexing stings like they were insects.

They could clearly hear somebody laughing from somewhere high in the trees. None of them doubted it was White Ghost. The mountain men remained frozen in their tracks, waiting to see what the large black bear did next. But the captain charged the beast on his own, ignoring the danger, and used his saber to end its life. It was dead before its head hit the ground. Seconds later, the body followed. Capt. Forrester's eyes were all lit up and scary, and he had blood up to his elbow.

"Now, what are we gonna do with the baby bears?" Levi asked, worried. "We can't leave 'em out here to be somebody's dinner."

"There's nothing we can do about that, pard," Rusty said, putting his hand on Johnson's shoulder. "Mother Nature has a way of workin' things out. It was that danged Indian that left the cubs motherless. Not us. We were just protecting our own lives. You can't bring 'em with us 'cause we're already chasing a dangerous outlaw. Even if you could, what would you do when they're bigger than you? It just ain't meant to be, boy. At times, life's ugly like that."

The cubs first ran to their mother. They sniffed her dead body, and then suddenly, they were aware of the strangers. They bolted for the bushes and disappeared as quickly as they appeared. Any hopes of saving them instantly vanished. All the men knew first would come the vultures and then the predators looking for the orphaned cubs. It was hard to watch, but these were the ways of the mountains. Every animal's loss was another's gain in the forest.

"Come on," Joseph said as he looked around, wide-eyed. "Let's get out of here. I'm getting the creeps with that crazy Indian out there. He seems to know what we're gonna do before we do it."

"Don't get all in a rush, now," Rusty whispered. "We've gotten through one trap, but that don't mean there ain't another one waitin' for us behind the first. Remember, this renegade is a hardened warrior, and he loves to play games with his victims. That's what this is —all a big game to him."

"What he doesn't know is that he's going to be the victim when he acts up on my watch," the captain seethed.

Everything seemed to set Will off lately. Even if it was just a couple of little bear cubs that had to pay the price, he was ready to strangle White Ghost by the neck with his single hand. Now, all they wanted to do was catch up with him and give him a dose of his own medicine.

They climbed past the place from where the gunshots came. Rusty and Levi found the Indians' tracks and even the rock they fired from. Rusty sniffed the air, but he was upwind to White Ghost. That meant he would know where they were, and they wouldn't have any idea of where he was hiding. He had planned it like that. Yet they knew he was out there waiting on them to make a silly mistake, and it was only a question of time until they did.

Rusty heard the arrow whistle past his ear. He didn't

even have time to duck. The projectile was clearly intended for him, but it missed its mark by no more than an inch. Rory Breaker took the arrow in his side, spinning him around like a top. When he looked down, he was surprised because the long white arrow he expected to see wasn't there. It had been shot with such force that it went into his side, luckily missing any vital organs, and out the back, just like a bullet. The wound was a through-and-through. If it didn't get infected, it would heal.

When Rory stopped spinning from the arrow's force, he looked puzzled. He had one hand over the entry wound in the front and his other hand covering the hole in the back. Virgil jumped straight in and began to administer first aid. The cowboy held back the scream as Virgil forced an alcohol-soaked cloth all the way through the hole. He grabbed the bloody rag at the back and pulled it through, cleaning the wound as best as he could. Virgil sprinkled gunpowder over each hole and lit a match. The fizzling heat melted the skin, closing the wounds. Then Lovejoy wrapped a long bandage around Breaker's waist. He was a little stiff but determined more than ever to carry on. Now, he had a grudge to settle.

As Lovejoy worked on their wounded man, the others stood guard. Pistols filled their hands as their eyes carefully traced across the land before them. It was all uphill from there on out, and the path looked challenging to approach, even on foot. Their heads tilted back as their eyes followed the cracks and crevices that allowed the Indians to climb so high. Most of it was rock faces and canyons.

As they climbed, low clouds hung around the

mountains below them. They felt like they were trespassing on dangerous ground, feeling like the signs were everywhere. Dark clouds passed overhead, moving shadows across the valley below. As the mountain men climbed higher, the path narrowed and steepened until both the men and horse struggled to keep their footing.

Sparks flew from iron horseshoes as they clacked against the stone trail. Vultures made lazy circles overhead. Whoever succumbed to the wilderness or their fellow man would have their bones picked clean by the scavengers. All that would remain were their bleached-out bones, jaw, and teeth, with the odd patch of hair or feathers.

The silence was broken by a choir of coyotes. It was like a stark warning that once they made a step more they were at the point of no return and there was no turning back. They were all physically and emotionally committed. They would follow this through or die.

Tricky Games

There was an eerie silence as they climbed above the donut-like clouds on the higher snow-covered peaks. Nobody in the group said a word as they crawled to the next ledge. The only sounds were from the horses. Their lungs sounded like tired locomotives, and the clopping of hooves echoed on stone paths across the ravine some two hundred feet below. Still, they struggled their way higher.

"The lake is farther away than I remembered," Rusty said, leading his horse. They both struggled to make the last three yards to the top. "Then again, I was bein' chased by hostile Indians. They ran me all the way to Hidden Lake, and I was so parched, I nearly took a drink. What saved me was the red color; then I noticed my horse shy away out of the corner of my eye, and I knew then and there that it was poisoned. It didn't get that color on its own. Why, once I had a look, I found animal and bird skeletons all along the bank. All that was left was bleached-out bone. I figure if anything can survive that water, it be vultures. Them and, of course, White Ghost. That's his home now."

The red color came from dense iron deposits, and a deadly algae poisoned the water. It was lethal to all animals, although the vegetation appeared to thrive on it. It was one of the mysteries of the Rocky Mountains. Green trees and bushes were lush and inviting, but the water was as deadly as a bullet. That was why nobody bothered White Ghost and his warriors. Nobody wanted the land they claimed as theirs. Maybe the man-ghost knew of a secret, unpolluted spring. The Blackfeet warriors were said to live in a deep complex of caves on the side of the mountain at the back of a canyon.

Others said they lived behind a waterfall where there was none. There were so many stories about White Ghost that it was impossible to separate fact from fiction. Especially now, since he was considered immortal and no more than a ghost. That was when the wild stories exploded, and his fame stretched far and wide. Now, parents used his name to scare their children when they were bad. He was the boogeyman incarnate; everybody in the mountains had heard his name, which they linked with death and suffering.

Suddenly, arrows began to appear in the dozens. At first, the men didn't know what they were, as they floated in the air so high above. They watched as they arced across the sky. Then, they began to thud into the ground around them. It was hard to tell how many archers there were or exactly where the arrows came from. Some of the Native Americans could shoot as many as three arrows a second. All the projectiles had the trademark albino feathers the Blackfoot war chief used exclusively—nobody else dared copy him.

Black flint arrowheads tied to dogwood shafts guided by white feathers hung in the sky like falling stars as a second volley was followed by a third. The projectiles seemed to be shot from high above and then lingered in the air until they changed their trajectory from up to down. As they sped for Earth, they gained momentum, finally striking hard.

The mountain men had nowhere to hide but under their horses. They huddled down, vulnerable to their unseen enemy. Two arrows hit their marks, but luckily, they burrowed deep into saddles instead of the horse flesh or men. The remains of ten dozen arrows lay scattered, buried in the ground or broken on the rocks. Again, it was apparent they were shooting blindly. The mountain men wondered what White Ghost was up to. Everybody assumed all four warriors were behind all those arrows. Then again, nobody was sure of anything with his rascal. With every turn came the unexpected.

It was apparent they were shooting wildly, hoping they might injure somebody to weaken the entire group. With every wounded man, it slowed down the group and made them more vulnerable. With his wound, Rory struggled with the climb, but it was too steep to ride the horses, and they didn't dare leave them behind. Nobody wanted to lose their animal, which was a sure thing if they abandoned them with White Ghost around. He would immediately kill them just for good measure and to assure escape was even more difficult. Especially once he had them in his trap.

The arrows stopped falling as quickly as they started. There was no sign of any Blackfeet Indians, although they all had proof they were there. The Indians continued to stay well ahead of the mountain men or any plan they might consider. Rusty had no choice but to follow, or they might disappear again, only to surface a year or more later. Now that they had undertaken the task, they all knew they had to follow it through. That meant no matter what happened, they couldn't turn back. They had all silently made a deal with themselves and God. It was him or them, and it was as simple as that. It all ended there on the mountain one way or the other.

WHITE GHOST and Black Crow carried baskets of arrows to a boulder high on the cliff but still out of sight of the mountain men. Their longbows lay on a rock as large and flat as a dinner table. From this point, they could aim just over the ridge, knowing the path was directly below. If they could kill one or two men or even a couple of horses, it would weaken the party as a whole. At the worst, they would anger them more, hopefully making them reckless in their decisions. At this point, one false move could cost one of them their lives. The Blackfoot war chief was tracking the men's every activity. He could smell and sense where they were, even when he couldn't see them.

The war chief made an ugly snicker. It wasn't quite a laugh because he frowned. He assessed the new situation and carefully selected his path every inch of the way. They were getting closer and closer to Hidden Lake. Maybe only a surprise or two more before they were there. He knew he wouldn't have a problem luring them to the water's edge, but he wasn't sure if they would be foolish enough to enter the caves alone. That was what he wanted, but he would kill them just the same if they didn't. Or maybe capture one and let his screams lead them to him. The ugly snicker came again. Black Crow ignored it, like many things his war chief said or did. He knew he was a mere mortal, so how would he ever understand spirits and ghosts?

The war chief was happy with their progress. All along, he had planned to lure the White men to the lake and his territory. They would never escape, even if they managed to split up. He would make sure they never left this part of the Rocky Mountains, and if he was lucky and killed one or two on the way or even injured more men, that was fine, too. The more damage he could inflict on them on their way to his trap would make them more manageable once they were in his clutches.

Every move that White Ghost made, he did so with great deliberation. It was as though he were planning a life-and-death game of chess. The Indian war chief was an expert tactician, tracker, and an even better killer. He was not only skilled at his job of taking lives, but he took great joy in his actions, even though nobody had ever seen him smile.

Black Crow never questioned his leader's orders, no matter what they may be. Nor did he allow himself to become distracted with things others did or said. For him, the world spun around his master, and nothing else mattered.

For a moment, Black Crow wondered how it was going with Nuka and Scar. They were able-bodied men, but when they weren't with their leader, it wasn't the same.

Nuka was rash and flew off the handle when alone with the others. Black Crow believed Nuka secretly wanted to be their war chief. Sometimes he simply bullied his way through situations. For him, it was brawn over brain. He was just glad his war chief sent Scar with his younger brother. Sometimes Nuka was as unpredictable as White Ghost himself.

Often, White Ghost asked him to commit a crime with no rhyme or reason, although he never questioned his boss. He chose to blindly follow his leader, just like Scar and Nuka. Despite White Ghost's despicable reputation, all three had unconditionally sworn their allegiance to the war chief. Nobody knew why they forfeited their lives for such a man, but they almost followed him like he was a god or a spirit. Any of the three, if not all, would gladly give their lives to save White Ghost. For them, it was payment enough to be in his presence. They felt blessed by the Blackfoot war gods and wouldn't have it any other way.

White Ghost had always promoted such stories. The more he appeared like an evil spirit, or even a ghost, the more successful he seemed. He wouldn't settle for less; whatever it took to dominate anyone he ran across. He found that he had half the battle won if they were already terrified even before they saw his evil-looking face. The more people spreading lies and exaggerations, the easier it was for people to believe the stories. If you told a lie enough times, most of the population would eventually think it was at least partially true, and others would swallow it, hook, line, and sinker.

Black Crow and his leader had already envisioned Rusty Steel chained to his cavern walls. He could almost hear the screams echo throughout the network of caves made by some ancient Indian culture a millennium ago. The cross-work of caverns was so vast, even the war chief hadn't explored them all. It was easy to get turned about and lost in the labyrinth of tunnels. Only he and his three warrior braves were party to where their homes lay in the maze of stone rooms. They were all carved out by hand to smooth, rounded surfaces. There wasn't a sharp corner in the network.

A hundred long shafts hollowed out in the stone provided the light that pointed at various spots of the sun's arch. That way, they had daylight piped in from outside all year around. The illumination system was so sophisticated that even the stars and the moon lit up the larger rooms at night. How many people lived in this ancient village? It must have been long before the lake's water became poisoned. Prosperity was evident in the construction of such a feat of humankind. Perhaps the lake's tainted water drove them from such a beautiful place.

After finishing both baskets, the Blackfeet Indians turned and fled even higher. They never gave any of the men's party members the chance to get a glimpse of their presence, other than the arrows that littered the trail. White Ghost believed these types of maneuvers were partially what made people believe it when he claimed to be a ghost. He often attacked without allowing his enemy to see him. He had a whole host of tricks up his sleeve to prove what he said was true. At times, even he wondered.

His three faithful followers believed every word he said. Was it eventually true, or was it all a ruse developed by the war chief to become an important man? Did he want everybody to be afraid of him? He would rather them be frightened of his presence than not knowing he existed. For him, that would be a fate worse than death.

He actually feared anonymity as a young man, but that was long ago—long before he became known across the Rockies. But there was a time when he felt he went largely unnoticed. This was something that he didn't tolerate any longer. It had been a long time since anyone dared to ignore him. He had killed the last man who had, and he was ready to kill anyone else who may.

The Magician

"You couldn't pour water out of a boot if the instructions were on the heel. When you're out of your depth, you should man up and admit it," Rusty growled. "I tell ya, we need to swing around wide so White Ghost ain't sure where we're at. So far, he's known our every move, ain't he? It's time we throw a wrench in the works and put 'im off his feed. At the moment, I ain't all that sure of who's chasin' who. What I do know is that neither he nor I have a handle on things, and the first one that does will dominate the situation."

"Remember, I was a trapper and mountain man just like you long before I became a sheriff. Maybe even before Angus and all," Sheriff Walker retorted. "I always stick to the trail. Then, at least, we know where he should be and where we're goin'. Then, I never get lost. It's just like followin' a map."

"Spoken like true city dandy and greenhorn." Rusty snickered. "I bet you don't even know exactly where you are right now. Would you have been able to get this far alone? I know all of them stories of how you lived like me, but with you, it didn't stick. It takes a special kind of man to survive in the mountains, and there's no room for errors. Maybe folks listen to what you've got to say back in Kansas, where you're a big shot, Joseph, but I'm the boss out here. You don't live with these Indians all year around like we do. You learn or die up here, so you follow my footsteps like the others and be as quiet as a sheriff can possibly be. Politicians—you're all alike. You never stop waggin' your jaws and complaining about one thing or another. And mark my words, White Ghost ain't ever where you expect 'im to be. He'll come at us when we're off guard, just like until now."

"I ain't no politician," Joseph retorted. "How can you say such a thing to a friend? I thought you liked me, Rusty."

"If I'm not confused, sheriffs are elected, ain't they?" Steel changed his tone. "Of course, I like you, or you wouldn't be ridin' along with us or stayin' in my home, now would ya?" Small curls appeared at the edge of his lips. He was baiting his old friend out of habit. Even he had to admit he was getting more cantankerous as time passed. "It's just... out here, the most experienced man takes the lead, and I'm more like White Ghost than any of ya. Ain't that right, Levi? He and the captain know. Now's not the time to be testin' our skills or trying to learn something. When you're chasing a bad outlaw like White Ghost, there ain't no room for mistakes."

"Step aside if you've got wax in your ears, sparky," Angus grumbled as he pushed past Joseph. "I always say, learn quick or be left behind. But be forewarned, those that loiter become easy pickings for the ghost Indian."

"Come on," Levi whispered to the sheriff, smiling.

He stifled a laugh. "They're just gettin' grumpy with age. They don't mean no offense, but they're right. Rusty is the best mountain man in the Rockies, and I may be the second. So, today, you're gonna have to take a back seat, Sheriff. When we're up on the peaks, we follow seniority, and everybody does exactly what the leader says. We're lucky to have Rusty with us today. He can smell a buffalo pass wind from a mile away, and there ain't a better man when it comes to trackin' somebody as dangerous as that Blackfoot Indian."

The sheriff was obviously angry; his face was as red as a beet, but he bit his tongue to keep the peace. The words dared to walk right out his mouth on their own, but he refused to allow a squeak to pass his lips. He swallowed his pride, even though it tasted like crow. He dragged his horse off the trail and into the bushes behind Steel, but he grumbled as he walked.

As they climbed, the trees began to grow shorter and were more sparsely scattered across the face of the mountain, and rock replaced grass and dirt. Supposedly, beyond the summit, there was a crystal-clear lake with a natural red glow. Its color left it shrouded in mystery. Nobody knew why.

Of course, there were as many stories as there were storytellers. One and all had an opinion. But lately, more and more people agreed. It had something to do with White Ghost, even though the lake was said to have gone poison long, long ago. Well before any Blackfeet or Crow arrivals. But still some said it was tainted by the blood the outlaw war chief spilled.

As they climbed closer to their destination, they saw a trail of smoke in the distance. It started at the top of the trees and curled high into the sky. The tracking party exchanged looks. Who would be making camp there where it was so dangerous? Only a fool would take such a chance. This part of the mountain was nearly uninhabited, and with good reason.

"Who in the world would be makin' a fire way the heck up here?" Joseph asked. "Only a moron would do such a thing."

"Or maybe that clever Indian, that's who," Rusty replied as his eyes narrowed. "I wonder what that rascal's up to now. You just never know when you're dealin' with White Ghost. Move around wider, boys, and stay close together. He may be tryin' to pick us off one at a time. Let's give 'em plenty of room. Maybe we can get ahead of 'im and see exactly what's goin' on."

"Keep an eye on that smoke, but don't forget to look everywhere else, too," Levi added. "There's more than just the war chief out there. Three more dangerous warrior braves are with 'im, too, and I assure you they won't be daisies. I wonder why they haven't already had a go at us. It just don't make any sense."

"You just keep it in your head that for him, it makes sense, so we best find out what he's plannin' before he can set his traps," Rusty said. "I reckon that's what the smoke is about. Still, he's actin' funny. He's sort of actin' like maybe he's on his own. I've always heard he was really up-front with his ways. So, it ain't quite like him to be beatin' around the bush so much. Maybe he's waitin' on his men for something. I wonder what it could be if that were the case."

"Now we're just takin' potshot guesses in the dark, ain't we?" Sheriff Walker spat. "And here I thought you knew exactly what you were doin'."

"You might spend your time tryin' to help us figure

out what this rascal's gonna do instead of lookin' for things to criticize," Angus growled. "A guest ain't supposed to act like you're actin', Sheriff. It makes it difficult to be a kind host."

"Maybe you've never been in the Army, Sheriff, but following orders is elementary to a successful mission," the captain said. "In the service, we don't talk back to our officers. We get our orders and follow them to the letter."

"Where the heck is Rory?" Walker asked. He was beginning to feel ganged up on. Still, he was too stubborn to admit Rusty was right. "I best check that wound to make sure it ain't started bleeding again."

WHITE GHOST PILED wood on the growing fire. He had chosen perfect specimens to make more black smoke. When he had the kindling roaring, he stacked the green logs on top and waited. Minutes later, clouds of dark smoke squirreled into the sky. The soot contrasted against the clear blue, making it impossible not to see. He looked up as the first traces passed the treetops. In a few minutes, it would be visible for miles and miles. There wasn't a breath of air, so the smoke floated straight up toward the heavens, identifying exactly where the camp was.

When he was sure the flames had caught and the fire wouldn't go out, he disappeared into the forest. Four bedrolls were spread out around the fire, shaping a cross. A pot of beans was bubbling beside the embers. Steam rose from four tin cups. He wanted to keep the mountain men behind him, but he didn't dare attack without his other two men. When Nuka and Scar returned, they would set the trap and capture them all, then take the next week enjoying their suffering while they tortured them slowly, one strip of skin at a time. They had plenty of spikes driven into the cavern wall with chains to hold their prisoners.

These weren't their first visitors. There had been scores before, but not so many of the caliber of Rusty Steel and his gang. This was going to be a special occasion. It would also send a bolt of fear through the mountain population. When he defeated what was arguably the White man most like the local Indians, his fame would grow even wider. The old mountain man was even an official member of the Crow tribe. Killing this one was what White Ghost was looking forward to, so everything had to be perfect. Anybody who interfered with his plans would die shortly after.

This wasn't the first time they had tortured captives for long periods of time. Hours, days, and even weeks passed before those captives had succumbed to their injuries. That was why the renegade Indian was an expert at prolonging death while the victims suffered the unimaginable. White Ghost planned to enjoy every minute of Rusty Steel's slow demise. He was still debating how he wanted to kill him. Maybe he would dismember him one piece at a time. Finger by finger, hand by hand, arm by arm, then toe by toe, foot by foot, and leg by leg. Or perhaps he would skin him like a buffalo, leaving the carcass in the sun to rot and die while he was still alive.

Black Crow waited for White Ghost just outside the fake camp. They stuffed bedrolls with leaves, so they appeared occupied. The smell of baked beans rose on puffs of air beside the orange embers. It filled their senses, making locating the campsite easier for the frontiersmen. This was an active camp for all appearances, but it couldn't be further from the truth. It was all a deception and a ruse designed to test the enemy's skill. The ghost warrior observed from the shadows where it was impossible to see. His eyes lit up like lighthouses.

He moved a matchstick from one side of his mouth to the other. He squinted his eyes as he watched and waited. His brow was as dry as a bone, despite the hot midday sun. He was so in control he even managed to adjust the rate of his heartbeat and slowed down his body to nearly a full stop. Not a muscle moved. He didn't even appear to breathe.

"Let's see how clever these mountain men really are," White Ghost whispered. His most trusted brave crept up behind him.

White Ghost towered over Black Crow. His best brave was a squat, bowlegged Indian but had lived with the Comanche, so his horsemanship skills were second to none. He was also as faithful as a follower could be. He would happily die for his war chief. As far as Nuka and Hook Scar went, the war chief wasn't so sure. He did believe they would follow him to the ends of the earth, but he also knew what they had done to the women in the past. White Ghost was as evil a man as ever walked the planet, but he didn't rape captive women, not even when it was done by his brother. His father was taken from him by White men when he was young, and his mother rejected all new suitors to honor her husband's memory.

This kept the spark alive inside White Ghost, too. For his mother, no one could ever equal his father. It was a belief he followed. Nobody knew why the war chief had that little white pot on his otherwise black soul. But he frowned on it when done by others just the same. Strangely enough, the same women he would later torture and kill. None of it made any sense, but who was brave enough to ask such a question of a man like the ghost warrior? So far, he had chosen to ignore the actions of his other two warrior braves, but the last time it got messy, and it was difficult not to see something right under your nose.

White Ghost and Black Crow hid patiently, waiting for the mountain men to check the campsite's surrounding area. They watched as all seven men checked every crook and cranny. The men even looked into the shadows. But nobody was clever enough to see the notorious Blackfoot Indian when he didn't want them to. White Ghost watched as the drama played out. He eyed the White men closely. He was surprised when he saw a Black man, too. It was the first he had ever seen, although he had heard of them. Some said they were forced to live with the White men and did their chores. Indian tribes often did the same with their captive males from other tribes. He wondered why they were thought to be different.

The women and children they captured were used to further populate their tribe. With the White and Black men came diseases that were more lethal to the Indians than the Easterners' rifles and pistols. They couldn't see that enemy, and it struck them down just as sure as a lead bullet. The common cold and measles were the worst of the unseen killers. Simple and nonthreatening for the people who brought the sicknesses with them, they had become accustomed to and had developed their own antibodies against such common diseases. The Indian population had no such defenses and fell like bowling pins by unseen enemies.

Finally, three of the men tracking snuck into the camp while the others waited on all four points. White Ghost pulled out a spyglass and brought it to his eyes. At first, the fuzzy objects became more challenging to see, but instantly, they appeared so close he felt he could reach out and touch them. The renegade Indian immediately recognized Rusty Steel, although they had only seen each other once. He was sure Rusty would remember him too, though. Both their presences created electrical waves like heat from a fire. It was all but impossible not to notice such men.

They had their eyes peeled. He could hear hammers cock in the near distance. Sweat glistened on the faces of the frontiersmen. None of them were calm and collected like White Ghost, not even Black Crow. Then again, Black Crow believed his war chief was immortal, and he was no more than his human servant. No one expected the leader to be afraid. That would also prove him to be mortal, which was the last thing the war chief wanted. The more shrouded in mystery were his surroundings, the more powerful he became.

White Ghost looked through the spyglass, and he saw the frontiersman Steel. Beside him stood a giant of a man. *That must be Levi Johnson, his new apprentice,* the war chief thought. There was supposed to be an Army captain, too. He would be the most dangerous. Finally, the White men used their rifles to poke the leaf-filled bedrolls. The old man obviously already believed there was no one there. Puzzlement showed on their faces as they carefully crept through the camp, looking for danger.

Rusty stopped when they found nothing but some warm beans and heated water in cups. It was obviously all a trick to put them off something, but what? He knew the Indians prepared this ruse for a good reason. He also knew all he had to do was wait, and he would discover what it was. Hopefully, the folly wouldn't cost them their lives.

All the mountain men froze in their tracks. They knew they had stepped into another trap, but they still didn't know what it was. They anxiously waited as their hearts pounded between their ears and their faces beaded in sweat. They even held their breaths. They felt it would happen at any moment now.

White Ghost plucked the wooden match from his lips and used his thumbnail to spark it to life. It snapped and cackled as a yellow-blue flame accompanied by the smell of sulfur appeared at the end of the stick. He lit a tinder ball laying on a broad leaf and pulled his bow from his back. A long arrow was waiting against the tree. The smell of kerosene was strong in the air—soaked bandages wrapped around the shaft.

He set the arrow, drew back the bowline to his jaw, and let it fly. It looked like an orange tracer as it raced through the sky. The mountain men looked up with their mouths hanging open. The burning arrow made its arc, then finally stalled and turned for Earth.

The frontiersmen watched as it came crashing down toward them. They all prepared to duck and run until they finally saw it wasn't aimed right at them but off to one side. And why was there only one arrow?

When the projectile landed, flames flashed around

them, and a ring of fire closed a circle encompassing the seven in flames. They found themselves trapped in the mocked-up camp. White Ghost had fooled them again. They hadn't noticed the earth soaked with a ring of flammable liquid around the campsite. The mountain men had made another mistake, and now they prepared for the attack, but it didn't come. At least not immediately.

White Ghost watched and chuckled. Now, he saw how he could easily outwit the trespassers and capture them all as he had planned. They were like putty in his hands. Had he had his three warriors with him, he would have taken them then, but it was always best if he didn't have to transport captives much distance—especially with the current terrain and them all dangerous men.

The shorter they had to travel after being caught and tied up, the less chance of one of them getting free and wreaking chaos. The ghost watched as he stifled a chuckle. At least that was what he wanted people to think—that he was a ghost, whether it be true or not. That was still to be discovered and proven. White Ghost's lips were sealed, and nobody dared ask such a violent man the question. They knew it would be signing their own death certificate.

He watched as the men inside the ring of fire panicked. Gun barrels poked out in every direction, but they had no idea where he was. Bullets began to zip through the leaves and slam into tree trunks nearby. The war chief calmly closed his spyglass and nudged his right-hand man. Then, they seemingly vanished in the blink of an eye. One moment, they were there, and the next, they weren't. Still, the mountain men acted like fish caught in a trap until they saw nobody coming to capture or kill them. This left them even more confused as their confidence diminished, and the first hint of fear crept into the least experienced men.

Soon, the fire died down as the flammables burned out. As soon as the men believed nobody was out there waiting to bushwhack them, they ran for the cover of the forest and hid in the bushes, waiting for nightfall. It was too dangerous to move around right now. They knew White Ghost was out there playing games and planning more mischief. The next mistake could cost them all their lives. They had already made too many.

White Ghost had the upper hand. They all knew that if things didn't change soon, they would be caught in one of the war chief's traps and might not get out the next time. The ghost of an Indian raced up the difficult climb like he had been doing it all his life. He hardly broke a sweat and right behind him came Black Crow only slightly out of breath.

Three Cabins

Flames lashed out from the massive fireplace, caressing the logs like fingers. Wood crackled and popped as steam puffed from nearly dry logs. Waves of dry heat came from the chimney and rippled across the room, creeping into the corners and making them as warm as toast. With a glance outside, they saw it had snowed again, although it was light and barely covered old tracks in the large yard.

A zigzag fence enclosed the compound, and a corral and some stables were at the end. The women sat at the table inside the first of three cabins. Their wavy images were visible through the glass panes. Yellow light glowed in the only window. Outside, snowflakes floated through the air.

They stayed in the biggest cabin because McFarlin's sod-and-log house had the best fireplace, cookstove, and the largest porch where they all gathered after breakfast and of an evening if it wasn't too cool. This was the first time the girls had been alone together. It provided them some time to become closer and discover each other's secrets and ambitions.

It was also an opportunity to ask and answer unsolved questions and confirm if Dahteste's guesses were accurate or if she was completely mistaken. She wondered if there was a spark of love between the captain and Miss Betty. The rest of the men didn't seem to notice the way she did. Still, she wasn't completely sure.

Angus had built his home over two decades earlier. Even he couldn't remember how many years it had been. For those who lived in the mountains, the precise month and year slowly became less and less relevant. They only paid attention to the seasons, some of which were as dangerous as the hostiles and wild animals. It wasn't long after Mountain Dennis Breed had built his log cabin when Angus arrived. They were the first White men to live on this land. They were the very first to settle on the mountain permanently. The others came with time; even a few had left this world too early and departed for greener pastures in the heavens above.

Of course, the land wasn't theirs. Crow Chief Hachta chose to allow them to trespass because they bartered, bringing them steel tools, coffee, tea, sugar, and gunpowder—all things they had become accustomed to having and had little access to purchase or trade. Like the Indians said, the land didn't belong to them; they belonged to the earth, so permission didn't mean they owned anything. They were only just tolerated until the negatives outweighed the plusses. The frontiersmen residing in the compound did everything within their power to secure a long future, but it would all depend on the coming encroachment on Native American land.

Betty Crockett sat at the table across from the Crow woman. Despite Dahteste being a war chief, she treated the White woman with equal respect. She suspected she might soon become the captain's wife, and everybody looked up to Will Forrester. He was the envy of half the warriors in the mountains and many more on the plains.

Nor was it lost on the local American Natives that the small Crow Indian woman was married to the second most famous trapper and tracker in the Rockies. Her husband was Levi Beaver Johnson, and Rusty Steel was his mentor. He was also Chief Hachta's White blood-brother. Despite their different cultures, the odd couple had proven to be a match made in Heaven.

"How did you know when you were in love with Levi?" Betty asked. Dahteste's eyes were puzzled. "Or maybe I wanted to ask when did Levi know?"

"I don't think either of us know exactly when it happened," Dahteste replied as she pondered the question. "I'm not so sure White women feel the same things Crow women do, but I guess we must. Or don't we?"

"I believe that when it comes to some things, both men and women are the same the world over." Betty smiled. It was such a relief to have somebody to talk to. "It doesn't matter if you're red, black, white, or yellow. We must all feel love equally. Showing it is another thing, though. We may all portray it differently, perhaps in our own manners. I haven't lived around Indians long enough to give an educated guess."

"I know very little about the ways of White people, like you and those who live back east," Dahteste replied. "I know I live here in the compound, but Chief Hachta told me that mountain men were different than most White men and lived more like Indians than the other people from Kansas and beyond. Have you ever been in a city where the houses are on top of each other? Is it really true?"

Betty laughed and said, "Yes, I have, and it's true, all right. For you, it must sound terribly confining. I was born and raised in the mountains of Tennessee back east, but there weren't any cities in my county. I've seen all the cities from across the eastern part of the United States, though. It reminded me of anthills. Hundreds of people live in the same clump of dirt, but they call it multi-story housing. They say a thousand people work in a single building in places like New York City. I can't even imagine that myself."

"If a thousand people live in a building, how many people live in such a city?" Dahteste asked, amazed.

"I recently read that three hundred fifty thousand people live in New York City," Betty replied. "I bet you can't even imagine so many people. Actually, neither can I."

"So, that's enough of...what do you call it? Small talk?"

Miss Crockett laughed and said, "All right. What do you want to talk about now?"

"What is happening between you and the captain?" Dahteste asked. Indian women, especially war chiefs, got right to the point. "Do you want him to be your man or not?" Her questions were short and clear as a bell.

Betty blushed a deep red. She wasn't so shocked by the question but by how Dahteste boldly went right at it. It caught her off guard. She knew Dahteste was different, being a war chief and all, but still she surprised her. When she spoke, she didn't seem like a little Indian woman any longer. She almost seemed bigger than life.

"I don't know what to say," Betty replied. "That's a question I didn't expect so quickly."

"It's simple," Dahteste replied. "Say the truth." Her eyes twinkled with mischief.

Betty took a moment and looked down at her hands. She traced her finger around the rim of her cup. She wondered if letting her deepest feelings be known was a good idea. The Crockett family wasn't the type to take their dirty laundry out in public, but then again, Dahteste was almost like family, and the truth was busting, trying to get out. Now that Betty had been asked, she could hardly hold it back. Still, something told her to be careful, or she might get hurt. It wouldn't be the first time a woman threw herself at a man only to be turned away.

"I'd ask you to keep it a secret, but I don't know if Crow Indians have secrets or not," Betty slowly started. "Of course, you do. How silly of me. To tell the truth, I'm a little afraid to tell you what I feel. If I do, my secret wish might not come true."

"That's all right." Dahteste smiled. "You just told me all I need to know. It showed in your eyes and the color of your face before you spoke. The reason I asked was I wondered if you knew men needed a good push. They might not do what you wish if you don't help them on their way. I asked Levi why it was this way, and he didn't know what I was talking about. But I'm pretty sure you know what I mean, don't you, Betty Crockett?"

Betty nodded, but the puzzled look stayed. "What

do you think I should do?" She ground her teeth and her mouth was a hard line.

"If you sit back and do nothing, you will lose him. If you want to hunt an animal, you need to make a solid plan and be patient, and you don't stop until you capture your prey. I think you have already waited far too long. I could see it in your eyes back in Oregon City. With the captain, it's harder to say, but he hasn't taken off running away yet, so that's a pretty good sign to start off. What you can't do is wait for him to propose to you, or you'll be waiting forever."

"What?" Betty exclaimed wide-eyed. Her face turned a darker shade of red. "You can't be suggesting that I propose to him, can you? I've never even heard of such a thing."

"And why not? In the Crow tribe, a woman can ask a man to marry her. You live in the Rocky Mountains and not in Tennessee anymore. Life is different here. Maybe the difference is good for you. He can only say no, then you'll have your answer. If he says no, you can go down the mountain in the spring and look for another man at the Rendezvous or head back east. If he says yes, he was going to say yes anyway, so we'll have a wedding. We have plenty of cabin space. Levi and I always have our teepee to get away from everybody. You may need a teepee for you and the captain, too. I can help you make one."

"A teepee?" Betty asked, already overwhelmed. Suddenly, she felt nervous talking about her dream. Until now, she had kept her true feelings to herself. The Crow woman had somehow sensed and observed her passion. Now, she felt Dahteste was going too fast for her to keep up. "Propose? Me—propose to the captain? I can't imagine how I would ever get up the nerve. I just wouldn't even know where to start."

She felt her head spin around and around as things seemed to go out of control. She grabbed the jug of corn liquor from the center of the table and pulled the cork. She splashed a large dose into her coffee. She blew on the cup to cool it off, then gobbled it all down. The harsh liquor and steaming coffee burned her throat, and she coughed, then nearly choked it back up. Here, eyes darted around for escape. She almost lost it for a second. Then she locked eyes with her Crow Indian friend and it was all better.

She saw the love in Dahteste's eyes. Betty's panic dissolved as fast as it appeared, and she sighed in relief. There was something soothing and reassuring in the war chief's eyes. Suddenly, she seemed wise far beyond her young age. Betty had panicked for nothing. But her Crow friend was right. If she didn't move first, she may regret it for the rest of her life. She was going to have to do something and do it fast.

She placed her hands flat on the table to ground herself and asked, "How do I go about proposing to him? I need all the help I can get. I can hardly get a moment alone with him as it is. How will I get him alone long enough to ask him to marry me? I know he cares, but I don't know if he loves me. But every time I have a moment with him, he runs off to put out another fire. I don't like having to share my feelings with the others. I can't even consider it unless we're alone."

"The moment you ask him, I promise you'll have your answer for better or worse. You'll see it in his face. Then, at least, you'll know." Dahteste laughed. "Don't worry anymore. You can worry until you make yourself sick, but it never changes anything. You've decided what you need to do. Now forget about all this fretting, calm down, and be a warrior. Let's make our war plan. First, we have to figure out how you can get him alone and all to yourself."

Suddenly, they both found themselves laughing until they got a stitch. Their laughter echoed against the canyon walls and back again as the wind blew snowflakes across the yard. It was good to hear such joy in the compound. Maybe there was going to be a wedding after all.

Betty wondered if the captain could ever imagine what was just about to happen to him, and she laughed some more. Of course, he had no idea, nor would anyone else in the camp expect such a thing. Then again, back a few months prior at the Rendezvous, several women chose new husbands based on their business success. How was this any different than that? At least she was already in love and knew the man she wanted. If he loved her or not would be revealed soon enough. She wondered if she was ready.

The men who had stepped off the porch returned, and the women instantly went silent. Suddenly, Betty realized she had just made a special bond with Levi's wife. They had conspired together, and now they had their first secret, and it looked like Dahteste was going to help her land the captain as her husband. The only two that knew it were her and Dahteste. This made it special; from then on, she knew the two women would become inseparable friends. They already felt kind of like sisters. The bond had already begun to grow.

The cabins were busy with activity. Mountain Dennis was the perfect host. Lt. Brad Holster slept in his log cabin with Cpl. Butch Sorely and Private Henry Blinds. Four men and two women were there to keep the horses safe and trespassers off their land. When Rusty, Levi, and the boys were there, friends were always welcome, but in the times they were living, no visits were allowed unless they came as a messenger from the big Crow camp a half day's ride away.

The Attack

Mountain Dennis Breed, Lieutenant Brad Holster, Corporal Butch Sorely and Private Henry Blinds waited in the compound with the women for the scouts to return. The three Army men stood guard while Mountain Dennis tried to appease the needy women. As soon as most of the mountain men left, they were like little girls asking for one favor after another. Of course, Dennis happily complied.

Maybe it was his easy-going nature and his enjoyment of doing little favors for the women. His wife died long ago, and he never sought to re-wed but still liked a female's company whenever the opportunity arose. This was special since it rarely happened in this part of the Rockies, and he had them all to himself. He was as busy as a honeybee as he buzzed around, allowing them their every desire. He felt like the luckiest man on the mountain, and it was all because he was left behind to care for Gus.

Grizzel still teetered on the edge of life and death.

Every day Betty and Dennis tended to the wound on his stump and used cold cloths to break his fever. Still, things were looking worse for the unfortunate mountain man. Even though they cleaned it daily, the wound began to smell bad again. The compound doctor thought it was just a matter of time, but Betty refused to have any such talk. She insisted they think positively and never gave in to negativity. Of course, at this point, Dennis would do anything the yellow-haired lady asked and played along but still he didn't believe it.

The mountain men spent most winters working and with little real fun. Just the presence of the pretty women changed this fall into a special event, though. The more they asked for, the happier Mountain Dennis was. He hardly paid attention to the military guards. It was rare that anybody had a go at the cabins anyway, mainly due to the significant Crow stronghold so close by.

The walls of the main cabin were nearly three feet thick and had heavy timber shutters and a massive wooden door. Angus's cabin was the chosen fort if things did go wrong. The shutters and front door even had gun slats, which they added after several hostile Indian attacks in the early days. The fact that they buried the house into the side of a mountain made it impossible to attack its flanks or rear.

It was a little fortress and all but unbreachable. They covered the roof in dirt and green grass, so it was impossible to burn out. Now, snow covered it, like its surroundings. This fact also made it hard to see from a distance, especially if snow covered the fence. Only the entrances were vulnerable, but achieving entry would cost many lives.

These attacks came mainly from the Blackfoot Indians, who also shared the mountain and the Yellowstone Valley below with the Crow, albeit as enemies. But the main cabin was almost impenetrable for anything less than a siege. Every possible danger was considered when Angus built his home, and together with Rusty, they had modified it to be a better fortress in defense of the odd occasion that someone did try to run them out.

The aging mountain man grinned like a monkey. Seeing both young women make fast friends despite their completely different cultures was good. At least Betty Crockett came from the forest and good stock like her uncle, Davy. This made the friendship easier to attain than if she had come from some big eastern city like Boston, New York, or Philadelphia. At least they had nature and the forests in common. Her uncle was so famous that even the Plains Indians had heard the stories and gossip. That included Dahteste, and she was eager to hear more about her favorite uncle.

They set out a semi-alert guard to protect the compound. The lieutenant changed men every seven hours and took one turn, including the graveyard shift. That was the hostile Indians' choice moment for attack. He believed it was the least they could do, since the mountain men had saved their lives, despite the fact that he had been searching for Captain Forrester all along. Sometimes, the world seemed so small it could fit on a napkin. They kept a large fire burning beside the porch and another inside at night. It kept off the early fall chill and provided enough light for the guards to easily see if someone was watching.

The Army men hoped against all odds somebody would pass by the compound and cabins before winter set in. They wanted to get back to their posts in Fort Leavenworth, Kansas. Especially now that their mission had run into a dead end, they were stuck there until somebody passed through on their way back east. They were still hoping to latch on with a late bunch of buffalo hunters who were returning with their hides. They were now acutely aware that if they struck out again on their own to find their way home, their chances of arriving were nil to nothing.

Dennis was as busy as a bee, but he didn't seem to appear to mind. He was hovering over two of the most beautiful women on the mountain. Of course, he was happy to just be around such beauties. One burned dark from the sun with coal black hair and the other a blue-eyed, blond beauty. He wondered if Betty would leave or stay. He kind of hoped she hooked up with the captain, but he saw little sign of any interest from Will.

Of course, he knew he was far too old for such a beautiful woman, but he daydreamed of having such a lady for a wife. Then again, that was for young men and not for older gentlemen. Levi had done well marrying Dahteste. He wondered if the captain even knew an available woman was in camp with them. Sometimes, he seemed to live in another world entirely.

Dahteste and Betty sat on the porch, munching on warm biscuits and sipping piping hot coffee. They were planning how Betty could catch the captain in a situation where he couldn't escape or called off to put out another fire. She would need him all alone for a few hours. How they were to work this out still remained to be seen. But now Betty clearly saw that she would wait all her life for nothing if she didn't act.

The captain was as brave a man as she had ever known, but he was like most men when it came to women. Either they were totally ignorant that the woman was in love with them or too shy to act on their feelings. It was surprising that men who faced death and hostile Indians almost every day of their lives were more afraid of a woman than a war party. Yet, she knew Will was at least curious but still, he didn't act on his feelings. That was the big difference between men and women.

The girls were obviously busy plotting and planning. This apparently made them happy because they would burst out in a fit of laughter every so often. Sometimes, it was a nervous laugh; others, it was pure joy. The women instantly became fast friends and now felt comfortable with each other. So, they shared stories and opinions of everything under the sun. They had endless conversations.

A few hours passed as the sun rose in the sky, and the light snow began to get sloshy underfoot. Suddenly, Dahteste stopped laughing and looked at Betty. Her face froze. It was as serious as death. She closed her eyes and took a deep breath. At first, a puzzled look crossed her face, but then discovery showed when she opened her eyes. She smelled Blackfoot Indians on the perimeter. If she wasn't mistaken, there were two warriors, if not more. She was sure there was more than one person.

Dahteste tilted her head and focused on her keen hearing but heard nothing unusual. Still, her senses told her they were there, and the smell of fear told her they were nervous, too. Maybe White Ghost wasn't with them after all, or perhaps it was some other group of warriors from another tribe. She was sure the ghost warrior wouldn't be nervous. She wasn't even positive he wasn't a ghost like most tribes believed. Some of them were her people. She wondered if a spirit even had an odor.

The thought that maybe they were from White Ghost's war party suddenly flashed through her mind, and she almost panicked. She looked at the soldier on guard, but he had no idea the compound was under threat. She pulled the pistol her husband Levi had given her, pulled back the hammer, and shot off a round into the sky. She meant it to shock the men in camp into action and to let the warriors out there hiding know that the jig was up, and they knew they were being stalked.

The Crow woman war chief suddenly vanished. Her bow and quiver disappeared with her. One moment, she was sitting beside Betty; the next, she was gone and had left Miss Crockett wondering what happened. Betty blinked her eyes in wonder. The second surprise came faster than the first. The woman war chief raced through the compound on her Appaloosa's back in a burst of flurry. She rode on the blind side of the horse, making her all but invisible to the braves waiting in the bushes. They could just barely see an arrow under her horse's neck.

White Ghost's soldiers opened fire with every rifle and pistol they had. Only when the last shot was made did their guns fall silent. Blue smoke made it impossible to see into the tree line as the attackers hurriedly began to reload.

Then Dahteste did the last thing they ever expected. She wheeled her horse toward the trees and single-handedly attacked the Blackfeet warriors head-on. Her war cry was frightening even to the veteran braves. They were caught off guard when the little Crow woman turned on them. She was as fierce as a honey badger. The enemy lost those first dear seconds due to their bewilderment. That was all the brave war chief needed to take the upper hand, and she was on them before they knew it. They never expected a woman to attack. They had focused on the soldiers. They didn't even consider the old mountain man a threat. Now, they had a wildcat in their midst.

Arrow after arrow flew from her bow, but still, they didn't have a clear shot. The edge of the forest looked like a pincushion in seconds. The stout Appaloosa fearlessly charged as more pistol flashes erupted from the bushes. But she and her horse were beyond fear. They were running on pure adrenaline. She didn't even notice the chunks of lead whizzing past her head. Still, they couldn't get a clear shot at the expert rider and archer.

Mountain Dennis was the first of the men to react. Almost as soon as he saw Dahteste run for her horse, he held a brace of pistols. He yelled to the officer to prepare for an assault. Miraculously, they all responded like a fine watch. Bullets followed the direction of the Crow war chief's arrows. They could hear the shots and projectiles slam and thud into trees and limbs. Then there was the sickening sound of lead against flesh. Bullets flew in both directions, but nobody had time to check for the wounded or casualties. There was no time to do anything but defend the compound and their lives with every ounce of strength they had.

Betty Crockett jumped from her seat and lunged for the door. As she slammed it behind her, she grabbed two rifles from over the fireplace, checked the load, and poked them out the gun slat after she closed the shutter. The recoil of the Tennessee long rifles nearly knocked her down, but one of her bullets hit its mark. She had only seen the flash of color among the leaves. The next thing she saw was a spray of blood. It covered everything near the downed aggressor.

They continued to fire long after no more bullets or arrows came from the other woods. There were no longer any gunfire flashes or movement either. Still, nobody was taking any chances, and they had plenty of powder and lead balls. Finally, Dahteste called out something in Crow Indian, and then she slowly rode her spotted horse toward the trees. Mountain Dennis followed on foot with a brace of pistols in his hands. Betty Crockett stood at the open shutter with a loaded rifle aimed at the bushes from where the bullets came.

Dahteste found Nuka and Hook Scar dead just behind the first line of trees. They had taken too big a risk of exposing themselves to a sudden attack. The war chief knew instinctively that if she hadn't attacked when they weren't expecting it, they wouldn't have had a chance. That was what she had been counting on. Again, the element of surprise won the battle.

Betty looked over at the boxes the Army men had been hiding behind. The wood was riddled with bullets, as were three blue uniforms. They had panicked and huddled together in the center of the camp, making them perfect targets. Only greenhorns would hide behind flimsy wooden cartons when the enemy used pistols and buffalo guns. Even the arrows penetrated their cover. At least they probably died in the first volley.

It was getting more dangerous to live in the mountains every day.

The experienced veterans had survived the short but deadly battle. Even Betty knew to take better cover than the soldiers. She wasn't a veteran Indian fighter like Dennis and Dahteste; she had learned on the journey across the country to Oregon City and back. Those who learned slowly or didn't learn enough didn't survive. The lieutenant, corporal, and private didn't know what hit them. Most of the bullets were aimed at them as the others picked off the Blackfeet killers. In a way, they had given their lives for the others by drawing the firepower away and allowing them to win the day.

The Blackfeet had thought they caught the mountain men unawares, and they were sitting ducks. They hadn't counted on Dahteste, Dennis, or even Betty. Even the soldiers had emptied their many weapons before they died, and every bullet counted. That was why the pioneers always carried four or even five flintlock pistols. When the shells finished, whoever was left standing won the fight.

Betty leaned the rifles against the wall, bunched her fists under her eyes, and burst into tears. She was strong but had seen enough violence to last for the rest of her days. Now, it had been White Ghost's men, and it seemed it never ended while living in the wilderness. There were enemies or dangerous threats at every turn.

Right then, she had doubts about living in the compound, even if she talked the captain into doing the right thing and marrying her. They both obviously needed it. She had felt lonely beyond belief ever since she met the captain, and he was lost and didn't even know it. She knew a little about his bout with amnesia and his demons but wanted to learn more and help him like he would help her with her loneliness. The men who were coupled in the Rocky Mountains were the happiest, although some were like Dennis, who had had his married life long ago and was happy enough to look back on what was and live what awaited him.

The Alarm

As soon as the Blackfoot tribe of White Ghost's youth heard he and his warriors were in the area, they sent out numerous three-man war parties to try to locate them quickly. They knew better than anyone how dangerous he could be. They hoped to keep him and his warriors away from the main camps or kill him if they could. Even his own people wanted him dead and buried, at least those who didn't believe he was a ghost and immortal.

Each and every man had declared that he knew it to be true, although half secretly doubted. A network of trails and paths connected smaller Blackfoot villages nearby. They, too, were encouraged to come to the main camp where it would be safer. The entire stronghold prepared for an attack. Heavily armed guards were posted at every entrance and angle. They had to make sure it was impossible for White Ghost to breach their barriers. Only then could they organize and prepare for such an enemy.

Even though this was where he was born and raised, now the members of his tribe all hated the white ghost for the curses and deaths he brought upon them. After a meeting with the chief and all three medicine men, they decided they would prepare for war. Not a war on some other Indian nation, but a war on one war chief and his three warrior braves—still, they would treat the threat of the four as though they were at war with the entire Sioux Nation, regardless of the number. It posed a personal threat to them and shamed them that he came from their village.

It seemed ridiculous for an entire camp with countless warriors to begin to plan for the defeat of four enemy braves. Of course, for many of them, one wasn't mortal. For those who did think he was a ghost, it would present its own difficulties down the road to his demise. But the leaders of the tribe had decided to try they must, and the chief declared all-out war. Smoke signals followed, warning all the hunting and war parties to return home as fast as possible. They ordered them to drop everything and come running for their lives. Nowhere was safe if the war chief run off the rails was nearby.

The smoke signals for WHITE and GHOST floated through the air like dark clouds, and they were seen far and wide. The elders believed they would need every able-bodied man they had, and there would be no exceptions this time. They all knew it was time for the ghost to die once and for all. Not to disappear, only to reappear unexpectedly and kill again, like he had so many times in the past.

The evil killer had more lives than a cat, but they swore this would be his last. He had died too many times before, only to return to kill, and the nightmare began all over again. They lost many members of their tribe to his knives, guns, or arrows. Only one Indian made white albino feathers, and they became his trademark. He was the most feared warrior in the Blackfoot Nation and maybe in the entire Plains.

Obviously, when one tribe sent up smoke signals, everybody on the same horizon saw them too—especially when the words were those of the Blackfoot Indian, whom all tribes feared and hated. Most of the other Indians also believed he was a ghost. Or, at the least, like many of the Crow Indians, thought he was different than them all in a strange and foreboding way. They were all very aware of how hard it would be to kill him. They all remembered how the stories said he had died so many times in the past.

Of course, Chief Hachta believed in spirits, as did the whole tribe. There were good spirits and bad ones, but the Blackfoot ghost was on a different level altogether. He killed senselessly and without apparent motivation. He was full of bloodlust from an early age, and it cursed him and his tribe alike. These exact two words were re-sent by other tribes in their languages, relayed by smoke signals. In an hour, every living being on this side of the Rockies knew that danger could lurk in every shadow.

The Blackfeet, Shoshone, and Crow Indians knew there was always a member of each tribe who could read the others' signs—especially the two most dreaded words: WHITE-GHOST. They were enough to send ripples of fear felt by all humans across the mountains. Nobody was safe with that monster on the loose.

Other tribes saw the smoke signals sent by the

Blackfoot camp and continued to send out their own alarms. By the end of the day, it would be known for hundreds of miles. The Eastern Shoshone, Crow, Blackfeet, Chippewa Cree, Assiniboine, and Sioux war parties responded. Small and large groups of men stealthily crept across the mountains, ignoring the other Indians. They knew they only had one target. White Ghost was so important that the different Indian nations set their differences aside to face the most pressing issue. The enemy of one and all. A killer who crossed all boundaries and murdered people from all tribes for no reason at all other than his own pleasure. There had never been another like him before. It was a long time coming for him to be dead and buried himself.

When asked when this all began and exactly when White Ghost was born, the past became hazy and elusive, and nobody could exactly remember the details. French trappers murdered his father; his mother had died of old age, but no one knew of any other relatives. All signs of his presence had been wiped clean by the tribe with each death. Yet again, he returned and threatened the everyday life of whichever tribe he chose at the time.

How to kill a ghost and keep him dead once and for all? Nobody even knew how many times the renegade war chief had supposedly died. The Blackfoot chief had witnessed a dozen but suspected more from conflicts with other tribes. Nothing was sacred for this godless man. He murdered women, children, and even babies as effortlessly as he killed a rabid dog. He slaughtered family pets before crying children, then killed the boys and girls before their parents' eyes. He seemed to like to lock gazes when he took a loved one's life. He always saw a look of wonder and confusion. All their faces looked to the heavens and asked, "Why?"

Over time, White Ghost became an expert on death —how to administer it and how to prolong it, too. His men simply observed as their boss did the dirty work. They knew they, too, were cursed by all the Indian nations and their gods, just like their leader, so they had nothing more to lose. Their only obsession was to keep their war chief happy and safe, and his singular obsession was the senseless murder of all those who crossed his path.

When War Chief Silver Wings rode out of the stronghold, a hundred painted Blackfoot warriors followed. Horses' hooves rumbled as they hammered the earth, and a large dust cloud followed. They were all armed to the teeth with the best weapons they possessed. The chief posed a striking figure. A wide band of white hair grew from his temples like little wings, but the rest was black, just like his bottomless eyes.

The chief wasn't exactly sure where he was going but had heard the rumors and stories for years. There was an isolated, secret place where White Ghost lived that no one dared visit. It was named Hidden Lake. There were many stories of strange things happening in this isolated stretch of mountain and forest. They say the lake was beautiful with a hint of red tint, but the water was poisonous for all animals, just like the men who lived nearby. It was the perfect home for evil men. Despite the beauty, he had heard that demons infested every nook and cranny.

Usually, he would send out scouts in twos or threes to check ahead for other hostile tribes. But the smoke signals had called a truce until White Ghost died. So, initially, they rode with abandon, with a specific direction in mind. When they got closer, they would have to tread more carefully. That is, if this hidden lake even existed. The renegade Indian war chief's entire life was shrouded in mystery.

When Crow Chief Hachta saw the smoke signals relayed from a small Blackfoot camp, he sounded the alarm. Every man, woman, and child had heard the words White Ghost throughout their lifetimes. The parents used the name to scare the children when they were bad. They spent many sleepless nights thinking about the dreaded baby killer. Now, they had seen the signals, and they said he and his three warriors were on the mountain. So, the chief assembled and personally led a significant war party. The Crow tribe had also lost too many lives to this man, who was considered a demon even by his people.

Chief Hachta sat on his pony with a long lance in his fist. A hundred horses shifted their hooves restlessly behind him as they waited impatiently. Warriors sat astride animals, struggling for control. Finally, a medicine man slowly walked his horse and pulled up by the chief. Then Hachta raised his lance, signaling to move, and they all began as one. Like a giant snake, they slithered their way out of the stronghold and higher into the mountains.

As they journeyed through the day, they saw other large war parties climb on paths across the valley, all heading for the same destination. How many tribes had sent out men to hunt down the outlaw Indian? Nobody knew for sure, but no one had ever seen so many large war parties simultaneously. Especially since they were after a common enemy and had no ill intentions for each other. If it took them together to defeat the monster, then so be it. After it was all said and done, they could resume their lifetime grudges.

All the tribes understood the threat White Ghost proposed to their children's future. Lately, he had taken to swinging infant babies by their feet and popping their heads open like watermelons against walls, posts, and, at times, even trees. By the time he and his three warriors left the crime scene, nobody was alive, not even the babies. Still, he frowned on rape. The man made no sense at all. The White men believed he was insane. The fact that he had always been a dangerous warrior just made him that much more successful. If practice is made for perfection, he could be the best murderer in the United States, especially in a land with little to no law at all.

WHITE GHOST and Black Crow squatted by an open fire before the mouth of the network of tunnels and caves. The war chief sat with his eyes spread wide as he glared into the flickering flames. Shadows danced on their faces, making them even more foreboding, especially with the war chief's white paint.

Both warriors rocked back and forth as they murmured a war song. They used their hands to pat their thighs in lieu of drums. Black Crow, too, had seen the signals in an array of Indian languages floating across the sky all day. Some smoke signals were very similar, and others identified the tribe immediately, especially to the trained and expert eye of a tribal chief. Or a war chief like his leader.

Neither man had the slightest idea of what happened to Nuka and Scar, but they now assumed they were dead. If they were alive, no matter what, they would have returned as their leader had ordered. Of course, even though they sometimes did things forbidden by the war chief, they also knew firsthand how fierce his fury could be if they directly disobeyed an order. Years prior, there had been six warrior braves besides White Ghost. They had all seen how easily they died at the hands of their leader.

The other three had been loyal but acted sometimes without orders or their leader's consent. For the man-ghost, that was unforgivable, and he killed the three one at a time. Those remaining knew well what their futures would be if they followed suit.

The two Indians waited patiently. Both knew that soon, there would be more enemies than they could count. When White Ghost had yet again reappeared, he had poked a stick in a hornets' nest. He knew all his enemies would be after him this time. But then again, they would be on ground that he knew like the back of his hand. As he had done in the past, they could lose any number of men deep in the caves beside him. The tunnels ran for miles and had various levels. Even the war chief didn't know all the tunnels and where they went.

But he knew enough to cause the men after him to have nightmares, and then he would pick them off one at a time. If it was a hundred to die, then that was what it would be. Overwhelming numbers never fazed the war chief. He always counted on his factors of fear and terror. Nobody would come after him totally confident. He didn't know the man alive who didn't know fear. Even he remembered it in his distant past.

The Red Lake

"What we've gotta do is find someplace to hide once we're close enough, and then Levi and I can go out on our own and locate the cave these rascals live in," Rusty whispered. "Once we've got the lay of the land, we can decide how we go about movin' forward. I aim to prove to everybody he ain't no more of a ghost than I am. If we can, we'll hang 'im, but right here where he lives. The same goes for the three that ride with 'im. Do you have any objections to that, Sheriff Walker? Lately, you seem to have a complaint about everything else."

Joseph Walker didn't like sitting back and taking orders. He had always been a take-charge kind of man. However, he really didn't know exactly where they were, but Rusty Steel obviously did. The aging mountain man never seemed to lose his bearings or sense of direction, even under canopies of trees that nearly blocked out the sun. So, for the time being, Walker listened to what was said and followed orders, even if it rubbed him wrong. There were too many chiefs here and not enough Indians in this group for his liking. But he would give the old mountain man a chance to see if he was still up to the task of taking on such a dangerous Indian.

"If you want me to make it legal to hang 'im, I reckon I'm your sheriff. Out here, we're all the law there is. The judge and jury are all wrapped into one. Nobody's gonna complain if we kill this one. He's as wicked as they come, and his death is long overdue. I wouldn't care if it *was* illegal. Given the chance, I reckon I'll kill 'im myself."

They finally crawled up a gravelly steep grade, scrambling to the top. When their eyes peeked over the ridge, they saw a large lake. Red snowcapped mountains reflected in the strange-colored water. It seemed void of any type of life except the dense vegetation surrounding it. There wasn't a drop of air. Trees towered over them motionless at the water's edge. A light snow covered its banks.

"Move back down to that stand of trees," Levi whispered. "If y'all try to hide out here, they'll spot ya for sure. Wiggle into those bushes and stay put until we sort this out. And make sure you don't make a move if you don't want that rascal to catch ya."

Joseph huffed and puffed as he looked at Johnson with narrowed eyes, but Levi just smiled. He knew it got the sheriff's goat to have to take orders from such a young man, but he and Rusty knew nobody else in the mountains had their skills. It sort of came naturally to them both, speeding up the learning process. They were like sponges for information about the wilderness and the people who lived there.

Together, they could track a snake across a red lake or a crow across the sky—they were that good. Rusty could follow most men by only using his sense of smell.

Still, he stayed far enough away from them so they couldn't hear them walking. And he did it all moving from shadow to shadow and the hard places to see, rarely getting noticed.

Everybody but Rusty and Levi crawled deep into brush and brambles. A bear would have a hard time getting to them. When they settled in, there wasn't a trace that they were there. Hopefully, White Ghost wouldn't have the same powerful sense of smell Rusty did. The mountain man even bragged that his was nearly as good as a dog's. They could only hope that White Ghost's wasn't.

"As long as y'all don't make a move or a sound, you'll be fine," Rusty whispered. "If we're not back in a week, you know somethin' went wrong." Rusty's eyes were full of mischief.

"In a week?" Rory Breaker asked. The blood drained from his face, and he began to shake like a leaf. Ever since he was wounded with the arrow, he had been feverish off and on.

"Oh, he's just joshin'." Levi chuckled. "He jokes like that to lighten things up. You might as well stop worryin' anyway. Worry never changed the outcome of nothin'. Worry as you may, it'll either work out or it won't, and nothing can change it. Try to enjoy your rest in the bushes. Catch a few winks of sleep. You're probably gonna need it."

Then the two men turned on their heels and vanished into the trees. It was so abrupt it left the men waiting all speechless—especially the sheriff. Joseph suddenly realized Rusty and Levi did have skills he didn't and wondered what more they had up their sleeves. He stood there scratching his head, wondering how they disappeared so fast.

Five men hid in the bushes while two more snuck around the red water. Dead, bleached-out trees dotted the banks, but no fish were visible in the clear, tinted lake. Not even a tadpole stirred on the muddy bottom. Apart from the lack of life, they heard grizzly bears come there to die, much like the elephants of Africa wandered off to graveyards to breathe their last breaths. It was a graveyard for all types of animals, including humans.

As they moved toward the lake, they found huge bleached-out skeletons of massive beasts they could only assume to be some type of bears. This just made the place appear more foreboding than before. They could feel the evil seep from the pores in the earth.

Rusty grabbed Levi's arm, stopping him in his tracks. He closed his eyes and took a deep breath. He stood still as a rock for a moment before wrinkling his nose and nodding.

"It's him, all right," Rusty whispered as he blinked his eyes. "White Ghost is in smellin' distance, so this must be where he lives. I'd remember that smell anywhere, even after so many years. Did you know that your sense of smell memory is stronger than regular memory? What you smell as a child will come back to remind you when you're an old man, but it will be as fresh and clear as the first time. Tread carefully, buddy. We're in enemy territory."

Of course, the Indians believed evil spirits lived on the lake, which was why it was red and deadly poison. Some thought it was from the blood of many lost lives to the evil demons living there. Each tribe had a slightly different version, but they all said the same thing. It was a place they needed to avoid. They could feel the sin seep up from the dirt they were walking on.

Cold chills ran up Rusty's and Levi's spines. They shot from one tree to the next, avoiding the lake's edge where there was no vegetation and no place to hide. They tried not to risk being seen before they were close enough to plan or turn back for reinforcements. No matter what, they had no intentions of leaving this lake with White Ghost still alive. Although they advanced, clueless about what was coming, they didn't hesitate. They both knew that could cost a man his life.

That was when they saw the black holes at the end of the water. From a distance, water appeared to run right into the cavern's mouth. Were there three entrances to the same network of tunnels, or were they three separate caves? Still, they looked too close together. This must be where White Ghost hid when he was supposedly dead. There must be some other source of water not too far away.

It looked like minerals tainted the water's color, and the algae was responsible for poisoning it. Nobody knew what was true and what wasn't. At this point, it was anybody's guess. All they knew was that the evil Indian was close enough to smell, so they assumed they would be face-to-face in seconds.

All the tribes' elders and the medicine men said to avoid Hidden Lake. It was taboo for six of the tribes that lived in this part of the mountains. What better place for a man like White Ghost to reside and hide? Most Indians didn't really believe the place even existed. They thought it was more of a ghost town, like the war chief with the painted white face.

The closer they got to the edge of the lake, the slower they crept. Now Rusty led the way, keeping a sharp eye out for trouble. When he held out his arm, they both stopped dead in their footsteps. Rusty knelt and looked closely at the hemp string. He gently flicked it with his finger, and it was as tight as a drum. He shifted his eyes to the tree above them, and Johnson's followed. A spiked post hung, ready to swing down and bash in a man's skull.

Rusty Steel grabbed a stick and set the trap, and it swung down, making a swipe at the path they were following. It swayed back and forth like a pendulum until it stopped. All the time, the hemp rope squeaked on the high limb. They exchanged glances. Sweat covered their faces.

They veered wide of the sprung trap and continued even more carefully than before. It almost felt like White Ghost was taunting them, or maybe he somehow even had his eyes on them. He seemed to be one step ahead of them at every turn. Now they were even more aware they had to be careful and not to step into another one of his clever traps. Rusty had found this one, but how many more were there?

In the distance, a slash cut into the mountainside. Below that were the black holes in the rock; they appeared so smooth they looked manmade. The whole formation seemed to form a natural cathedral. Red streaks of mineral deposits scarred the face of the rock above the openings, making them look strangely like church steeples.

Rusty had heard there was a network of caves somewhere by the lake. Easier to find they could not have been unless there were more than those visible. Maybe somewhere where there was fresh water available. Perhaps an underwater spring. He wondered if this, too, was some trick. At this point, they no longer knew what was real or false.

The idea that maybe the Blackfoot war chief was a ghost began to sneak into Rusty's consciousness. He had never believed in such frivolous fantasies, but now he started having doubts. He had never been led by the nose, regardless of who the enemy was. This time, he appeared to have met his match. So far, everything he did, the Blackfoot ghost was one step ahead of him.

They moved deeper into the forest as they neared the canyon wall and the far bank. They wanted to stay out of sight of the cave openings. If they could get above them, they could watch any activity from the cliffs without being seen.

They didn't see a living animal other than the perpetual vultures circling endlessly overhead. The Indians had to be inside one of the caverns, if anybody was there. The place appeared to be uninhabitable for any living thing. Was it possible the earth there was poisoned, too? Maybe the prolonged presence of such an evil man had made the lake and caverns a home for devils and demons.

As soon as Johnson and Rusty reached the water's edge and looked down on the lake, the captain came up behind them. Levi whirled around with his pistol cocked, but Rusty had already smelled him.

"I figured this was one you better sit out, boss," the captain said. "Today will be a hard nut to crack, so it's best to leave it to the young men. We've already lost too many old friends this year, and I don't intend to lose another."

"And who made you the boss of this outfit?" Rusty growled. "Now you're actin' like the sheriff. And why ain't you back in the brush, hidin' like I told ya to?"

"It's not that at all, my old friend," the captain said. "Don't we always let the best at the task lead the way? Just like you said to Sheriff Walker. Unfortunately, I'm the best killer of us all, so today, I've got to be the leader. I promise as soon as Levi and I assess the situation, we'll come running back, and we can decide what to do next. But if we run into trouble, it will be best if I'm there regardless of the situation."

Will's deep blue eyes pleaded with Rusty as Levi watched in wonder. Neither he nor the captain had ever questioned any of Steel's orders. Rusty had always had the last word in the past, but it was true his young friend was the man for the job. It was also time they made their old neighbors stop risking their lives before there weren't any of them left. The young men turned and dropped over the top and slid down to the bottom. Then they raced for the back of the lake and the tunnels.

Black Crow

When Black Crow turned back around, White Ghost had vanished. They had just been talking seconds before. He had asked him a question, and then he was gone. He rubbed his eyes with his fists and blinked, then stared again into the fog, but White Ghost wasn't there. When he looked down, there weren't even any footprints in the snow; what he didn't see made him shudder. Had his leader really been there at all? He knew that ghosts did strange things, but he suddenly got a bad feeling. He felt sure his war chief had just abandoned him.

Was that possible after all they had been through together? Why else would he vanish without a word? They had already accepted that something fatal had happened to Nuka and Scar. Otherwise, they would have been back long before now. For men like them, only one thing could have stopped them. The only reason they wouldn't follow orders was if death came knocking on their door. This he felt his war chief knew, just like he did. White Ghost must have felt the demise of his own brother. Any ghost should be able to do that.

Black Crow closed his eyes, but he couldn't feel the presence of the war chief like he always had. There seemed to be a void of smells despite the pines. He felt strangely alone—maybe even vulnerable. He wondered what was going to happen next. This time, things had appeared like they were going according to plan, but the last part of the scheme had seen a few hiccups. The traps they set didn't fool any of the mountain men nor injure anybody. They had hoped to reduce their numbers, or at least their horses, but the clever frontiersmen had survived, as did their animals.

And now their numbers appeared to be the ones reduced to two from four. Now, two men were left to take on seven. Then again, if his leader felt it was what they should do, who was Black Crow to question his desires?

The problem was that old Rusty Steel could smell the Indians before they even got close. He was impossible to surprise and capture. Now that he knew they were there, he hardly showed himself for more than fractions of a second. Not even enough time to take a bead with a rifle or a bow. Black Crow knew because he had tried. The White man shifted between the shadows as though he had Indian blood.

He must have been mothered by a pack of wolves, Black Crow thought. *How else could a mortal man have such a sense of smell?*

That was when it hit him. Maybe this Rusty Steel wasn't mortal, either. Perhaps he was a spirit like his leader. And the sizable young mountain man who ran with him must be his pup. A chill suddenly ran up

Black Crow's spine, and he knew he was doomed. How else could the old man evade every booby trap and follow them like a bloodhound? No mere man had the smell of a wolf. Only Steel did, so was he a man, or was he a spirit like his Blackfoot war chief?

He was just beginning to suspect there were more spirits involved than he had believed existed. Maybe that was why White Ghost fled. Or was he out there sneaking up on Rusty Steel, poised to kill him at any second? He thought about it, but he just didn't feel it. Now, he didn't know exactly what to expect. All he knew was that he was alone and would have to surrender or fight to the death against countless numbers. He shivered involuntarily.

Right then, a loneliness grew in Black Crow's dark heart like he never felt before. He couldn't even sense the slightest presence of his chief or blood brothers. He had always expected to die defending White Ghost in some honorable act of bravery and wasn't ready to die alone. Who would know or care what happened to him in the end? He would be deprived of the honor of dying like a hero. To an Indian, how a man died was as important as how he lived. In some cases, even more so. A brave death could turn you into a legend.

Would anybody miss him or even notice he was gone? Would there be anyone to tell his story? If his leader had fled for good, there was no reason for anybody to remember him or what he had done. He wondered where his spirit would go when he died. He knew death was imminent. It was only a matter of minutes before they found him. He knew there would be too many to hide from. Still, he planned to take it like a man.

Black Crow did not plan to give his captors the pleasure of seeing him cry or scream. He would take his death like the brave warrior he always professed to be. He had never shied away from danger or possible death, and he had no plan to start now. He had died many times in his mind's eye and had done so bravely—but never alone. That shook him more than he expected. He always thought he would fight to the end with his leader behind him and his two blood brothers by his sides. It had been that way for years, or was it decades?

It left him feeling like his life and, even more, his death would be all for nothing. He had only been a tool of revenge against his leader's countless enemies. He would be forgotten tomorrow, and his name would never be mentioned again. This last fact made him gasp. He had always believed the Blackfeet elders would sing about him in their songs. Of course, they would sing of his terrorizing war cry and extreme acts of violence against his enemies.

Just the same, they would sing his name. That was of great importance to any brave who strived to achieve fame. Long ago, he knew he wasn't the kind of warrior to follow any leader. When he met White Ghost, he instantly understood. It had changed his life's direction and given him something to fight for—to live for. Even if it was senseless killing, he still complied with his spiritual leader's orders, which he followed to the letter.

He hid in the dark of the tunnel near the opening. He had to make a mad dash and try to get over the ridge of the lake where he would be safe. His heart hammered between his ears, and his breath came short and fast. Sweat glistened on his face as he struggled to stay calm. Just a few more minutes and he could reach safety. All he needed was a little luck.

He pulled a knife and a pistol. He didn't notice he was squeezing the grips so tightly. He crouched, ready to make the mad dash. He took three deep breaths and ran for the other side of the lake. It had always given him the creeps. It looked like bloody water. Then, he was suddenly up and running for all he was worth—through the dark tunnel and suddenly into the bright light.

The Tunnels

Levi and the captain neared the end of the red lake. A foreboding smell came off the water. When they got close to the openings in the side of the cliff, they immediately knew they were manmade, although it looked like it had been a millennium ago. Levi edged to the opening with his back to the stone wall and peeked around the corner. He saw what he hadn't expected. The massive room was a vast dome, and the stone was as smooth as a baby's butt. All three openings entered the same room and then came a maze of passageways.

"This isn't a good spot to perch out here in the open," Forrester whispered. "We've got to move, quick."

The top of the passageways were as smooth as glass. Steps were carved into the stone to climb up or down the inside of the mountain. A dozen corridors apparently ran out to a network of rooms and tunnels. It gave the feeling that they were never-ending and ran deep into the earth forever.

As soon as they saw it, the sight of some unknown technology from eons ago humbled them. They noticed holes burrowed high into the walls and ceiling that reached all the way to the outside, somewhere above. Indirect sunlight spilled into the caverns. Some advanced tribe must have lived there a thousand years ago. Now, the caves sounded empty, even though they knew they weren't. Numerous tunnels branched out from the first main room. They didn't dare linger and take the time to check out the other openings. They knew they had to move quickly if they wanted to remain unseen.

Somewhere in there, White Ghost and his three warriors were lurking. Levi wondered if the Indians already knew they were near. He was starting to feel edgy and uncomfortable. They felt they couldn't wait any longer. He waved his hand at the captain and ducked into the diminished light, but still, the men could easily see where they were going. In a flash of less than two seconds, the two friends crossed the dome's floor and ducked into the darkest tunnel. Suddenly, they could barely see three feet in front of themselves. It got darker the farther they went.

"Stop," the captain whispered as he carefully listened for any sounds. "At this point, your guess is as good as mine, so let me lead the way. The saber gives me the advantage of a longer reach. We can barely see where we're going anyway." A matchstick moved from side to side and across his mouth and under the captain's blond mustache. "It's a helluva thing, tracking a man to kill."

"Uh-huh," Johnson replied. "So, what's new?"

Forrester drew his saber. Levi held two pistols in white-knuckled fists. They began to inch forward, certain the famous war chief would be waiting for them just around the next corner. They could feel the danger in the air. It was so thick you could cut it with a knife. Their hearts pounded between their ears, and their shirts stuck to sweat-covered backs. Johnson nudged his friend's shoulder and then took another step into the darkness. The tunnel lightened, and they came to another sizable dome-shaped room.

Levi's eyes shifted suddenly, and he shouted, "Beside you! Look out!"

Their bodies came alive when they heard the shot from a tunnel on their left flank. Levi instinctively went for his booted long gun. The captain's hand swung his saber down and back toward the threat, but a sword was no match for a rifle, and he was too far away. There was no time to draw a pistol. It all depended on Levi.

Johnson drew his weapon in his mind, planning his motion and the bullet's trajectory in an instant thought. Now he saw the man hiding in a tunnel entrance. He had a rifle in his hands, too, pointing his way. Will ducked, and the bullet hit the crown of his cavalry hat. That was too close for comfort. Black Crow looked at them wide-eyed for the briefest of moments, then disappeared down the dark network of caves.

Levi's rifle roared, but they saw it hit stone and then ricochet down the passageway. The outlaw Indian turned long enough to glare at Johnson but didn't see the captain beside him. Maybe White Ghost wasn't the most dangerous man in the wilderness. Perhaps it was a close friend. Still, the warrior brave had escaped.

Now, it was a game of cat and mouse, but they only saw one outlaw. There would be three more someplace. They had no doubts about who this one was. He was one of White Ghost's gang members. They held their breaths and crept down the cave in the direction he escaped. It got darker and darker as they neared the end. It was something they felt more than they saw because in two more steps, it was pitch dark again, and they couldn't see their hands before their faces.

Some gravel stirred beside them. Then Forrester felt fingers clawing through his shirt and wrapping around his neck, trying to get a good grasp, but he dropped his saber in the attack and struggled to resist with his one hand. Due to constant use, his muscle-wrapped arm resisted, but still he floundered.

The captain pushed himself back and out of the assailant's clutches, rolling to the ground to get out of reach, and gracefully rose to his feet in one clean motion. For a one-armed man, he was as graceful as a ballerina. He closed in again and swung hard, hitting Black Crow square in the jaw. He staggered and started to fall, but he grabbed the wall, pushed himself off, and fled into total darkness. The captain grabbed his saber from the ground, and he roared his frustration.

Beaver Johnson dropped to his hands and knees, using his fingers to claw the dirt to release his fury as he screamed in anger. He rocked back and sat on his heels. His eyes followed the black hole where Black Crow had disappeared. A light shone brightly at the end of the tunnel. They wondered if they had lost the killers for good, so they carefully backtracked to where they entered. They didn't dare take another route for fear of another ambush or getting completely lost in such a labyrinth of tunnels.

WHEN BLACK CROW came racing out of the cavern's mouth, he ran straight into three hundred warriors. He slid to a stop, nearly falling into the gravel with his eyes popping out of his head. Of course, he froze. What was he to do? In the end, he hadn't been quick enough.

The painted Indians slowly neck-reined their ponies toward their common enemy. When they got their first glimpse of Black Crow, he wore a stiff-brimmed Army hat pulled low, shading his eyes. When the light reached them, they highlighted his weather-cut features. The renegade's stare followed the long line of braves. It appeared to never end. He snarled at the warriors. It was obvious he wasn't scared.

"Now that you have me, what will you do with me?" Black Crow asked, his mouth a gash as he tried not to gulp for air. His controlled voice told nothing of what he was thinking. Not a hint of body language gave his thoughts away—only the quick movement of his chest.

"You already know why we're here," Hachta said. "You know what we're going to do, too. So why the questions?"

Black Crow slowly breathed in and out and calmly said, "I swear on the spirits I was just following White Ghost's orders just like any other warrior brave would. If you look deep down inside, I'm no different than most of your braves."

"None of my people are like you," Hachta spat angrily. "Not like Scar or Nuka, either, not to mention White Ghost. But I must admit that none of you are as evil as him. Still, that is no excuse for your actions, and for that, you must pay. Just like the rest of your people will pay with their lives. Do you think you can escape such a massive war party? Do you take us for fools?"

"Just make it quick," Black Crow spat. He tried to smile and almost made it, but the Crow chief saw through his façade.

"I promise you, it will be so slow you'll beg to die," the Blackfoot Chief Silver Wings hissed. It sounded like a viper.

"Drop your weapons!" Hachta screamed. As he said it, Black Crow was already getting dragged across the snow.

They surrounded him while two braves held his hands, but he didn't struggle. He was too proud for that. Instead, he spat at his captor's feet. A war club instantly came from nowhere. It stung against his face, and his jaw hung like a broken hinge. The tip of a lance jabbed into his back. They dragged him to the nearest tree, holding each arm, but he walked with his head high, despite his imminent future. He expected no mercy because White Ghost and his band of warriors had shown none when they killed their victims.

"This one is a hard-bitten, weathered veteran, so don't trust him for a second," the Blackfoot chief warned.

Hachta's eyes hadn't left Black Crow's. Despite his broken jaw, the renegade Indian smiled. He spat again. It was a bloody red against the white snow.

Black Crow thought, *I'm going to die*. He repeated it in his mind. *I'm going to die*, but the words seemed to slow down as the fact sunk in. *All right, I always knew this day would come. Come on, think straight, and control your emotions. You're a Blackfoot warrior brave, after all.* But he felt alone just the same.

Regardless of all his bravado, he was nervous, and he didn't like it at all. He couldn't entirely accept and believe what was happening to him. He forced himself to buck up and take it like a man, but still, it saddened him that he would die alone. His dream of a hero's death was just about to vanish. He thought about his mother and father—something he hadn't done for decades. He thought about a prayer, but what spirits would listen to a man like him?

The chief motioned to his men waiting by a tree. They slid down from their horses and pulled Black Crow to his feet.

Black Crow locked eyes with the chief and said, "Goodbye, for now. Who knows what will happen in our next lives, in the spirit world." Their eyes held lingeringly.

"Get him up!" Hachta growled.

The Crow chief turned on his horse blanket as he slid the weapon out. His pony sidestepped nervously. It kicked at the snow and threw its head. He cradled the large rifle in his arms. His face was cold and held no emotion.

Hachta had believed that Black Crow would have been in a panic by now, pleading for his life. Most men who tortured and murdered women and children were more afraid to lose their lives, but not this brave. He was at ease as they lifted him onto a pony. He sat as still as a stone when they walked him toward a tree.

They looped a noose over a low limb; the other end they tied to the trunk. Uncertainty clouded the renegade's eyes. Two granite-faced Crow warriors stared down the stony captive. One slipped the noose around his foot, and suddenly, he was flying in the air. When his ankle nearly reached the branch at the top, they secured the rope as he hung upside down.

Hachta and Silver Wings walked over to the dangling body with skinning knives in their fists. Revenge sparkled in their eyes. They had waited years for this moment. Today, they would kill White Ghost and his men, too. Still, some of their men believed he was a ghost. Would he vanish yet again only to return later to kill?

"Tie off his other hand and legs, so he can't move," the Blackfoot chief ordered. "I like to make nice thin strips when I skin a man." He sounded like he had plenty of experience.

Despite Black Crow's bravado, he eventually folded and succumbed to the pain. As they cut away his skin in three-inch strips, soon his body was all red dermis. The epidermis was completely removed. It was when they doused the body with alcohol that the renegade lost control and howled like a wounded beast. It even sent chills up the warriors' backs. Then they covered him in kerosene to make a final fire.

The war chiefs got caught up in the moment and forgot about time and their primary target. The warriors enjoyed acquiring their long-awaited restitution—especially the men from his tribe. The day began to wane when they remembered. But now, was it too late?

They left the burning body to smoke and smolder in the growing afternoon. They jumped back on their horses and rode the short distance to the end of the lake. They were after Nuka, Scar, and of course, their leader, White Ghost.

Ghosts & Spirits

Levi and the captain crept along the water's edge. They had spent a lengthy time figuring out how to get out of the tunnels safely, but now they were on the trail of the War Chief White Ghost. From a distance, they had seen Black Crow's future. They believed it was better if all White men stayed away from Indian business, so they watched from afar but didn't allow even their friend Hachta to know they were there. He appeared angry and cross.

That wasn't the disposition you wanted when dealing with Indians. It was best to be humble and mind your own business. Especially when they were torturing and killing an enemy. It was a dangerous time to be near an angry war party. Especially for a couple of White men.

They believed non-natives should have no interest in what was about to happen to a warrior whom the tribes considered a traitor. Levi was aware that there was always some warrior brave with an axe to grind over an old grudge, and both mountain men knew to avoid problems when possible. So, they tiptoed around the torture nearly as soon as it began. But they had seen enough to know they captured one of them and that he would quickly face the consequences.

Nobody had seen the other two warriors. There were no tracks of more than two men, no matter where they looked. Could it be possible that two had gone AWOL and vanished under the threat of certain death? So, why did Black Crow choose to stay? There were too many Indian warriors on the mountain for anybody to get away. It was just a matter of time before they located the leader. Johnson had seen his tracks all around the lake, so he didn`t doubt that he was nearby.

The loose gravel shifted and crunched under their feet. They felt they sounded like two buffalo as the noise echoed across the still pond. The moon reflected off the red water into their eyes, making them glow in the dark. As they neared the end of the lake, it appeared to be shrouded in fog. Still, a strange light bounced off the surface. It seemed that smoke covered the water in the far corner. As they came closer, they believed they saw a wavy image that cast a heated glow like a hot brown aura. It was outlined in a thin, red, wavy line.

They stopped, rubbed their eyes, and looked again, but the image, if that was what it was, was blurry and hard to see. One moment, it appeared, it would clear, and they would see a detailed outline only to fall back into wavy lines. Maybe it wasn't even real. At this point, they doubted almost everything. They felt no religious man was protected from the demons on such poisonous ground. All human beings trespassed on this land at their own peril.

Levi had a brace of pistols in his fists, and the moonlight flashed off the captain's saber. Their hearts hammered between their ears and sweat glistened on their faces as they crept even closer. With every step, they felt the danger build to nearly unbearable measures. Neither man had ever been this tense, not even when they fought the Comanche warriors back in Kansas almost two years prior.

Something was foreboding about War Chief White Ghost—even though they had never considered him anything but a human being. Doubt began to worm into their brains, and the tension doubled. It was the first hint that the lie may actually be accurate, but they continued to resist.

Still, their logic refused them to acknowledge such things as ghosts, but their souls were already darkening as the poison seeped in—even Capt. Forrester began to doubt, and he was the strictest Army man Johnson had ever known. White-knuckled fists wrapped around their grips. Their eyes narrowed as they focused on the wavering image.

"Do you see that?" Levi whispered.

"I'm not sure what I see," the captain replied, "but I think it's White Ghost."

They waited silently, but all they could hear was a nearby waterfall. Ripples raced across the water, reflecting light off the tiny red waves of liquid.

Suddenly, they saw War Chief White Ghost standing huge before them. He appeared twice the size they had remembered. He seemed to be immortal or maybe even a ghost. It looked like he was walking on water. Up close, he seemed bigger than life. Levi fired once, then twice as flames flashed and gun smoke spewed from the barrels, but the image of the Indian before them belly laughed at their bullets.

He didn't appear fazed by the lead slugs. Johnson dropped his spent pistols and drew two more from his belt. More bullets raced from the barrels and seemed to pass right through the Blackfoot warrior. He continued to laugh at his aggressors. He obviously wasn't afraid of either. Gun smoke made it even harder to see the fuzzy image.

Then the captain got a crazy look in his eyes. Even with the threat before them, Levi couldn't help but notice. It was something he had never seen before in all the months they had traveled, explored, and fought together. The giant mountain man went to stop his friend, but all he grabbed was an empty sleeve, and it slipped right through his fingers. Before he could stop the captain, he disappeared into the foggy haze. The only sound was of crunching gravel. The sound echoed across the lake, repeating the gravelly footsteps until there were many.

Then Levi thought he heard the swoosh of a large blade, maybe even a saber. He drew his last pistol and pulled a Bowie knife from his boot. With a weapon in each fist, he was ready to make his last stand and stepped forward. He assumed the captain had fallen since he didn't hear anything more. The numbers of the compound were dwindling fast.

A thought shot through his mind. Would he ever see Dahteste again? His heart cried out, but he knew he couldn't turn back now. Will had made that impossible. He could hear her voice as clear as a bell, but in his memory, he couldn't quite see her face. Things were becoming hazy, making him doubt everything.

Would the captain have a chance to marry Betty, or would they be denied that, too? Both answers seemed evasive, and their adopted home seemed too far away ever to return. Even their friends' faces became blurry and hard to see in his memory. Levi wondered where Rusty was. They had split up hours previously but hadn't caught sight since; had he, too, fallen to the white arrows of the ghost warrior?

He knew if anyone could care for themselves, it was his teacher, Steel. But everyday life in the wilderness was tricky business, so when the forest was so full of dangerous and hostile Indians, a man had to stop and think. He or any of them could lose their lives at the drop of a hat. That was proven recently when they lost three of their own. Were they just about to lose more or had they been lost already?

"Are we on a one-way road to hell?" Levi barely whispered, but still, it sounded too loud. "Lord, help me." He walked into the fog. It was so thick it parted like cloth. "Are you out there, Will?" His voice echoed off the canyon walls. Then he heard running water. It splashed somewhere behind the mist.

That was when Beaver Johnson discovered that White Ghost's image was a reflection against a curtain of water at the end of the lake. He saw the flash of polished metal glint off the moonlight to his left on the banks. As the Indian stood at the water's edge, his image reflected off the red-tainted mirror and onto the haze of mist and moisture. It made him appear to be a ghost and gave the illusion he was walking on water. Levi had wasted his bullets on a reflection.

Johnson watched as White Ghost turned his gruesome face, and they locked eyes—it sent a bolt of electricity up his spine. At the same time, the captain silently crept up behind the Blackfoot war chief, but Levi didn't realize Will was there. Levi winked and smiled at the ghost warrior momentarily, leaving him slightly puzzled. This wasn't the face the war chief expected to see. The captain stepped out of the fog and lobbed off White Ghost's head in one swift movement. He proved once and for all that he was mortal and made of flesh, blood, and bones just like them.

Forrester picked up the head by the hair. He had no intention of White Ghost ever returning to the living again. They would put the head on salt and take it back to the Crow camp in a canvas sack. Then they would let Chief Hachta stick it on a pike to display and prove the "ghost" was dead to one and all. The Indian gossip would do the rest. Then they could let the stories die, too, and put the evil man in his grave with his companions once and for all.

Suddenly, five tribes of Indian warriors descended on Hidden Lake, with their faces painted for war. When they saw White Ghost's hair wrapped in the captain's fingers, their chins dropped to their chests. They saw that the mountain men had already ended their nightmare, and the ghost wasn't a ghost after all. Nervous laughter rippled through hundreds of warrior braves. The horses felt the tension in their riders and shifted their hooves and sidestepped. Many nickered or groaned and a couple screamed at the smell of blood.

Right then, nobody even remembered they were enemies in the past. As one, they had saved the day, of course, with the help of the mountain men. They had a common adversary, but even his life had ended.

Warm blood still dripped from the bodyless head.

Since the blood had drained from his face and the cut was so clean, it looked more like a clay figure. Now, he was no more than a head of an image of what once terrorized the entire Rocky Mountains. His old, fierce features had lost all their evil power, and now his eyes were blank and empty. His mouth gaped open as a sliver of blood ran down his chin and dripped into the contrasting color of white snow.

It was confirmation enough to prove to the medicine men that he was no more than flesh and blood like all human beings. There was nothing immortal about him at all. He died and probably didn't even know that death had silently crept up on him and taken his life away so fast he didn't realize it had happened. The last he knew, he was still laughing at the White man. Johnson would never forget the look in White Ghost's eyes. Who was the clown now?

Captain Forrester stood by the water's edge. He still had White Ghost's hair clutched in his fingers. He knew that each of the tribes would want the prize, but if he offered it to them now, it would probably end the delicate truce that White Ghost obliged them to adopt. He locked eyes with Chief Hachta and then with the man he believed to be the Blackfoot leader.

He nodded to each leader of the war parties, then drew the skull in his hand as far back as possible. He catapulted it with a long arc as the ball of hair sailed over the water. Finally, it splashed into the middle with a plop. They could see it sink for the first few yards, then it drifted toward the bottom.

No one dared jump into a poisoned lake to retrieve his head. Chief Hachta instantly saw the wisdom in the captain's actions, as did the Blackfoot and Sioux leaders.

It avoided a conflict just waiting to happen. Maybe this White soldier was more like Rusty Steel and Levi Johnson than they had believed. All the Indian tribes on the mountain gained a new respect for Captain Will Forrester. He was the first soldier they ever trusted, and now they were in his and the mountain men's debt.

The warrior braves shouted in an uproar, angry because the White man denied them the ultimate trophy. The chiefs slowly wheeled their horses around and retreated to a safe distance. The body of White Ghost, less his head, would join that of Black Crow for eternity.

After a few moments, the braves settled down, followed their leaders, and waited for new orders. All they had to do now was dispose of the body and ensure it never came back among the living like the self-proclaimed ghost had done a dozen times before.

But the Shoshone, Crow and Blackfoot leaders had different plans for the body. It was to be buried so deep even the coyotes and wolves couldn't dig it up. They all wondered what would happen to his head. Some talked of ways to retrieve it, but most of the warrior braves were just happy the threat was over and their children were safe. After White Ghost's reign of terror, that should be enough for everybody.

Proposals

Will smiled as his stallion pranced while Betty bounced on his lap. Her arms wrapped around the captain as she snuggled her face in his neck. Her feet made little kicks in the air, showing her delight. She noted the salty smell of manhood as they headed for a stand of wild high-bush cranberries. The first flurries were fresh on the ground so they could be the last fruit of the season. Soon, heavy snows would follow, and they would be confined to their small stretch of land and strings of traps in the surrounding streams and creeks.

In the darkest months of the Rocky Mountain winters, they stayed inside. They only ventured out to collect firewood or use the outhouse. That made for cold seats in the early mornings. That was when they worked and cured the furs they had trapped in the fall and early winter. Will wondered if he would return to the Rendezvous next summer. Most things that happened this year had been wrong—even bad. Maybe if it wasn't for the Squirrel Clan, they might have been able to enjoy themselves. Still, the constellations had aligned, and things happened, changing everybody's future.

Currently, the following summer seemed like a long time away. A lot had happened in a short period of time. It changed the lives of all the members of Rusty Steel's compound. Many of those changes weren't for the better and weren't undoable. Others were fortunate gifts of life and happiness. Each of them came out of this wiser and slightly more scarred. It was inevitable when living in the wilderness.

When the mountain men returned from killing White Ghost, they were surprised to find the women and Dennis were responsible for killing his Blackfoot warriors, Hook Scar and Nuka. The poor dead soldiers were all buried, and their graves stood just outside the compound. Three mounds of fresh dirt marked their demise, and inexperience had cost them their lives: that and a frivolous mission. If things kept going like they had been, they would soon have their own cemetery full of family and friends.

If they had brought home Syracuse Sam, Portland Pete, and Yosemite Bob, there would be six graves instead of three. Little by little, their members were being whittled down. Then again, new blood was being pumped into the small community. It appeared that Miss Betty Crockett was there to stay. At least until she saw whether things would work out with the captain; time would tell if there was a romance there or not.

When they arrived at the cranberry patch, Betty gracefully slid off the captain's lap, and he stepped down from his black stallion. He reached for the berry basket, but Betty grabbed his hand and pulled him to her. He opened his mouth to protest, but she covered it with hers. Will instantly relaxed, and they melted into each other's arms. Until then, they had guessed, and Betty had even hoped against all odds that the feeling would be there. The moment of truth had arrived, and it was more magical than she had ever imagined. She quickly swept Forrester off his feet. At least, she hoped she had. Now came the bold part.

She held his face close to hers in her hands and smiled. He could feel her minty, warm breath on his face. The captain was fixated and appeared as though he couldn't move. She knew she finally had his undivided attention, and he couldn't run off to put out any fires.

"I won't get down on one knee because I refuse to make a fool of myself, but I may be bold enough to ask you to marry me." Her eyebrows raised in question as she cocked her hip and waited.

Will just blinked in wonder. It was as if he got a hint of what was happening but didn't quite understand. He shook his head, puzzled, unsure of what he had just heard. Of course, he must have misunderstood. He wiggled his little finger in his ear and frowned in confusion.

"Well, are ya gonna answer or not, Will Forrester? I'm not gonna wait on you forever."

"Did you ask me a question, or am I hearing things?" Will asked, puzzled. "I didn't quite understand what you're talking about."

"Do I have to spell it out for you?" Betty laughed at his discomfort. She knew it was just about to get worse. "I'm askin' you to marry me, Captain. I know if I wait for you to get around to it, the Indians may have killed me by then, so I decided not to linger."

"Why, I've never heard of a woman proposing to a man!" He shook his head like he was still too confused to understand. To him, it seemed almost against the laws of nature.

"You can stop batting those big blue eyes of yours, darlin'. I have no plans to get back on that horse until I have an answer. Better yet, until I have a promise."

Now, the captain finally understood, but he was still shocked. He had never heard of a woman asking for a man's hand in marriage. Then again, they were a long way from civilization. He wondered if the Indian women were so bold. He didn't know what to think. What he was just asked was unheard of back in civilization. But then again, where was it more civilized? Back in the big eastern cities or there with the Native Americans?

"Well, I'm still waitin'," Betty said as she impatiently tapped her toe. "If you're having a hard time deciding, let me tell you what I'm going to do if you say *no*."

Will's face drained, and he turned as gray as a ghost. She had never talked about leaving before, so he never even considered it. Now, he suddenly felt he didn't like the idea, and maybe she might just slip through his fingers. She had his full attention.

"If you don't want to marry me, I'm gonna ask Dahteste to take me to the Crow village. I will stay there with Pine Needle for the winter. Angus is beatin' around the bush so I can stay there instead. Then, when Chief Hachta sends his men to the Rendezvous next summer, I'll go with him and find a new husband there. I do not intend to leave the Rockies, so you can get used to that. If you don't want to marry me, I'm sure at least there will be a hundred men to pick from at the next fur trappers' meet.

"Of course, they won't be my Captain Forrester, but at this point, I'm willing to sacrifice to settle in this wonderful place, regardless of whether it's with you or not. I will just have to live with the sacrifice. I suppose, in the end, it's more about *where* I am more than *who* I'm with. But of course, I want to be with you if that's possible, but we have to feel it both ways. One-way love doesn't work. At least not for me."

Will opened and closed his mouth like a beached fish. He was more puzzled than ever, and he felt pressed for time like never before in his life. Not even while back in New York, studying at West Point. When Betty said she was ready to take another husband if he said no, he remembered how the mountain men and miners lined up for the seven women from the Squirrel family.

They were mostly ugly or homely ladies with shocking red hair and freckles. Still, they had so many suitors they had to thin them out first to the richest and most reliable and the widows had their pick. He remembered how over a hundred rugged men lined up, and there were another hundred that weren't brave enough to try.

But to the lonely mountain men, they were treasures to be cherished, and they fell all over themselves, hoping to be one of the husbands. To them, it hadn't even mattered which one. The ladies had had their choice of any man there. He believed he wouldn't even make the grade in such a situation.

With a couple of women to every hundred men, it made for slim pickings for most males in the West. Then, love hadn't been involved at all. It was all for practical purposes, at least for the Squirrel women. Then again, anything was better than the situation they had been in.

Betty let her hands slide down Will's cheeks and lay her palms flat on his chest. She kissed his cheek, lay her head on her hands, and impatiently waited. She had to remind herself to breathe. She knew she was taking a big chance, but it was the only way. Miss Crockett was thirty years old, going on forty, and she wasn't getting any younger. If she wanted to start a family, she didn't have much time. Her heart raced in her chest as she waited. Seconds seemed like minutes, and that first minute felt like it lasted half her life.

"Yessum," Will finally said. He started to laugh, both because it sounded funny, and he felt happy. The most complicated thing he had ever contemplated in his life just got made as easy as pie. "Will there be anything else, ma'am?" His eyes twinkled in delight. "I suppose the decision got made for me, didn't it?"

He walked to his saddle and pulled the pigging string securing a rolled-up blanket. He gently laid it on the ground, making far too much fuss straightening it out. It was apparent he was killing time for lack of knowing what to do next. They lay down beside each other for the first time as a couple in love.

"Do I have to do everything?" Betty asked, leaning over her beau.

She kissed Will full on the lips as she explored his mouth. At first, he was shocked and didn't know if he quite liked it, but his physical response was so apparent that he obviously did. It was so new to him that he felt like a clumsy boy. Of course, Betty was a grown woman, already widowed by a wicked man. Forrester was like a kid in a box full of new toys and didn't know which one to pick.

"I think Rusty better get out his ship's log and marry us this afternoon. I want to keep you an honest woman. Mrs. Forrester—that sounds splendid, doesn't it—Mrs. Forrester, I mean."

Their laughter filled the forest. They stayed there all day, discovering new things about each other. They requested that the ship's Captain, Rusty Steel, do the honors that very night. It was becoming a habit for the old riverboat skipper to get out his logbook and captain's hat and marry another couple. If this kept up, the compound would soon be infested with little human critters.

Jump the Broom

The following day, a foot of snow covered the ground. Any signs of people or animals were wiped clean. Snowflakes as large as quarters floated in the cool air. Crows cawed in the trees. It was crisp and clean, and a fresh new season was upon them. Soon, the grizzly bears would go into hibernation, and travel would become impossible. But today, the sun shone brightly overhead, and the temperatures rose, if only for a few hours.

Snow was sprinkled across the trees and the mountains. Rays of light reflected off the sun and the white peaks. Warmth radiated from the fiery disk penetrating the cool morning, making for a perfect day. There wasn't a cloud in the sky, although the moon was still visible in the daylight.

Every chair on the porch was vacant. The door and window to the cabin were open, letting in cold air. Betty had found a fiddle stored in Syracuse Sam's cabin. She surprised everybody when she claimed to know how to play. Smoke billowed from the kitchen chimney.

Another fire roared in the fireplace, but nobody was around.

They were shocked when Rusty Steel approached the couple with an old blue skipper's hat. He had a Bible in his right hand and his sailor's log in his left. This was the second wedding he was to perform in the compound. He had recently married Dahteste and Levi Johnson. Now, he was going to marry Betty Crockett and Will Forrester.

Dahteste had invited her closest friends from the Crow stronghold a half day ride away. Angus was with his Crow wife, too, and everybody was laughing and acting like a bunch of kids. Betty's face glowed, and her cheeks were as red as roses. Her blue eyes sparkled like diamonds and held a hint of mischief. Angus gave the bride away, and Levi was Will's best man.

Joseph and Dennis got a little tipsy before the ceremony and began dancing the jig in the snow. Everybody laughed when the sheriff slipped and fell on his backside. Steam came out of his ears as he growled while staggering to his feet.

"I bet you fools would dance on my grave if I died," Sheriff Walker spat. But despite himself, he began to laugh, too. It was contagious.

They had all survived the dangerous White Ghost, and now a new family was being formed. He looped his arm in Dennis's, and they danced a polka. Each time they made a turn, they nearly slipped on the ice.

Soon, Mountain Dennis was back and busy as usual with the ladies' demands. Now Pine Needle had discovered how to sweet talk the vulnerable man, and they all enjoyed his attention. Levi and Rusty laughed at how the women controlled him, but he didn't mind what they thought because he was having the time of his life.

Everybody stopped dancing and laughing when Rusty Steel cleared his throat and began the ceremony. It was short and to the point. The skipper didn't loiter when it came to his duties. He squinted at the small print of his little Bible and began. When he finished, Virgil Lovejoy read a few words from his tattered Good Book.

Halfway through his dedication to the newlywed's marriage, his friends began to hem and haw. Virgil was aware that he was long-winded, but he carried on just the same. He believed whenever a religious man had the opportunity, he should shower his friends with the words of the Gospel, even if they resisted. He chuckled as he continued to read, despite their impatience.

When it was over, Mrs. Betty Forrester grabbed a broom she had handy just for the occasion. She and Will jumped the broom as was custom back in Tennessee. This was how people who lived too far from a preacher wed. Many people had no more ceremony than that. For Betty, this and the Christian wedding tied the knot once and for all. Again, the party started up but now in full earnest.

As Dahteste's family pounded drums and danced around the fire, Betty pulled out the dusty fiddle and began to tune it. In a couple of minutes, she was playing *Turkey in the Straw*. The Crow musicians took a while to catch on, but soon, they were beating to the rhythm of the happy melody. Then everybody was dancing with Joseph and Dennis. Leather-wrapped feet pounded the snow until it melted where they celebrated.

After they finished the religious part of the wedding,

they all retired to Rusty and Angus's porch to eat and drink for the rest of the day. Joseph and Dennis were soon snoozing in the corner. They had gotten too drunk too quickly and now were already fading, and the party was just beginning.

Rusty ducked inside, pulled out two labeled whiskey bottles from his secret stash, and brought them to the table. Angus had made a large cornbread, and they put a candle in the middle, so it looked like a cake. Steaming wild turkey sat on a large tin platter with a small bucket of gravy beside it. Sweetcorn, wild onions, pine nuts, a variety of wild berries, and dried mushrooms filled pie pans, and a bucket of fresh water and a ladle sat on the floor.

"Why does the kitchen smell like apples?" Angus asked as he waited for Betty to get out of his way. He was fussy about his kitchen unless it was Virgil who knew how to cook better than him anyway.

"Don't you ever make anything in the oven, you old fool?" Betty laughed. "You don't have to cook everything in a frying pan. What you smell is fresh apple pie. Now get that silly candle out of the cornbread, ask Dennis for the figures, and get out of my way."

Everybody took in a deep breath. It smelled like cinnamon. They all eyed Mountain Dennis. Was he conspiring with the women? He grinned as he pulled a wooden carving from his pocket. He had whittled a little figure of a big man and a little woman out of balsa wood he had bought at the Rendezvous. From the top protruded a baby bird feather.

They said the wood came from Ecuador and was as light as air and simple to carve. He even cut out the eagle feathers in Dahteste's hair and Levi's beard in great detail. Everybody laughed and cheered except Angus, who felt he got betrayed. But his anger was fleeting, and soon, he was eating pie with a shot of quality whiskey and had a grin on his face. For them, this was a memorable feast.

After the meal, everybody asked Betty to play one last song. It turned out her skills with the fiddle were everything she claimed. She played it so well that their hearts sang with the music floating from the magical bow and strings. It took them to the clouds and back as her fingers gently pressed the frets. She played *Meet Me by Moonlight* by J. Augustine Scott and their souls soared with the angels.

Hours later, the captain and Betty sat together one minute, and the next, they were gone. Somehow, they had snuck off without anyone seeing them. Fresh smoke came from the draft at the top of the teepee minutes later. Soon after, the lodge lit up like a candle.

When Rusty noticed, he chuckled. "The newlyweds are consummating their marriage. I still can't believe Betty proposed marriage to the captain. Of all the gumption, she's got more than most."

Hoots and cries echoed in the compound, bouncing off nearby canyons. But the new couple paid them no mind and even expected it from friends like them. They were just happy for them is all. They were more like brothers and sisters than friends. The party on the porch continued until the wee hours of the morning, despite the couple's absence. In the Rockies, you celebrated whenever you had the chance.

The teepee glowed, making silhouettes of the inhabitants. It was a fuzzy, hard-to-see image, but everyone knew they were there just the same. Smoke continued to curl out the draft, but they tied the flap tightly, and no visitors were welcome. Murmurs and whispers were barely heard, with the occasional burst of laughter.

In the last hours, the three original compound dwellers were the only ones left. They discussed the old times and what would come with two newly married couples. But they didn't mind because, as Rusty always says, the road behind them is long, but the road ahead gets shorter daily.

That night Gus Grizzel succumbed to his injury. White Ghost could still claim another soul, even if it was from the grave. The following morning Angus, Rusty, and Dennis quietly buried him. Virgil said his last rites. They saw it fitting for him to pass quietly. He sure had suffered enough while he was still alive. The frail skeleton of a man they buried was a shadow of what he once was. It would have been better if he had died with his friend, Fred Barns, then he wouldn't have suffered so.

Peace & Quiet

A big black dog snored, curled up on the feet of its master. Rusty Steel patted his head and grinned. They heard the door to the outhouse slam behind the buildings. Mountain Dennis walked their way, buttoning up his pants. His thick winter moccasins squeaked in the fresh snow as cheroot smoke floated around his head.

Angus sat silently, puffing on his ceramic pipe and warming his hands with his steaming cup of coffee. He stared blindly into the distance. It was an easy guess what was on his mind. Pine Needle had arrived just in time for the wedding. Now, she wanted him to head back to the Crow stronghold to spend the winter like years past. But he didn't know if he could stay cooped up in the teepee after such a wild and exciting summer. He believed he would need a few weeks to slow down. But how was he supposed to tell that to his Crow wife?

"I wonder what else unexpected will come our way this winter?" Rusty asked. "I swear, ever since I invited Levi and the captain to come and live up here with us, life has been a whirlwind. At least there's never a dull moment."

"Oh, I think you made a fine choice." Angus smiled as his thoughts returned to Earth. "Now we're all one big happy family and not just a few old men lost in the wilderness. I figure in short order, there'll be rug rats crawling around on the floors and in the dirt." He laughed at the thought. "I think both the boys found themselves some mighty fine wives."

"I believe they have brought a breath of fresh air to the compound," Dennis said. "Things were gettin' kind of stale before they got here, that's for certain. Ya sure as heck can't say we've been exactly bored or nothin'. I've barely been able to catch my breath."

Smoke squirreled from all three chimneys and the small teepee in the middle of the compound, too. Levi and Dahteste had loaned it to the newlyweds, and they hardly left their warm, cozy refuge. It had already been two days since the wedding, but the boys still suffered from the party.

"When I was a young man, I hardly had hangovers." Rusty chuckled. "Now they last for three days." The laugh made his head throb as he held it in his hands.

"What happened to Levi and Dahteste?" Angus asked. "I ain't seen 'em all morning."

Dennis turned his head toward the far cabin and observed, "There's plenty of smoke comin' from the fireplace. I reckon they're takin' advantage of some time alone, too. I guess it's just us old farts again. Just like it was before they came. Now that I look back, I don't know how we got on without 'em."

Joseph tapped his pipe on his boot, spilling the ashes on the floor. He sipped his coffee, looking at Rusty over the brim. He was still ticked off how Steel bossed him around. He wasn't used to being told what to do. Where he was from, sheriffs led the posse.

"No, there were three more of us before they came," Rusty huffed. "Too many people have died of late. Now that Gus has died, too, we have four graves in the garden."

"But that ain't the boys' fault," Angus said. "It's all of them Easterners that's gettin' the Indians all worked up. They won't stop trespassin' on their land and killin' their game. I'd feel the same if I were them. This was gonna happen whether we brought Levi and Will up here or not. Why, I wouldn't have it any other way. Maybe it ain't such a good idea for you to bring a hundred wagons across the South Pass and West, Joseph. You're kind of gettin' close to home, ain't cha?"

"There y'all go again, pickin' on me for no good call. You know the South Pass is almost three weeks' walk from here, that is, if you know where you're goin'. Half the people that come up to these parts end up lost."

"That's precisely what we mean," Rusty joined in. "It used to take a man six months to find us up here, and now they'll only be three weeks away. There's bound to be a number that get lost and end up here where they ain't welcome. Ain't that right, Angus?"

"If you're gonna hack on me all winter, I'll find myself somewhere else to sleep," the sheriff grumbled.

"I wonder how the trappin' is gonna be this winter," Rusty pondered. "If it's as good as last year, we'll be headin' back to the trappers' meet again. With the one this summer, it makes fifteen in a row. Every year when the Rendezvous ends, I always say I'll never go back, but when the time comes around again, I can hardly wait to return."

"I reckon the grass is always greener..." Angus laughed.

"The one this year was a doozy." Dennis chuckled. "As it is, I liked to have a heart attack."

Angus disappeared momentarily and returned with a cast-iron frying pan full of steaming biscuits and a fresh pot of coffee. Brown bubbles spewed from the spout, filling the air with the aroma. "Go fetch the butter, Dennis. I just made a fresh batch from goat's milk yesterday."

They broke open biscuits the size of fists. Then, generously scooped butter and spread it on the steaming buns. It instantly melted. Angus grabbed the jug and dosed the coffee with a splash of whiskey to fight off the morning cold.

Rusty looked over at the sun, and it said ten o'clock. It didn't look like they were going to see much of the couples today. They were building their nests for winter.

13TH AWAKENING

THE SOUND OF A WATERFALL SPLASHED AGAINST ROCKS IN the distance. The remains of a fire scarred the earth. The distant hint of burning flesh seemed to linger in the air. The snow-white ground was clean of prints. Birds dove from the sky toward the water to have a sip but turned up at the last moment when they sensed the water was poisoned.

What looked like a burned-out tree stood at the end of the trail. A misty haze lingered at the back of the poison lake. Three caves loomed like the monster's eyes, inviting trespassers to disaster. At the end of the lake, the water seemed to approach the tunnels.

The setting sun blushed and rose on the horizon, shooting the last rays of light toward the heavens. Sunlight slanted through shiny leaves reflecting light. Stars began to roll out like a carpet from the eastern sky.

Lightning bugs danced in the distance as mosquitoes buzzed in the air. Snowflakes as big as ears began to fall everywhere as the temperatures dropped. The earth was hard and frigid.

Two mounds of fresh dirt were piled high on the ground. The Plains Indians usually didn't bury their dead like people from other cultures, but nobody wanted to take any chances with these wicked men. They planted White Ghost's body twelve feet deep in the ground along with his accomplice, but nobody ever found his head. To make sure some shaman or speculator didn't remove his body, they covered it with heavy stones.

On top was a layer of freshly turned dirt. The smell of earth filled one's senses. There were no markers on his or Black Crow's graves, and the men present at his burial were sworn to silence. No one dared break the code, or the curse of White Ghost could return to kill their families.

The Rocky Mountains Indians didn't bury their dead like the Indian tribes from back east in Ohio, West Virginia, and Mississippi. There, local tribes used Indian mounds for burial sites. The Crow tribe lay their dead on a scaffold in the open air. This they refused the two renegade killers. Their souls would never see the sun, dooming their spirits forever.

Other than the piles of earth, everything looked fresh and clean. Nobody could imagine what happened there only days before. Though, later, they would sing it in all the tribes' songs—how enemies had come together for a common cause and had gained victory. Still, there was no mention of Black Crow, Nuka, or Scar, as expected. They even used White Ghost's name sparingly. Most people wanted to forget his existence. They were just happy the nightmare was over so there was no reason to remember.

A rat scurried across the mountain of brown dirt,

blending in with its surroundings. It abruptly stopped, stood on its hind legs, and sniffed the air in all directions.

The rodent sensed no intruders and nibbled at something at its feet. For a hungry rat, everything was food. His friends tempted their fate and slowly climbed the mound. In seconds, a dozen furry rodents were busy eating bugs and worms.

Four fingers wiggled, loosening the dirt around the little creature. The rat froze for a second, but nothing happened, so it resumed eating. It happened so quickly; if you blinked, you would have missed it.

The white hand snatched the rat and dragged it under before it had time to squeal. Its companions were oblivious of its capture. What was it, and who would be next? That was the question that they asked later, but nobody would have the answer.

A Look at Book Eight:
Out in the Cold: A Western Double

Some men chase glory. Others just want to make it home alive.

Out in the Cold

Rusty Steel and Angus McFarlin head deep into forgotten country—cold-water streams they haven't trapped in over a decade. Determined to prove they've still got grit, the old mountain men face the brutal Rockies head-on. But when a blizzard hits and strange tracks appear in the snow, they begin to wonder what stalks them—weather, man, or something worse.

Back at the compound, the cold outside has nothing on the heat inside. Betty Forrester and Crow war chief Dahteste are at odds, and their husbands—Levi and Will—struggle to keep peace as tensions mount. Two proud women, one tight cabin, and no room to back down.

Rocky Mountain Fever

With winter breaking, Rusty and Angus finish curing their prized pelts—but trouble's never far. When smoke rises near the compound, Levi and Rusty investigate. What they find sparks gunfire and bloodshed.

Gold fever has come to the high country, and with it, desperate men ready to kill for a stake.

AVAILABLE JANUARY 2026

About the Author

Born in 1886 in Southern Ohio, Ash Lingam grew crops, raised cattle, and doted on the young boy. Ash's family was among the early settlers in pre-Revolutionary America. He has traced his lineage back to around 1746 when his ancestors immigrated from Europe to the aspiring American Colonies.

A retired marketing executive, Ash devotes his spare time to training police dogs and writing novels. He has found his niche in the Western, historical fiction, and adventure genres. With his vast vault of experience, he never runs out of sources for new stories. He has lived in eleven different countries and worked in a total of forty-six to date, Ash has written approximately 130 novels, short stories, and poems. More than one hundred of his eclectic titles help the American frontier come alive for his readers.

https://www.ashlingam.com/

www.ingramcontent.com/pod-product-compliance
Lightning Source LLC
LaVergne TN
LVHW040215110826
845146LV00005B/1295